HACKERS

Edited by Jack Dann & Gardner Dozois

HACKERS

EDITED BY
JACK DANN & GARDNER DOZOIS

ACE BOOKS, NEW YORK

This book is an Ace original edition,
and has never been previously published.

HACKERS

An Ace Book / published by arrangement with
the editors

PRINTING HISTORY
Ace edition / October 1996

The Putnam Berkley World Wide Web site address is
http://www.berkley.com/berkley

ISBN: 0-441-00375-3

ACE®
Ace Books are published by The Berkley Publishing Group,
200 Madison Avenue, New York, NY 10016.
ACE and the "A" design are trademarks
belonging to Charter Communications, Inc.

PRINTED IN THE UNITED STATES OF AMERICA

10 9 8 7 6 5 4 3 2 1

ACKNOWLEDGMENTS

The editors would like to thank the following people for their help and support:

Susan Casper, who helped with the computer stuff; Janeen Webb; Ellen Datlow; Michael Swanwick; David G. Hartwell; Kathrine Cramer; Darrell Schweitzer; Tom Dupree; Martha Millard; Sheila Williams, Scott L. Towner; Sharah Thomas; Merilee Heifetz; and special thanks to our own editors, Susan Allison and Ginjer Buchanan.

CONTENTS

PREFACE

No one knows exactly when the term "hacker" came into the language, although it was certainly being used in small elite circles of what would eventually become the computer industry as far back as the mid-sixties. Even twenty years ago, few people outside of that fledgling computer industry would have known what you were referring to if you talked of "hackers," and that would have included most avid science fiction fans, and even the majority of science fiction writers—even many of the so called "hard science" SF writers who pride themselves on staying technologically *au courant*.

By the middle of the seventies, a few of us were vaguely familiar with the basic concept of hacking in its most general sense, although mostly what we heard of in those days were "phone phreaks," a specialized form of hacker who pirates telephone service; as long ago as 1967 or 1968, one of your editors can recall someone telling him about a friend who had made a "black box" or "whistler" that enabled him to make long-distance calls without having to pay for them—but, since this was before even the term "phone phreak" had come into common parlance, there was no *word* to describe someone who engaged in that sort of activity. "Hacker" had yet to surface from the tightly closed ranks of the *cognoscenti*.

Today, of course, after the explosive expansion of the computer industry, which has put personal computers into a respectable percentage of all Amercian homes; after the "Cyberpunk" revolution in science fiction, which brought writers such as William Gibson and Bruce Sterling to wide attention outside of traditional genre boundaries; after a follow-up flood of books and stories and comics and even songs and tapes and CDs; after big-budget movies such as *Sneakers* and *War Games*, cult movies such as *Johnny Mnemonic*, and even weekly television shows such as *Max Headroom*, *Nowhere Man*, *Deadly Games* and *The X-Files*, just about *everyone* knows what a hacker is, at least in the most commonly accepted sense: someone who illicitly intrudes into computer systems by stealth and manipulates those systems to his own ends, for his own purposes.

Usually, in these scenarios, the hacker is up to no good when he intrudes into those computer systems. Usually, in fact, his goal is to perform an act that is illegal, immoral, or both: to commit a white-collar computer crime (transfer ten million dollars to a personal bank account); to commit an act of espionage, either industrial espionage or the old-fashioned political kind (steal the restricted designs for the new product line, steal the secret plans for the new terror weapon); to commit an act of sabotage or technological terrorism (crash the telephone system or the power grid, make an atomic power plant melt down, cause nuclear-armed missiles to be fired at Someone Somewhere). And so on.

This is, of course, a somewhat limited conception of a hacker. Although some hackers *do* commit some of the above acts, mostly computer crime and computer fraud of one sort or another (pirating phone services is still big, as is the stealing of other people's credit card numbers), not all hackers are computer criminals, by any means. Many of today's foremost captains of industry were once scruffy teenage hackers, and many of the people who will one day pioneer new industries or new technologies, or explore as yet unimagined new frontiers of scientific knowledge, are scruffy teenage hackers *right now*. Nor, as the stories in this anthology will show you, are computers the *only* thing that can be hacked. In the future, for good *and* ill, clever hackers will be hacking DNA, viruses, or even the basic nature of humanity itself—indeed, some of them have *already* started doing so.

It should also be kept in mind that hackers are not always driven by venal goals such as money or power. Money, in fact, is often the *least* potent of a hacker's motives, far outweighed by the desire to discover secret knowledge for its own sake, to explore the parameters of technologies that are new enough that no one as yet can be quite sure *what* can or cannot be done with them, to push the edge of the envelope . . . and then, when a new edge has been established, further out, to push it again. Hackers are *experimenters*, not content to passively accept a service as a consumer, always wanting to be in active *control*—which is why you will find no Virtual Reality or computer-sex stories here (for those, you must go to two other Ace anthologies, *Isaac Asimov's Cyberdreams* and *Isaac Asimov's Skin Deep*); instead, hackers are always driven to explore, manipulate, meddle, alter, rearrange, improve, upgrade, adapt, and change things around until they better suit their own needs.

All this, *plus* the kind of restless, impatient, sometimes amoral or egocentric spirit that chafes at any kind of restriction or boundary, the kind of spirit (either "free" or "outlaw," depending on how you look at it) that bristles resentfully at other people's laws, rules, regulations, and expectations, and relentlessly seeks a way to get over or under or around those rules. The something that does not love a wall. In other words, very much the same sort of spirit that drove the people who, for good *and* ill, opened up the American West, the kind of spirit that produced farsighted explorers as well as cattle rustlers and horse thieves, brave pioneers as well as scurvy outlaw gangs, and that built the bright new cities of the Plains at the cost of countless thousands of Native American lives.

Today, poised on the brink of the twenty-first century, society may be about to change again in fundamental ways, and hackers will drive much of that change, for good and ill. Never before has so much power been in the hands of so few, those elite individuals who have the knowledge and the ability to manipulate the very structures that hold society together in this complexly interrelated Information Age. Will they bring the infrastructure of that society crashing in upon itself in flaming ruin, inflicting upon us acts of terrorism on a heretofore unimaginable scale, or will they be the trailblazers who will lead us to a new kind of society, one wherein the individual enjoys more personal freedom—and thus, inevitably, more individual responsibility—than was ever before possible in the history of the human race?

Only time will tell. Only the future will know—but, in the meantime, *you* can get a *taste* of that future, or, rather, a taste of one of the many *different* futures that *could* come to pass, simply by turning the page, and reading the stories that await you. . . .

BURNING CHROME

William Gibson

Although it has aesthetic antecedents in stories such as Samuel R. Delany's "Time Considered As a Helix of Semi-Precious Stones" and James Tiptree, Jr.'s "The Girl Who Was Plugged In," the stunning tale that follows may be the first real hacker story ever written, the first to explore some of the darker future possibilities of the then-emergent computer community . . . which makes it all the more ironic that it was written not on a computer, but on a battered old manual typewriter. It's a story that has been imitated hundreds of times since, not only in print science fiction but in comics, movies, and even weekly television shows—none of which takes anything away from the elegance and power of the original. As you shall see, this prototype hacker story is still *one of the best ever written. . . .*

Almost unknown only a few years ago, William Gibson won the Nebula Award, the Hugo Award, and the Philip K. Dick Award in 1985 for his remarkable first novel Neuromancer—*a rise to prominence as fiery and meteoric as any in SF history. By the late eighties, the appearance of* Neuromancer *and its sequels,* Count Zero *and* Mona Lisa Overdrive, *had made him the most talked-about and controversial new SF writer of the decade—one might almost say "writer," leaving out the "SF" part, for Gibson's reputation spread far outside the usual boundaries of the genre, with wildly enthusiastic notices about him and interviews with him appearing in places like* Rolling Stone, Spin, *and* The Village Voice, *and with pop-culture figures like Timothy Leary (not someone ordinarily much given to close observation of the SF world) embracing him with open arms. By the beginning of the nineties, even most of his harshest critics had been forced to admit—sometimes grudgingly—that a major new talent had entered the field, the kind of major talent that comes along maybe once or twice in a literary generation. Gibson's short fiction has been collected in* Burning Chrome. *His most recent books are a novel written in collaboration with Bruce Sterling,* The Difference Engine, *and a solo novel,* Virtual Light. *Born in South Carolina, he now lives in Vancouver, Canada, with his wife and family.*

It was hot, the night we burned Chrome. Out in the malls and plazas, moths were batting themselves to death against the neon, but in Bobby's loft the only light came from a monitor screen and the green and red LEDs on the face of the matrix simulator. I knew every chip in Bobby's simulator by heart; it looked like your workaday Ono-Sendai VII, the "Cyberspace Seven," but I'd rebuilt it so many times that you'd have had a hard time finding a square millimeter of factory circuitry in all that silicon.

We waited side by side in front of the simulator console, watching the time display in the screen's lower left corner.

"Go for it," I said, when it was time, but Bobby was already there, leaning forward to drive the Russian program into its slot with the heel of his hand. He did it with the tight grace of a kid slamming change into an arcade game, sure of winning and ready to pull down a string of free games.

A silver tide of phosphenes boiled across my field of vision as the matrix began to unfold in my head, a 3-D chessboard, infinite and perfectly transparent. The Russian program seemed to lurch as we entered the grid. If anyone else had been jacked into that part of the matrix, he might have seen a surf of flickering shadow roll out of the little yellow pyramid that represented our computer. The program was a mimetic weapon, designed to absorb local color and present itself as a crash-priority override in whatever context it encountered.

"Congratulations," I heard Bobby say. "We just became an Eastern Seaboard Fission Authority inspection probe. . . ." That meant we were clearing fiberoptic lines with the cybernetic equivalent of a fire siren, but in the simulation matrix we seemed to rush straight for Chrome's data base. I couldn't see it yet, but I already knew those walls were waiting. Walls of shadow, walls of ice.

Chrome: her pretty childface smooth as steel, with eyes that would have been at home on the bottom of some deep Atlantic trench, cold gray eyes that lived under terrible pressure. They said she cooked her own cancers for people who crossed her, rococo custom variations that took years to kill you. They said a lot of things about Chrome, none of them at all reassuring.

So I blotted her out with a picture of Rikki. Rikki kneeling in a shaft of dusty sunlight that slanted into the loft through a grid of steel and glass: her faded camouflage fatigues, her translucent rose sandals, the good line of her bare back as she rummaged through a nylon gear bag. She looks up, and a half-blond curl falls to tickle her nose. Smiling, buttoning an old shirt of Bobby's, frayed khaki cotton drawn across her breasts.

She smiles.

"Son of a bitch," said Bobby, "we just told Chrome we're an IRS audit and three Supreme Court subpoenas. . . . Hang on to your ass, Jack. . . ."

So long, Rikki. Maybe now I see you never.

And dark, so dark, in the halls of Chrome's ice.

Bobby was a cowboy, and ice was the nature of his game, *ice* from ICE, Intrusion Countermeasures Electronics. The matrix is an abstract representation of the relationships between data systems. Legitimate programmers jack into their employers' sector of the matrix and find themselves surrounded by bright geometries representing the corporate data.

Towers and fields of it ranged in the colorless nonspace of the simulation matrix, the electronic consensus-hallucination that facilitates the handling and exchange of massive quantities of data. Legitimate programmers never see the walls of ice they work behind, the walls of shadow that screen their operations from others, from industrial-espionage artists and hustlers like Bobby Quine.

Bobby was a cowboy. Bobby was a cracksman, a burglar,

casing mankind's extended electronic nervous system, rustling
data and credit in the crowded matrix, monochrome nonspace
where the only stars are dense concentrations of information,
and high above it all burn corporate galaxies and the cold
spiral arms of military systems.

Bobby was another one of those young-old faces you see
drinking in the Gentleman Loser, the chic bar for computer
cowboys, rustlers, cybernetic second-story men. We were
partners.

Bobby Quine and Automatic Jack. Bobby's the thin, pale
dude with the dark glasses, and Jack's the mean-looking guy
with the myoelectric arm. Bobby's software and Jack's hard;
Bobby punches console and Jack runs down all the little
things that can give you an edge. Or, anyway, that's what the
scene watchers in the Gentleman Loser would've told you,
before Bobby decided to burn Chrome. But they also
might've told you that Bobby was losing his edge, slowing
down. He was twenty-eight, Bobby, and that's old for a
console cowboy.

Both of us were good at what we did but somehow that
one big score just wouldn't come down for us. I knew where
to go for the right gear, and Bobby had all his licks down
pat. He'd sit back with a white terry sweatband across his
forehead and whip moves on those keyboards faster than
you could follow, punching his way through some of the
fanciest ice in the business, but that was when something
happened that managed to get him totally wired, and that
didn't happen often. Not highly motivated, Bobby, and I
was the kind of guy who's happy to have the rent covered
and a clean shirt to wear.

But Bobby had this thing for girls, like they were his
private tarot or something, the way he'd get himself
moving. We never talked about it, but when it started to look
like he was losing his touch that summer, he started to spend
more time in the Gentleman Loser. He'd sit at a table by the
open doors and watch the crowd slide by, nights when the
bugs were at the neon and the air smelled of perfume and
fast food. You could see his sunglasses scanning those faces
as they passed, and he must have decided that Rikki's was

the one he was waiting for, the wild card and the luck changer. The new one.

I went to New York to check out the market, to see what was available in hot software.

The Finn's place has a defective hologram in the window, METRO HOLOGRAFIX, over a display of dead flies wearing fur coats of gray dust. The scrap's waist-high, inside, drifts of it rising to meet walls that are barely visible behind nameless junk, behind sagging pressboard shelves stacked with old skin magazines and yellow-spined years of *National Geographic*.

"You need a gun," said the Finn. He looks like a recombo DNA project aimed at tailoring people for high-speed burrowing. "You're in luck. I got the new Smith and Wesson, the four-oh-eight Tactical. Got this xenon projector slung under the barrel, see, batteries in the grip, throw you a twelve-inch high-noon circle in the pitch dark at fifty yards. The light source is so narrow, it's almost impossible to spot. It's just like voodoo in a nightfight."

I let my arm clunk down on the table and started the fingers drumming; the servos in the hand began whining like overworked mosquitoes. I knew that the Finn really hated the sound.

"You looking to pawn that?" He prodded the Duralumin wrist joint with the chewed shaft of a felt-tip pen. "Maybe get yourself something a little quieter?"

I kept it up. "I don't need any guns, Finn."

"Okay," he said, "okay," and I quit drumming. "I only got this one item, and I don't even know what it is." He looked unhappy. "I got it off these bridge-and-tunnel kids from Jersey last week."

"So when'd you ever buy anything you didn't know what it was, Finn?"

"Wise ass." And he passed me a transparent mailer with something in it that looked like an audio cassette through the bubble padding. "They had a passport," he said. "They had credit cards and a watch. And that."

"They had the contents of somebody's pockets, you mean."

He nodded. "The passport was Belgian. It was also bogus, looked to me, so I put it in the furnace. Put the cards in with it. The watch was okay, a Porsche, nice watch."

It was obviously some kind of plug-in military program. Out of the mailer, it looked like the magazine of a small assault rifle, coated with nonreflective black plastic. The edges and corners showed bright metal; it had been knocking around for a while.

"I'll give you a bargain on it, Jack. For old times' sake."

I had to smile at that. Getting a bargain from the Finn was like God repealing the law of gravity when you have to carry a heavy suitcase down ten blocks of airport corridor.

"Looks Russian to me," I said. "Probably the emergency sewage controls for some Leningrad suburb. Just what I need."

"You know," said the Finn, "I got a pair of shoes older than you are. Sometimes I think you got about as much class as those yahoos from Jersey. What do you want me to tell you, it's the keys to the Kremlin? You figure out what the goddamn thing is. Me, I just sell the stuff."

I bought it.

Bodiless, we swerve into Chrome's castle of ice. And we're fast, fast. It feels like we're surfing the crest of the invading program, hanging ten above the seething glitch systems as they mutate. We're sentient patches of oil swept along down corridors of shadow.

Somewhere we have bodies, very far away, in a crowded loft roofed with steel and glass. Somewhere we have microseconds, maybe time left to pull out.

We've crashed her gates disguised as an audit and three subpoenas, but her defenses are specifically geared to cope with that kind of official intrusion. Her most sophisticated ice is structured to fend off warrants, writs, subpoenas. When we breached the first gate, the bulk of her data vanished behind core-command ice, these walls we see as leagues of corridor, mazes of shadow. Five separate landlines spurted May Day signals to law firms, but the virus had already taken over the parameter ice. The glitch systems gobble the distress calls as our mimetic subprograms scan anything that hasn't been blanked by core command.

The Russian program lifts a Tokyo number from the unscreened data, choosing it for frequency of calls, average length of calls, the speed with which Chrome returned those calls.

"Okay," says Bobby, "we're an incoming scrambler call from a pal of hers in Japan. That should help."

Ride 'em, cowboy.

Bobby read his future in women; his girls were omens, changes in the weather, and he'd sit all night in the Gentleman Loser, waiting for the season to lay a new face down in front of him like a card.

I was working late in the loft one night, shaving down a chip, my arm off and the little waldo jacked straight into the stump.

Bobby came in with a girl I hadn't seen before, and usually I feel a little funny if a stranger sees me working that way, with those leads clipped to the hard carbon studs that stick out of my stump. She came right over and looked at the magnified image on the screen, then saw the waldo moving under its vacuum-sealed dust cover. She didn't say anything, just watched. Right away I had a good feeling about her; it's like that sometimes.

"Automatic Jack, Rikki. My associate."

He laughed, put his arm around her waist, something in his tone letting me know that I'd be spending the night in a dingy room in a hotel.

"Hi," she said. Tall, nineteen or maybe twenty, and she definitely had the goods. With just those few freckles across the bridge of her nose, and eyes somewhere between dark amber and French coffee. Tight black jeans rolled to midcalf and a narrow plastic belt that matched the rose-colored sandals.

But now when I see her sometimes when I'm trying to

sleep, I see her somewhere out on the edge of all this sprawl
of cities and smoke, and it's like she's a hologram stuck
behind my eyes, in a bright dress she must've worn once,
when I knew her, something that doesn't quite reach her
knees. Bare legs long and straight. Brown hair, streaked
with blond, hoods her face, blown in a wind from somewhere, and I see her wave goodbye.

Bobby was making a show of rooting through a stack of
audio cassettes. "I'm on my way, cowboy," I said, unclip-
ping the waldo. She watched attentively as I put my arm
back on.

"Can you fix things?" she asked.

"Anything, anything you want, Automatic Jack'll fix it."
I snapped my Duralumin fingers for her.

She took a little simstim deck from her belt and showed
me the broken hinge on the cassette cover.

"Tomorrow," I said, "no problem."

And my oh my, I said to myself, sleep pulling me down
the six flights to the street, *what'll Bobby's luck be like with
a fortune cookie like that? If his system worked, we'd be
striking it rich any night now.* In the street I grinned and
yawned and waved for a cab.

Chrome's castle is dissolving, sheets of ice shadow flickering and fading, eaten by the glitch systems that spin out
from the Russian program, tumbling away from our central
logic thrust and infecting the fabric of the ice itself. The
glitch systems are cybernetic virus analogs, self-replicating
and voracious. They mutate constantly, in unison, subvert-
ing and absorbing Chrome's defenses.

Have we already paralyzed her, or is a bell ringing
somewhere, a red light blinking? Does she know?

Rikki Wildside, Bobby called her, and for those first few
weeks it must have seemed to her that she had it all, the
whole teeming show spread out for her, sharp and bright
under the neon. She was new to the scene, and she had all
the miles of malls and plazas to prowl, all the shops and
clubs, and Bobby to explain the wild side, the tricky wiring

on the dark underside of things, all the players and their names and their games. He made her feel at home.

"What happened to your arm?" she asked me one night in the Gentleman Loser, the three of us drinking at a small table in a corner."

"Hang-gliding," I said, "accident."

"Hang-gliding over a wheatfield," said Bobby, "place called Kiev. Our Jack's just hanging there in the dark, under a Nightwing parafoil, with fifty kilos of radar jammer between his legs, and some Russian asshole accidentally burns his arm off with a laser."

I don't remember how I changed the subject, but I did.

I was still telling myself that it wasn't Rikki who was getting to me, but what Bobby was doing with her. I'd known him for a long time, since the end of the war, and I knew he used women as counters in a game, Bobby Quine versus fortune, versus time and the night of cities. And Rikki had turned up just when he needed something to get him going, something to aim for. So he'd set her up as a symbol for everything he wanted and couldn't have, everything he'd had and couldn't keep.

I didn't like having to listen to him tell me how much I loved her, and knowing he believed it only made it worse. He was a past master at the hard fall and the rapid recovery, and I'd seen it happen a dozen times before. He might as well have had NEXT printed across his sunglasses in green Day-Glo capitals, ready to flash out at the first interesting face that flowed past the tables in the Gentleman Loser.

I knew what he did to them. He turned them into emblems, sigils on the map of his hustler's life, navigation beacons he could follow through a sea of bars and neon. What else did he have to steer by? He didn't love money, in and of itself, not enough to follow its lights. He wouldn't work for power over other people; he hated the responsibility it brings. He had some basic pride in his skill, but that was never enough to keep him pushing.

So he made do with women.

When Rikki showed up, he needed one in the worst way. He was fading fast, and smart money was already whisper-

ing that the edge was off his game. He needed that one big
score, and soon, because he didn't know any other kind of
life, and all his clocks were set for hustler's time, calibrated
in risk and adrenaline and that supernal dawn calm that
comes when every move's proved right and a sweet lump of
someone else's credit clicks into your own account.

It was time for him to make his bundle and get out; so Rikki
got set up higher and farther away than any of the others ever
had, even though—and I felt like screaming it at him—she
was right there, alive, totally real, human, hungry, resilient,
bored, beautiful, excited, all the things she was. . . .

Then he went out one afternoon, about a week before I
made the trip to New York to see the Finn. Went out and left
us there in the loft, waiting for a thunderstorm. Half the
skylight was shadowed by a dome they'd never finished,
and the other half showed sky, black and blue with clouds.
I was standing by the bench, looking up at that sky, stupid
with the hot afternoon, the humidity, and she touched me,
touched my shoulder, the half-inch border of taut pink scar
that the arm doesn't cover. Anybody else ever touched me
there, they went on to the shoulder, the neck. . . .

But she didn't do that. Her nails were lacquered black, not
pointed, but tapered oblongs, the lacquer only a shade
darker than the carbon-fiber laminate that sheathes my arm.
And her hand went down the arm, black nails tracing a weld
in the laminate, down to the black anodized elbow joint, out
to the wrist, her hand soft-knuckled as a child's, fingers
spreading to lock over mine, her palm against the perforated
Duralumin.

Her other palm came up to brush across the feedback
pads, and it rained all afternoon, raindrops drumming on the
steel and soot-stained glass above Bobby's bed.

Ice walls flick away like supersonic butterflies made of
shade. Beyond them, the matrix's illusion of infinite space.
It's like watching a tape of a prefab building going up; only
the tape's reversed and run at high speed, and these walls are
torn wings.

Trying to remind myself that this place and the gulfs

beyond are only representations, that we aren't "in" Chrome's computer, but interfaced with it, while the matrix simulator in Bobby's loft generates this illusion . . . The core data begin to emerge, exposed, vulnerable. . . . This is the far side of ice, the view of the matrix I've never seen before, the view that fifteen million legitimate console operators see daily and take for granted.

The core data tower around us like vertical freight trains, color-coded for access. Bright primaries, impossibly bright in that transparent void, linked by countless horizontals in nursery blues and pinks.

But ice still shadows something at the center of it all: the heart of all Chrome's expensive darkness, the very heart . . .

It was late afternoon when I got back from my shopping expedition to New York. Not much sun through the skylight, but an ice pattern glowed on Bobby's monitor screen, a 2-D graphic representation of someone's computer defenses, lines of neon woven like an Art Deco prayer rug. I turned the console off, and the screen went completely dark.

Rikki's things were spread across my workbench, nylon bags spilling clothes and makeup, a pair of bright red cowboy boots, audio cassettes, glossy Japanese magazines about simstim stars. I stacked it all under the bench and then took my arm off, forgetting that the program I'd bought from the Finn was in the right-hand pocket of my jacket, so that I had to fumble it out left-handed and then get it into the padded jaws of the jeweler's vise.

The waldo looks like an old audio turntable, the kind that played disc records, with the vise set up under a transparent dust cover. The arm itself is just over a centimeter long, swinging out on what would've been the tone arm on one of those turntables. But I don't look at that when I've clipped the leads to my stump; I look at the scope, because that's my arm there in black and white, magnification 40X.

I ran a tool check and picked up the laser. It felt a little heavy; so I scaled my weight-sensor input down to a quarter-kilo per gram and got to work. At 40X the side of the program looked like a trailer truck.

It took eight hours to crack: three hours with the waldo and the laser and four dozen taps, two hours on the phone to a contact in Colorado, and three hours to run down a lexicon disc that could translate eight-year-old technical Russian.

Then Cyrillic alphanumerics started reeling down the monitor, twisting themselves into English halfway down. There were a lot of gaps, where the lexicon ran up against specialized military acronyms in the readout I'd bought from my man in Colorado, but it did give me some idea of what I'd bought from the Finn.

I felt like a punk who'd gone out to buy a switchblade and come home with a small neutron bomb.

Screwed again, I thought. *What good's a neutron bomb in a streetfight?* The thing under the dust cover was right out of my league. I didn't even know where to unload it, where to look for a buyer. Someone had, but he was dead, someone with a Porsche watch and a fake Belgian passport, but I'd never tried to move in those circles. The Finn's muggers from the 'burbs had knocked over someone who had some highly arcane connections.

The program in the jeweler's vise was a Russian military icebreaker, a killer-virus program.

It was dawn when Bobby came in alone. I'd fallen asleep with a bag of takeout sandwiches in my lap.

"You want to eat?" I asked him, not really awake, holding out my sandwiches. I'd been dreaming of the program, of its waves of hungry glitch systems and mimetic subprograms; in the dream it was an animal of some kind, shapeless and flowing.

He brushed the bag aside on his way to the console, punched a function key. The screen lit with the intricate pattern I'd seen there that afternoon. I rubbed sleep from my eyes with my left hand, one thing I can't do with my right. I'd fallen asleep trying to decide whether to tell him about the program. Maybe I should try to sell it alone, keep the money, go somewhere new, ask Rikki to go with me.

"Whose is it?" I asked.

He stood there in a black cotton jump suit, an old leather jacket thrown over his shoulders like a cape. He hadn't shaved for a few days, and his face looked thinner than usual.

"It's Chrome's," he said.

My arm convulsed, started clicking, fear translated to the myoelectrics through the carbon studs. I spilled the sandwiches; limp sprouts, and bright yellow dairy-produce slices on the unswept wooden floor.

"You're stone crazy," I said.

"No," he said, "you think she rumbled it? No way. We'd be dead already. I locked on to her through a triple-blind rental system in Mombasa and an Algerian comsat. She knew somebody was having a look-see, but she couldn't trace it."

If Chrome had traced the pass Bobby had made at her ice, we were good as dead. But he was probably right, or she'd have had me blown away on my back from New York. "Why her, Bobby? Just give me one reason. . . ."

Chrome: I'd seen her maybe half a dozen times in the Gentleman Loser. Maybe she was slumming, or checking out the human condition, a condition she didn't exactly aspire to. A sweet little heart-shaped face framing the nastiest pair of eyes you ever saw. She'd looked fourteen for as long as anyone could remember, hyped out of anything like a normal metabolism on some massive program of serums and hormones. She was as ugly a customer as the street ever produced, but she didn't belong to the street anymore. She was one of the Boys, Chrome, a member in good standing of the local Mob subsidiary. Word was, she'd gotten started as a dealer, back when synthetic pituitary hormones were still proscribed. But she hadn't had to move hormones for a long time. Now she owned the House of Blue Lights.

"You're flat-out crazy, Quine. You give me one sane reason for having that stuff on your screen. You ought to dump it, and I mean *now*. . . ."

"Talk in the Loser," he said, shrugging out of the leather jacket. "Black Myron and Crow Jane. Jane, she's up on all the sex lines, claims she knows where the money goes. So she's arguing with Myron that Chrome's the controlling interest in the Blue Lights, not just some figurehead for the Boys."

" 'The Boys,' Bobby," I said. "That's the operative word there. You still capable of seeing that? We don't mess with the Boys, remember? That's why we're still walking around."

"That's why we're still poor, partner." He settled back into the swivel chair in front of the console, unzipped his jump suit, and scratched his skinny white chest. "But maybe not for much longer."

"I think maybe this partnership just got itself permanently dissolved."

Then he grinned at me. That grin was truly crazy, feral and focused, and I knew that right then he really didn't give a shit about dying.

"Look," I said, "I've got some money left, you know? Why don't you take it and get the tube to Miami, catch a hopper to Montego Bay. You need a rest, man. You've got to get your act together."

"My act, Jack," he said, punching something on the keyboard, "never has been this together before." The neon prayer rug on the screen shivered and woke as an animation program cut in, ice lines weaving with hypnotic frequency, a living mandala. Bobby kept punching, and the movement slowed; the pattern resolved itself, grew slightly less complex, became an alternation between two distant configurations. A first-class piece of work, and I hadn't thought he was still that good. "Now," he said, "there, see it? Wait. There. There again. And there. Easy to miss. That's it. Cuts in every hour and twenty minutes with a squirt transmission to their comsat. We could live for a year on what she pays them weekly in negative interest."

"Whose comsat?"

"Zürich. Her bankers. That's her bankbook, Jack. That's where the money goes. Crow Jane was right."

I stood there. My arm forgot to click.

"So how'd you do in New York, partner? You get anything that'll help me cut ice? We're going to need whatever we can get."

I kept my eyes on his, forced myself not to look in the direction of the waldo, the jeweler's vise. The Russian program was there, under the dust cover.

Wild cards, luck changers.

"Where's Rikki?" I asked him, crossing to the console, pretending to study the alternating patterns on the screen.

"Friends of hers," he shrugged, "kids, they're all into simstim." He smiled absently. "I'm going to do it for her, man."

"I'm going out to think about this, Bobby. You want me to come back, you keep your hands off the board."

"I'm doing it for her," he said as the door closed behind me. "You know I am."

And down now, down, the program a roller coaster through this fraying maze of shadow walls, gray cathedral spaces between the bright towers. Headlong speed.

Black ice. Don't think about it. Black ice.

Too many stories in the Gentleman Loser; black ice is a part of the mythology. Ice that kills. Illegal, but then aren't we all? Some kind of neural-feedback weapon, and you connect with it only once. Like some hideous Word that eats the mind from the inside out. Like an epileptic spasm that goes on and on until there's nothing left at all . . .

And we're diving for the floor of Chrome's shadow castle.

Trying to brace myself for the sudden stopping of breath, a sickness and final slackening of the nerves. Fear of that cold Word waiting, down there in the dark.

I went out and looked for Rikki, found her in a café with a boy with Sendai eyes, half-healed suture lines radiating from his bruised sockets. She had a glossy brochure spread open on the table, Tally Isham smiling up from a dozen photographs, the Girl with the Zeiss Ikon Eyes.

Her little simstim deck was one of the things I'd stacked under my bench the night before, the one I'd fixed for her the day after I'd first seen her. She spent hours jacked into that unit, the contact band across her forehead like a gray

plastic tiara. Tally Isham was her favorite, and with the
contact band on, she was gone, off somewhere in the
recorded sensorium of simstim's biggest star. Simulated
stimuli: the world—all the interesting parts, anyway—as
perceived by Tally Isham. Tally raced a black Fokker
ground-effect plane across Arizona mesa tops. Tally dived
the Truk Island preserves. Tally partied with the superrich
on private Greek islands, heartbreaking purity of those tiny
white seaports at dawn.

Actually she looked a lot like Tally, same coloring and
cheekbones. I thought Rikki's mouth was stronger. More
sass. She didn't want to *be* Tally Isham, but she coveted the
job. That was her ambition, to be in simstim. Bobby just
laughed it off. She talked to me about it, though. "How'd I
look with a pair of these?" she'd ask, holding a full-page
headshot, Tally Isham's blue Zeiss Ikons lined up with her
own amber-brown. She'd had her corneas done twice, but
she still wasn't 20–20; so she wanted Ikons. Brand of the
stars. Very expensive.

"You still window-shopping for eyes?" I asked as I sat
down.

"Tiger just got some," she said. She looked tired, I
thought.

Tiger was so pleased with his Sendais that he couldn't
help smiling, but I doubted whether he'd have smiled
otherwise. He had the kind of uniform good looks you get
after your seventh trip to the surgical boutique; he'd
probably spend the rest of his life looking vaguely like each
new season's media front-runner; not too obvious a copy,
but nothing too original, either.

"Sendai, right?" I smiled back.

He nodded. I watched as he tried to take me in with his
idea of professional simstim glance. He was pretending that
he was recording. I thought he spent too long on my arm.
"They'll be great on peripherals when the muscles heal," he
said, and I saw how carefully he reached for his double
espresso. Sendai eyes are notorious for depth-perception
defects and warranty hassles, among other things.

"Tiger's leaving for Hollywood tomorrow."

"Then maybe Chiba City, right?" I smiled at him. He didn't smile back. "Got an offer, Tiger? Know an agent?"

"Just checking it out," he said quietly. Then he got up and left. He said a quick goodbye to Rikki, but not to me.

"That kid's optic nerves may start to deteriorate inside six months. You know that, Rikki? Those Sendais are illegal in England, Denmark, lots of places. You can't replace nerves."

"Hey, Jack, no lectures." She stole one of my croissants and nibbled at the tip of one of its horns.

"I thought I was your adviser, kid."

"Yeah. Well, Tiger's not too swift, but everybody knows about Sendais. They're all he can afford. So he's taking a chance. If he gets work, he can replace them."

"With these?" I tapped the Zeiss Ikon brochure. "Lot of money, Rikki. You know better than to take a gamble like that."

She nodded. "I want Ikons."

"If you're going up to Bobby's, tell him to sit tight until he hears from me."

"Sure. It's business?"

"Business," I said. But it was craziness.

I drank my coffee, and she ate both my croissants. Then I walked her down to Bobby's. I made fifteen calls, each one from a different pay phone.

Business. Bad craziness.

All in all, it took us six weeks to set the burn up, six weeks of Bobby telling me how much he loved her. I worked even harder, trying to get away from that.

Most of it was phone calls. My fifteen initial and very oblique inquiries each seemed to breed fifteen more. I was looking for a certain service Bobby and I both imagined as a requisite part of the world's clandestine economy, but which probably never had more than five customers at a time. It would be one that never advertised.

We were looking for the world's heaviest fence, for a non-aligned money laundry capable of dry-cleaning a megabuck online cash transfer and then forgetting about it.

All those calls were a waste, finally, because it was the Finn who put me on to what we needed. I'd gone up to New

York to buy a new blackbox rig, because we were going broke paying for all those calls.

I put the problem to him as hypothetically as possible.

"Macao," he said.

"Macao?"

"The Long Hum family. Stockbrokers."

He even had the number. You want a fence, ask another fence.

The Long Hum people were so oblique that they made my idea of a subtle approach look like a tactical nuke-out. Bobby had to make two shuttle runs to Hong Kong to get the deal straight. We were running out of capital, and fast. I still don't know why I decided to go along with it in the first place; I was scared of Chrome, and I'd never been all that hot to get rich.

I tried telling myself that it was a good idea to burn the House of Blue Lights because the place was a creep joint, but I just couldn't buy it. I didn't like the Blue Lights, because I'd spent a supremely depressing evening there once, but that was no excuse for going after Chrome. Actually I halfway assumed we were going to die in the attempt. Even with that killer program, the odds weren't exactly in our favor.

Bobby was lost in writing the set of commands we were going to plug into the dead center of Chrome's computer. That was going to be my job, because Bobby was going to have his hands full trying to keep the Russian program from going straight for the kill. It was too complex for us to rewrite, and so he was going to try to hold it back for the two seconds I needed.

I made a deal with a streetfighter named Miles. He was going to follow Rikki the night of the burn, keep her in sight, and phone me at a certain time. If I wasn't there, or didn't answer in just a certain way, I'd told him to grab her and put her on the first tube out. I gave him an envelope to give her, money and a note.

Bobby really hadn't thought about that, much, how things would go for her if we blew it. He just kept telling me he loved her, where they were going to go together, how they'd spend the money.

"Buy her a pair of Ikons first, man. That's what she wants. She's serious about that simstim scene."

"Hey," he said, looking up from the keyboard, "she won't need to work. We're going to make it, Jack. She's my luck. She won't ever have to work again."

"Your luck," I said. I wasn't happy. I couldn't remember when I had been happy. "You seen your luck around lately?"

He hadn't, but neither had I. We'd both been too busy.

I missed her. Missing her reminded me of my one night in the House of Blue Lights, because I'd gone there out of missing someone else. I'd gotten drunk to begin with, then I'd started hitting Vasopressin inhalers. If your main squeeze has just decided to walk out on you, booze and Vasopressin are the ultimate in masochistic pharmacology; the juice makes you maudlin and the Vasopressin makes you remember, I mean really remember. Clinically they use the stuff to counter senile amnesia, but the street finds its own uses for things. So I'd bought myself an ultraintense replay of a bad affair; trouble is, you get the bad with the good. Go gunning for transports of animal ecstasy and you get what you said, too, and what she said to that, how she walked away and never looked back.

I don't remember deciding to go to the Blue Lights, or how I got there, hushed corridors and this really tacky decorative waterfall trickling somewhere, or maybe just a hologram of one. I had a lot of money that night; somebody had given Bobby a big roll for opening a three-second window in someone else's ice.

I don't think the crew on the door liked my looks, but I guess my money was okay.

I had more to drink there when I'd done what I went there for. Then I made some crack to the barman about closet necrophiliacs, and that didn't go down too well. Then this very large character insisted on calling me War Hero, which I didn't like. I think I showed him some tricks with the arm, before the lights went out, and I woke up two days later in a basic sleeping module somewhere else. A cheap place, not

even room to hang yourself. And I sat there on that narrow
foam slab and cried.

Some things are worse than being alone. But the thing
they sell in the House of Blue Lights is so popular that it's
almost legal.

At the heart of darkness, the still center, the glitch systems
shred the dark with whirlwinds of light, translucent razors
spinning away from us; we hang in the center of a silent
slow-motion explosion, ice fragments falling away forever,
and Bobby's voice comes in across light-years of electronic
void illusion—

"Burn the bitch down. I can't hold the thing back—"

The Russian program, rising through towers of data,
blotting out the playroom colors. And I plug Bobby's
homemade command package into the center of Chrome's
cold heart. The squirt transmission cuts in, a pulse of
condensed information that shoots straight up, past the
thickening tower of darkness, the Russian program, while
Bobby struggles to control that crucial second. An unformed
arm of shadow twitches from the towering dark, too late.

We've done it.

The matrix folds itself around me like an origami trick.

And the loft smells of sweat and burning circuitry.

I thought I heard Chrome scream, a raw metal sound, but
I couldn't have.

Bobby was laughing, tears in his eyes. The elapsed-time
figure in the corner of the monitor read 07:24:05. The burn
had taken a little under eight minutes.

And I saw that the Russian program had melted in its slot.

We'd given the bulk of Chrome's Zürich account to a
dozen world charities. There was too much there to move,
and we knew we had to break her, burn her straight down,
or she might come after us. We took less than ten percent for
ourselves and shot it through the Long Hum setup in Macao.
They took sixty percent of that for themselves and kicked
what was left back to us through the most convoluted sector
of the Hong Kong exchange. It took an hour before our

money started to reach the two accounts we'd opened in Zürich.

I watched zeros pile up behind a meaningless figure on the monitor. I was rich.

Then the phone rang. It was Miles. I almost blew the code phrase.

"Hey, Jack, man, I dunno—what's it all about, with this girl of yours? Kinda funny thing here . . ."

"What? Tell me."

"I been on her, like you said, tight but out of sight. She goes to the Loser, hangs out, then she gets a tube. Goes to the House of Blue Lights—"

"She what?"

"Side door. *Employees* only. No way I could get past their security."

"Is she there now?"

"No, man, I just lost her. It's insane down here, like the Blue Lights just shut down, looks like for good, seven kinds of alarms going off, everybody running, the heat out in riot gear. . . . Now there's this stuff going on, insurance guys, real-estate types, vans with municipal plates. . . ."

"Miles, where'd she go?"

"Lost her, Jack."

"Look, Miles, you keep the money in the envelope, right?"

"You serious? Hey, I'm real sorry. I—"

I hung up.

"Wait'll we tell her," Bobby was saying, rubbing a towel across his bare chest.

"You tell her yourself, cowboy. I'm going for a walk."

So I went out into the night and the neon and let the crowd pull me along, walking blind, willing myself to be just a segment of that mass organism, just one more drifting chip of consciousness under the geodesics. I didn't think, just put one foot in front of another, but after a while I did think, and it all made sense. She'd needed the money.

I thought about Chrome, too. That we'd killed her, murdered her, as surely as if we'd slit her throat. The night that carried me along through the malls and plazas would be hunting her now, and she had nowhere to go. How many enemies would she have in this crowd alone? How many would move, now they weren't held back by fear of her money? We'd taken her for everything she had. She was back on the street again. I doubted she'd live till dawn.

Finally I remembered the café, the one where I'd met Tiger.

Her sunglasses told the whole story, huge black shades with a telltale smudge of fleshtone paintstick in the corner of one lens. "Hi, Rikki," I said, and I was ready when she took them off.

Blue. Tally Isham blue. The clear trademark blue they're famous for, ZEISS IKON ringing each iris in tiny capitals, the letters suspended there like flecks of gold.

"They're beautiful," I said. Paintstick covered the bruising. No scars with work that good. "You made some money."

"Yeah, I did." Then she shivered. "But I won't make any more, not that way."

"I think that place is out of business."

"Oh." Nothing moved in her face then. The new blue eyes were still and very deep.

"It doesn't matter. Bobby's waiting for you. We just pulled down a big score."

"No. I've got to go. I guess he won't understand, but I've got to go."

I nodded, watching the arm swing up to take her hand; it didn't seem to be part of me at all, but she held on to it like it was.

"I've got a one-way ticket to Hollywood. Tiger knows some people I can stay with. Maybe I'll even get to Chiba City."

She was right about Bobby. I went back with her. He didn't understand. But she'd already served her purpose, for Bobby, and I wanted to tell her not to hurt for him, because I could see that she did. He wouldn't even come out into the hallway after she had packed her bags. I put the bags down and kissed her and messed up the paintstick, and something came up inside me the way the killer program had risen above Chrome's data. A sudden stopping of the breath, in a place where no word is. But she had a plane to catch.

Bobby was slumped in the swivel chair in front of his monitor, looking at his string of zeros. He had his shades on, and I knew he'd be in the Gentleman Loser by nightfall, checking out the weather, anxious for a sign, someone to tell him what his new life would be like. I couldn't see it being very different. More comfortable, but he'd always be waiting for that next card to fall.

I tried not to imagine her in the House of Blue Lights, working three-hour shifts in an approximation of REM sleep, while her body and a bundle of conditioned reflexes took care of business. The customers never got to complain that she was faking it, because those were real orgasms. But she felt them, if she felt them at all, as faint silver flares somewhere out on the edge of sleep. Yeah, it's so popular, it's almost legal. The customers are torn between needing someone and wanting to be alone at the same time, which has probably always been the name of that particular game, even before we had the neuroelectronics to enable them to have it both ways.

I picked up the phone and punched the number for her airline. I gave them her real name, her flight number. "She's changing that," I said, "to Chiba City. That's right. Japan." I thumbed my credit card into the slot and punched my ID code. "First class." Distant hum as they scanned my credit records. "Make that a return ticket."

But I guess she cashed the return fare, or else she didn't need it, because she hasn't come back. And sometimes late at night I'll pass a window with posters of simstim stars, all those beautiful, identical eyes staring back at me out of faces that are nearly as identical, and sometimes the eyes are hers, but none of them ever are, and I see her far out on the edge of all this sprawl of night and cities, and then she waves goodbye.

SPIRIT OF THE NIGHT

Tom Maddox

Here's a fast-paced tale of romance and high-tech intrigue that shows that a hacker is at his most dangerous when he has nothing to lose. . . .

Born in Beckley, West Virginia, Tom Maddox now lives with his family in Olympia, Washington. Although he has sold only a handful of stories to date, primarily to Omni *and* Issac Asimov's Science Fiction Magazine, *he has been thought of from the beginning of his career as a figure of some note in the "cyberpunk" movement, and scored a major success in 1991 with the publication of his well-received first novel,* Halo. *He is currently at work on a new novel.*

W*e dropped out* of bright sunshine into gray fog and rough air. Two rows in front of us a woman said that EuroWeather was forecasting a beautiful May Day for Paris. Carol squeezed my arm, hard.

"We'll be there," I said. "Tomorrow."

Carol turned to me, smiling. Harsh interior lights showed lines in her face and gray streaks in her hair, but at the age of forty and after ten years of very close quarters, she still knocked sparks off me like steel off flint. I leaned over and kissed her neck just below the line of her jaw.

The plane slewed sideways, we broke through low clouds, and green Virginia countryside showed briefly before we touched lightly onto wet tarmac.

One of the airport's mutant reptile buses wheeled out to meet us, then felt with blind stalks for the side of the plane. Five minutes later we all filed aboard, and it rolled us through a gray gothic dream. There should have been trolls and dwarves riding the service vehicles, waving phosphorescent wands to guide us in. Instead there were the orange-suited workers in their yellow earmuffs and the somber geometry of the Saarinen terminal sitting half-hidden in the fog.

Shoulder harness in place, I read as Carol drove the rented Buick as though it were a GT Porsche, taking it across the three lanes of the Beltway and slotting it into a space that didn't seem to be there.

Charley Kelly's summary of our client's recent history didn't really tell me much Charley himself hadn't on the phone. Moshe Bergman had quit BioTron, one of your major multinationals, in a sort of high-tech huff after his work on biocomputers had been ignored, then scorned—there had even been talk of his having cooked crucial experiments. Now the irate Dr. Bergman was looking for investment capital to develop his process, which had all sorts of weird and profitable potential: eyes for the blind, brain implants, artificial intelligence.

That's where Econtel, Inc.—Carol and I—came in. Tipped by Charley Kelly, who heard about Bergman through a friend at BioTron, we had contacted Bergman and were ready to present him with an investment package. Our cut would be from five to ten points, depending on the extent of our involvement.

We were delaying a Parisian vacation for twenty-four hours to take care of this little piece of business. Then we had reservations on the Air France SST and plans to drive through Bordeaux in a rented BMW Electro.

"You're not going to believe this," I said. Carol was busy edging out a guy in a maroon Saab next to us who wanted to get off at the Key Bridge. "According to Charley, Bergman's hired himself a bodyguard."

"Whatever for?"

"Thinks BioTron is out to get him."

"Certainly—employing telepathic dogs, no doubt, to steal his valuable processes. Christ, I hope he is not a scientist nutter."

"Kelly says he's mildly eccentric, is all. Anyway, Charley's arranged for us to meet the bodyguard, who will answer all our questions. Ex-CIA, Charley says. Might be interesting."

"You can talk to the cowboy, I'll catch up on some sleep."

We checked into the new Hyatt in Alexandria—near National Airport and the shuttle to Kennedy, where we would catch the SST. The room had pink linen walls and bright Matisse prints; teak Scandinavian dresser, desk, table, chairs, and platform bed. I left Carol in the shower.

I hate driving, so I took the Metro to Silver Spring where I was to meet Bergman's bodyguard, a man named Oakley. He and Bergman were staying at a rooming house nearby.

We met at the Chesapeake Bay Crab Bucket. Just by the Georgia Avenue Metro, it featured yellow Formica and fly-speckled mirrors, and you probably wouldn't want a real close look at the kitchen, but the crab cakes were fine, and so was the Rolling Rock beer.

Oakley, on the other hand, seemed to be about ninety-nine percent pure neurotoxin. He made a point of letting me see his pistol, a "hot sight" Colt .357 he told me, almost as soon as we sat down. "Good weapon for this kind of work," he said, holding open his coat to flash the knurled butt end of the Colt.

He was in his middle fifties, a big man with rough skin, thick wrists and jet-black hair which had to have come from a bottle. He said he had retired from "the Company" two years ago but still trained attack dogs for them at a kennel in Falls Church. "Those suckers have got to be brutal," he said. "So you get them big, man, and you hurt them. Pick one up over your head and drop the son of a bitch on the ground. Lay him out good so's he can't breathe. Do it a few times and he knows who's in charge. Get him to do anything. And they do good work, man." He sucked on a Winston and looked at me with intent black eyes. "If Ramos had let me put the dogs in the dining room like I wanted to, they'd never have gotten to him."

I cut short his loving memory of his years with Alejandro Ramos. Other than admiring the sheer horror of it, I wasn't much interested in his Company scrapbook. I wanted to know about Bergman. I said, "What's happening here, Oakley? Is Bergman involved in some kind of corporate spy crap?"

"I don't know, man. The guy's a wimp, and when I met him, he was scared bad, so I figured I could make some easy change by stringing him along a ways. But that's not how it went. His condo out in Rockville was solid jammed with voice bugs. So I moved his ass out of there."

I put some cash on the table and said, "We're just businessmen, you know, trying to make a few bucks . . . think of us as pilot fish here in the water with the big corporate sharks. We do *not*, absolutely do not, fuck around with them."

"Look, I ain't telling you your business, but there's been nothing since I moved him. *Perfectamente nada*. So I figure I just flushed some old bugs—I'm sure BioTron runs routine surveillance on high-level employees. I really don't think anything's happening, man."

"Okay, we'll try it a little bit, just a taste. But if you find out any different—like something funny is going down— you come tell me, and *I'll* pay your fee. My wife and I, we're just not into killer dogs in the dining room, you know what I mean?"

"Sure, man, I'll let you know. But I don't think you have to worry. I've been running all the tricks, just to keep busy, and nobody's there. Believe me. . . ."

Carol was asleep when I got back to the room. I showered and crawled into bed beside her. In the curtained twilight I curled against her back. "Umm," she said and pressed against me. "What did you find out?" she asked.

She was awake now, so we discussed Bergman's problems. We agreed to go quick and dirty, to get the package out on the wire tonight if possible. Ordinarily we'd have spent at least a few days waltzing a client and lining up the most likely investors, but not this time. "I'll finish up the prospectus," she said.

She sat at the round teak table, face bright against the

gray sky, peach nightgown glowing under a hanging cylinder of chrome. While I settled in for a nap, she worked our hopped-up computer, a SenTrax Optix, and put the final touches on Bergman's package.

Some time later she crawled into bed next to me.

We were both beginning our final semester in graduate school at UCLA when we met. She was getting an M.B.A., and I was finally picking up the M.S. in Telecommunications that I had started five years before. Early marriages along the way had gone sour for both of us. No children.

We told each other these things and a lot else at the party in Santa Monica where we met. At the time she favored black sheath dresses and bright red nails, plastic talons two inches long which cut holes in the air as she talked. Simple, mean, and fetishistic—she punched all my buttons anyway. My knees shook when she leaned close.

Through that whole spring we talked. We walked among the trim green lawns and bright flowers of Westwood, where Japanese gardeners with an angel's touch groomed the property of the middle classes. Our previous plans—Data General for me, Bank of America for Carol—shrank to nothing.

Databanks, genetic tailoring, the Japanese space program, optical computers, weather satellites, the commodities markets—we talked of these things, and Carol sketched a possible world in the air with red nails.

After graduation we got a place in the Fairfax District, among the delis, kosher groceries, and Hebrew language newspapers. We started Econtel, Inc. in our living room and ran it there for the next few years—surfing the Third Wave, you might say, with an audience of bearded Hassidic Jews.

Later we moved to Berkeley and bought a two-story brown shingle that cost one hell of a lot more than I'd ever figured myself paying for a house or anything else.

I felt her gown sliding between us as she pulled it over her head, and there was the familiar hot light touch of her breasts against my skin.

• • •

Around ten o'clock Oakley showed up with Bergman, who turned out to be a tall, skinny fellow in a cheap suit and the kind of nasal New York accent that cuts to the bone.

He seemed content with the deal we presented. A fat budget for his lab to operate for a year if necessary—Charley had said, "By then, he's either cracked it or gone bust." Forty-nine percent of patent monies to his backer, forty-five to him, five to Econtel, one to Kelly.

A bit of chitchat, then everybody's signatures and thumb-prints went on the contracts. I set up the SenTrax and began by tapping into BIONET, the news service subscribed to by anyone interested in commercial bioscience. Potential investors might not be on it, but their scouts would be. An outline of the process, computer projections for the lab work, references to the NIH and Patent Office files—all were made available along with a financial summary.

The next few hours are frozen in my memory—the four of us blithe in the champagne glow that comes from putting a project out on the network, never mind that we weren't likely to hear anything for weeks. Bergman was being courtly in an awkward way with Carol, who was all dark blue silk and French perfume, and even Oakley seemed relaxed.

Then Oakley said he wanted to get some more equipment from the car; he'd checked the phone for taps but thought he'd sweep the room as well—I think we all smiled at this. "I'll go with you," I said. "I need to call a client—should have done it before we tied up the phone lines." Carol was talking to Bergman, and as I left she gave me a wink and a smile.

The glass-sided elevator dropped twenty stories down the side of the building. Oakley jittered with tension next to me—poor bastard, I thought, not happy unless in the grip of operational paranoia. Interior doors slid back, and we went out, Oakley right toward the parking lot, me left into the lobby.

In a pay booth in the deserted lobby—it was close to two in the morning—I spent half an hour explaining to F. L.

Daugherty—a metal-rich eccentric who lived in Boise, Idaho, where it was only eleven—that even blue-chips could take a turn for the worse.

I was alone in the elevator going back. Street lights made small jewels in the mist on the glass. Across the Potomac, the Washington Monument winked to drive airplanes away, the Jefferson Memorial sat bathed in floodlights. I thought that we had done fine—none of the maddening complexities that can turn a simple proposition into a long-term puzzle, just a quick hit and on to Paris. I could almost smell the buttery pastries and dark coffee. . . .

When I began to step into the hallway, there was Oakley in a crouch, his back to me, both hands extended in front of him holding the Colt .357. "What the hell is going on?" I asked, and he said, "They're snatching Bergman and your wife. Stay in the elevator—get the fuck out of here." The Colt jumped in his hand and made one of the loudest noises I've ever heard.

The doors slid closed, and I pressed *G* and descended to the ground floor, ears ringing.

When the doors opened, I sprinted across the lobby and out to the parking lot, where I stood watching the elevator go back up to the twentieth floor.

It was all so far away. I could just see an indistinct shape, someone in the elevator, then crazywork cracks spread over the glass, and the box began its quick trip down the side of the building. As it got lower, I saw that the glass was splashed with red. I ran back into the lobby.

Oakley lay with his back against the outside wall, bleeding from arm and face and torso. His pistol barrel pointed at me, then drooped. "Oh Jesus Christ," I said. The elevator smelled of burned gunpowder and was splashed with bright fresh blood.

"Go man," he said. "Now. They got them both."

"I'll call an ambulance and the police."

"No! Go away now. No police, or maybe your wife and Bergman are dead. Call 911, you want, tell them a shooting, but mostly get the fuck out of here."

The Metro station fifty yards away had closed, so I just

kept running. I passed under an overpass and turned left, ran
up a flight of cement stairs and stopped in front of the sign
that said *Amtrak*.

The station seemed centuries old, with its painted slat
seats and wood and plaster walls. Half a dozen people
wandered around the platform outside, and a young girl—
maybe twenty, sullen and pale, wrapped in a dark blue
cape—sat on one of the benches.

Three pay phones were against the wall—no privacy
booths. I dialed 911, then whispered, "There's been a
shooting—lobby of the Alexandria Hyatt." I listened long
enough to make sure the operator had heard me, then hung up
on his agitated questions.

One concession to the information age—a dark train
board with red LEDs gave station stops and showed the
southbound Miami Express was right on time—in half an
hour or so it would come into Alexandria. Behind an iron-
barred window, a dark-haired clerk asked if he could help
me. He was very cheerful. "Charlotte, North Carolina," I
read off the list of stops. I had to tell him something. I paid
the fare in cash.

I stood in the fog and drizzle about a hundred yards up the
platform, waiting for the train. Across the street, on a hill
that loomed above the station, a tall, spired building, lit up
by huge floodlights, stood foreshortened, grotesque . . .
mausoleum, civic building, some sort of pointless lodge or
temple. Soon a bright glow swished back and forth across
the tracks, and a slow-moving train fronted by three diesel
engines pulled in.

"To your left," the woman in red Amtrak uniform said when
I showed her my ticket. "Watch your step."

Soon after the train pulled out, I blanked. Sitting in a nearly
empty couch, I stared at a "Dining Car Other Direction"
sign at the end of the car and fell into a trance that I didn't
come out of until the train began to slow as it pulled into the
station at Richmond, Virginia a little after four A.M.

I got up and went into the vestibule between cars. A
few people waved from the bright platform as the train

pulled away. Rain spit against the glass . . . as it had the elevator . . . oh god, I thought, no—

The train had been moving quickly between opposite-moving lanes of a highway, but it slowed . . . I could see office buildings peeking over the top of an embankment. I pulled the release handle that freed the opening mechanism and cranked the door open, the steps out and down. I jumped out into the night.

Some more time got lost in there. I remember walking along the tracks in the narrow strip formed by double link fences, coming to where a trestle soared high over rocks and black water, then climbing the high link fence, and I remember a group of young black men standing in front of an all-night grocery who watched with predators' attention as I passed. Nothing else.

When the sun rose, I was standing on a street corner in front of a hologram arcade. A sign in the window read:

BEAT THE DEVIL
BOGART IN FULL HOLO!
SEE THE MOVIE—PLAY THE GAME!

The rain had stopped at some point, so I was merely damp and wrinkled. Still I waved at two cabs before one stopped, and then the old black man in the driver's seat was wary—he kept his window closed and yelled, "Where you going?"

"Airport."

"Needs to see me some money, ace."

I held up my wallet and spread it to show him credit cards and bills. He was to end up with a fifty dollar tip, my thanks for his buying my ticket to San Francisco on the 7:15 non-stop.

It was late morning when we got into SFO, and I dithered. I had to go home—not for clothes and comfort but for some things I really needed, for means to strike back. I took a shuttle bus into the city, then the BART train to Berkeley, where without thinking I got off at the Claremont Station and went down the steps to College Avenue.

And ended up in front of the Hardtack Coffee House. I

stepped through the dark glass door. Smells of coffee and tobacco smoke and an atmosphere not of day or night. Name your game: chess, go, backgammon, checkers, simulator, cini-max. Behind a nondescript white-painted stucco front, there was a huge room with square tables of dark wood, tops charred by decades of frenzied smokers, among them some of the best games players in Berkeley, some of the best in the world.

It was a trip into my past. Back when I was a silicon kid, one of the few places we could find people—in the flesh, that is—was the Hardtack. I must have been thirteen when I first discovered the hackers, phone phreaks, network bandits, all the computer cowboys living in the optic fibers, wave guides, old-fashioned copper wires. I tapped into HUMAN HEADZ, the most accessible of the underground networks, and began to meet them one by one. The Zork, from New Jersey, who would stack up long-distance tandems around the globe just to listen to his own voice echoing through the night. E-Muff, from Berkeley, a consistent thorn in the side of the U.C. Computer Police. U-3 Kiddo, a group from Portland who planned free gas and electricity for one month for all Bonneville Power Authority customers—power to the people.

Through them I was admitted to the inner circles and the gossip, rumor, and mad delusion that passed in the midnight hours. The Princess and Ozmo and Dwarf had gotten married over the net but had sworn never to meet in person—it was a purely spiritual connection that gave total intimacy through the wires. Frostie had disappeared in Paris, taken away by Interpol, and would never be heard from again. Bright Water the Hiroshima-Nagasaki group, had sworn vendetta against Boeing because their B-29s had dropped the bombs. Captain Muck had broken into a C^3 system at Omaha and planned to launch a first strike if he didn't—finally—get laid.

It was the heaviest fantasy trip going, until the Federal anti-hacking laws went into effect. Then it turned into something a little too heavy. Anyway the social dynamic had shifted, as another crop of adolescents discovered its own strange pleasures.

But for some the pirate life remained a lifelong obsession. Captain Crunch III, Blind Lemon—also known as The Whistling Kid—and Rolly the Deuce were among the perfect masters, silicon *sensei*, masters of solid-state zen.

Now I was looking for Rolly the Deuce, my one-time personal master, who had taught me some of the more arcane tricks and stood by when I tested them by accessing the FBI's Most Secret files. "Good work," he told me then, "but you won't stay with it." And he was right. By the time I went to college, I was pretty much out of it. I lacked the pure lunar drive that powered the great bandits.

We hadn't exactly stayed in touch. Rolly communicated in his own ways. A few Christmas Eves at the last stroke of midnight, the computer played "Jingle Bell Rock," and once, when Carol and I were printing out some stock figures from the Dow Jones, we got a page blank except for the message, "You're under arrest—violation of the International Meep Statutes. Glad to see you're in the money, but your bank's got lousy security. Love, Rolly."

Anyway, Jesse Woods, who had stayed in touch with Rolly, was playing speed chess with a well-dressed young guy, might have been a chump, might have been a pupil. There was a *beep* as the kid's hand punched the chrome button on top of his clock, an almost simultaneous *beep* as Jesse punched his. "Shit," the kid said, and he was almost out of his chair with tension, searching the board for a move as his right hand hovered over it, the same one he'd have to punch the clock with.

Beep beep beep beep and a bright red light flashed on the kid's clock. The kid slumped in his chair, then said, "I almost had an attack going," and he began setting up pieces. "Can we do it again?"

"No," Jesse said. "I've got a friend waiting."

Dull red snakes of hair dirty like the rest of him, fingernail on the littler finger of his left hand curving into a spiral, nose beaked and thin enough to be from a party

kit—Jesse was as usual a paragon of bizarre appearance, a
sight to scare prospective parents with.

I said, "You seen Rolly?"

"A little man. He's fucked up these days, you know?"

"What do you mean?"

"Sort of, I don't know, left behind."

"That's all right, Jesse. I need to see him. Where can I
call?"

"Nobody's got any of his numbers. He's hiding out, I
guess you'd call it. Thinks the FBI is on his case."

"Are they?"

"What do you think, man? That shit's all yesterday's
paper."

"So how do I find him?"

"He's in Oakland—" And he gave me directions.

"Good. Look, Jesse, you want to make some quick cash?
I need a few things picked up from home, and I can't do it
myself."

I had agreed to meet Jesse at Cody's Books on Telegraph
Avenue. He loved the idea of an anonymous transfer of the
plastic sheath of mini-CDs and the book-thick SenTrax Tele
that he had picked up for me at home. Jesse stuck his bundle
into one of the wooden slots at the front of the bookstore, and
I picked it up a few minutes later.

I walked out of Cody's figuring I had some time to kill.
There was no point in trying to get Rolly the Deuce until
after dark, not if I wanted him functioning at peak form.
He'd have been up all night, ghost dancing in the wires. So
I walked toward the campus and along the Avenue, where
the sidewalks were crowded with tourists and the multitude
of street sellers hustling them.

I stopped at an All-Bank Booth to pull all my and Carol's
liquid funds. I didn't know what was likely to happen next,
but I figured I might need chunks of money. The voucher
spilled out of the slot—when I put my signature and
thumbprint on it, it would turn into a very high denomina-
tion dollar bill. I noticed that it was made out to me

only—Carol's name wasn't on it. Her name wasn't on the account receipt either.

Why was that?

Inside the blanked silence of a street-side phone booth, I plugged in the old SenTrax Tele, long-time hackers' favorite. I ran a program that snagged and ghosted a raw tandem. Now I could call anyone I wanted, and the call would appear to originate through the AmerEx Trouble Line.

CREDITERM was my first call. Using my portable comp and a couple of sweet little utility programs, I accessed their credit records, the sacred books of plastic money. I asked for a read-out on Carol. **NEG REC/REQUERY?** Bullshit. Something peculiar *was* happening. I did it again. **NEG REC/RECONFIRM ID.**

Then I went to the NDB, the National Data Bank, where every citizen is caught in lines of electromagnetic force. Ran Carol's name again—first alpha access, which any inquisitive bureaucracy has its command, then the beta codes, which dig deep to pull up a mass of unverified, undigested garbage. **NO REF** *repeat* **NO REF READDRESS SOC SEC**.

Something ugly came into view then. Just a small dot on the screen, but getting larger—

So I ran the same trip on Bergman. **NO REF** *repeat* **NO REF.**

Negative evidence they call it, the dog that doesn't bark in the night. Great, but evidence of what?

Crowds surged around me on Telegraph Avenue, which was enjoying a resurgence of trade and popularity—nostalgia had taken hold for the twentieth century in general, the "gentle decade" of the 60s in particular. Flower children and all that, never mind the, uh, *war* that had been going on. Bright sunshine, blue sky, the hot hum of money changing hands. . . .

There I stood, and for the first time I got the feeling that Carol had gone much farther away than I had guessed. Fundamental law of our times: To exist is to be transformed into information, to have NDB files, credit ratings, to be significant data in the computers of banks, police. Corollary: To have no such files—

What kind of crazy-assed game was BioTron playing?

Rolly lived deep in Oakland, in the kind of neighborhood where people clear the street after dark so they don't interfere with the nighttime's quick and violent business. Here, if I saw a group of young men—black, white, yellow, or brown—looking me over, I'd run *now* and hope I had enough of a head start.

I buzzed Rolly's apartment, and he looked me over through the vidscreen and told me to come up. This was a climb through the usual sleazy stairways, past litter, peeling walls, bare bulbs. Rolly had always remained pretty much oblivious to his immediate surroundings; his real life was out in the networks.

When he opened the door, I stepped into a combination of Condo Grosso and Teletronics Heaven. Consoles and bubble boxes in tottering stacks, a bank of flatscreens, snarls of optic fiber and cable, inverted plastic boxes of connectors—all of it junk, kipple, the spill-off from Rolly's constant restructuring of his system, which would be behind a steel door in another room.

Jah rockers danced across the wall; the room reverberated with their slack-string bass and syntho-drums. Scattered around were stacks of empty pizza boxes, piles of tamale wrappers, beer cans, filled ashtrays, dirty clothes. Streamers of print-out were tacked to two walls. Brave New Silicon World.

He looked just as he did the last time I saw him—thinning hair plastered to his white skull, sallow skin, a roll of fat around his middle. The All-American boy, my friend Rolly.

I walked to the control console and punched off the Jah rockers. "Got to talk, Rolly," I said.

It all came out, and he just stood there, his eyes wide as he listened to the story of blood and pain that he knew—that all of us know—is out there, happening to somebody in the night.

"Man," he said. "Carol . . . I'm sorry."

And that's when I cried a little for the first time. I sat in an old chair and hammered on its stuffed arms and shook with sobs and yelled—

Then I told him *damage*. I wanted to be able to take it to the limit, and quickly, like piranha on a baby goat.

"I'm slack, man," he said, "slack—no chops."

That was bullshit, and he knew it. "I want to hammer these bastards, man," I said. He paced the floor, kicked empty boxes, dithered. Then he began to think about *how to do it*. "I brought my best shit, Rolly," I said, and waved the plastic sheaf of CDs. I had him.

One side of the room was filled with tented plastic—a clean room—where Rolly sat like a man with a congenital immune deficiency or a caterpillar in its chrysalis. In front of him were the flat silver rectangles of viewscreens; behind them, bare processor chips, small dark blocks on legs of fine golden filament. To one side were processor and bubble boxes, traditional cubes of multi-hued red, next to chrome-armed chip burners and flat black wave guide boxes. Connecting all were knots of flesh-toned cable and strands of optic fiber sheathed in carnival colors. Inside the clean room the whole multiplexed electronic package could lie open like an autopsied corpse.

He worked through the night, with me providing occasional suggestions and doing the routine work, the stuff that didn't require Rolly's level of cunning and artistry. He sweated, and his face was red; he played his keyboards like a virtuoso and kept his modems alive most of the night as he called in favors from all over the country.

Lethe, a seventeen-year-old girl from Long Island, had a sweet set of monetary transfer access and com codes. Johnny Too Bad in Austin had played games with the Stock Exchange and had worked out a very slick series of burns. Anon-Al, a translator at Fort Meade for NSA, had the real prize—a piece of killer software cooked by some Agency hotshots to demonstrate how any databank could be turned to hash. It should work once on just about anything. Or on everything. He hit these fellow souls within the first two hours, and from there it rolled

I sat much of the night back in the front room, sitting in the old stuffed corduroy chair, pulling stuffing out of a tear and thinking. I kept returning to what the silicon kids called a "K-9 anomaly"—a program doing things it was never intended to do and shouldn't be capable of. A werewolf program.

For instance: BioTron could have nailed us at the Hyatt (no problem there, as we were using standard industrial encryption and unscrambled lines), and they *might* have been able to remove Carol from our checking accounts, but they *couldn't* have pulled Carol and Bergman from CREDITERM and the NDB—no way. Negative evidence all right, of the impossible.

I thought, screw it. No accounting for the weirdness of The Real.

Early the next morning we had located BioTron's heaviest clandestine hitter, the guy who would have ultimate control of any operation like this one. Using programs out of a switch-and-dummy box hooked to a local switchboard in Buenos Aires so that a backchase was impossible, we addressed a message to T. Edward Shales, BioTron's counter-intelligence chief without portfolio.

Our message was pretty simple: let's deal; if you don't want to, we've got some bad economic news for you. Have a look at LiveSoft Projects, we told him; its stock will have *disappeared*, and it's going to cost someone a hell of trouble to bring it back. Then think about the implications.

We got the usual "don't know what you're talking about, never heard of such terrible happenings" reply within an hour. Rolly skimmed it off the B.A. dummy, and we both had a sour laugh.

Then we waited for hell to freeze.

By nine o'clock that night brimstone had turned to solid ice, and we both were ready to collapse.

Finally, BioTron's reply. On the tape, T. Edward Shales himself—heavy and solid and anonymous—sat in dark-suited splendor and said, "I believe you got a problem, really I do. But we are not it. I did not authorize the incursion you describe, and I can categorically state that no one else in this corporation did. In short, you have got some disinformation here somewhere.

"Dr. Moshe Bergman was an employee of ours, but his period of postresignation surveillance showed nothing important. We are also aware of the man Oakley, who as you say has been shot—his short-term future appears uncertain, according to the George Washington University Hospital computer.

"Frankly, however, we thought Bergman was of no further concern to us. Now, however, we do have an interest in this affair. Should you wish our assistance, we can perhaps negotiate terms. We would be particularly interested in quick restoration of LiveSoft's portfolio."

That tape hurt me. Remember, putting the crush on BioTron was all I had, and I saw that I couldn't. They were ignoring me; despite what we had showed them, we appeared to have no leverage. I said, "Rolly, I want to do it tonight. I want to hit them like we planned."

"No, man. It's like uh . . . shit . . . nuclear deterrence. Like, when you've got to use it, man, then shit—" Like many silicon kids, Rolly had an uncertain grip on words—Carol said they were people who had no native language.

It came to me all at once then, and I don't know whether I believed it or not. But I had to have him, I couldn't do this myself.

So here's what I told Rolly, and you've got to understand, I was driven by my need and dancing in the dark. I worked with questions like these: What if I was right the first time, and BioTron *couldn't* have done these things? What then if T. Edward Shales wasn't lying?

I told Rolly that we had hold of something strange, not BioTron but the spirit of our times, the living essence of the information age. We are its senses, the datanets its nervous system and memory, all the interchange among systems its consciousness. Not a werewolf program, but Gaia in silicon, born of wire and electromagnetic wave—new life, new being.

"Do you really believe that?" he asked. I had shaken him,

he was seeing the descent of some testing angel into the dark night of his soul.

And I did for a moment, nodding, as I reached to him out of my absolute need and said, "It's all that makes sense." The datanets were the key, I said. Gaia must have been brought into being by the saturation of the planet with information, and the nets are the loci. I said that INFINET was crucial, and its creation was the point of transformation, the birth of Gaia. So that's where we would go after it.

I told Rolly I was going to use Gaia's senses, its nervous system and memory, against it.

Early the next morning I was back in the nether world I had first discovered as an adolescent, where space, time, and identity are blurred, "real time" is just a choice among others, and what really matters is the flexible, multi-dimensional spacetime of the networks.

Using BART, I covered the Bay Area. From one station to another I would go, then out to find a pay phone. Pop the phone receiver into the computer's blue-green modem, a silver disk into the computer. RUN the programs, disconnect, go.

I was sowing choas. Gaia couldn't tell good data from bad, so the programs I fed into it were just the usual stuff of its perceptions.

Banque Nationale de Paris and Credit Lyonnais, Bayerische Vereinsbank and Deutsche Bank, Frankfurt, Barclays and National Westminster Bank, Citibank and Bank of America, Union Bank of Switzerland, Dai-Ichi Kangyo Bank of Tokyo, Hongkong and Shanghai Banking Corporation—I forget how many others, but I was forming the heaviest conglomerate that ever hit the markets and exchanges to make some heavyweight purchases: BASF Aktiengesellschaft, Chiyoda Chemical, Dupont, ICI, Standard Oil of New Jersey, Sony Corporation, and BioTron itself, oh yes . . . run the programs, promise payment in cash, stock, options. Stocks, futures, currency, you bet. We made pretty good efforts to corner the silver market—the Hunt brothers would have been envious—pork belly and potato futures. . . .

Some purchases and manipulations would go through, some wouldn't. And pretty soon someone was going to figure out that there was some strange and illegal action taking place. Confusion—markets scrambled, stocks, futures, and currencies in disarray. At one level, just another tender of our bona fides, a promise to Gaia—we can touch you; at another level, *diversions*.

I was really after INFINET, the network of networks, but I couldn't hit it straight on. It was too well defended without more lead time than I'd had. But some of the older auxiliaries did just fine. We got in.

INFINET had programs which allowed it to read from and write to everything that was in its member networks, which included about every civilian network in the world, along with the low-to-medium parts of military networks such as ARPANET. I was planting into INFINET that lovely hostile software that NSA had created.

If it's triggered, INFINET and the member networks will disappear in the world's biggest information crash. The only uncertainty regards the military nets—how good are their countermeasures? Well, we may find out.

All night long we had put the programs together, and now I planted them. READ, WRITE, LIST, ERASE—one instruction's just like another to a computer. Garbage in, pal, garbage in.

Remember those tapes—we've all seen them—of buildings getting torn down? Silence and slow motion is the way I like to see it happen, masonry and invisible iron frame looming high and still, then disintegrating and dropping straight into itself, turning into no more than a pile of rubble where a building used to stand, just something for the dump trucks to carry away.

Doesn't matter how big the building is, or how strong. You just find the right spots and plant your charges. . . .

So I planted my charges, then went home.

I took the house computer out of its passive mode, told it yes, I was answering calls, and sat in the study. Was everything I had said to Rolly a con and delusion?

I watched the slow turn of our light sculpture. It was a copy of the Charles Cohen "Illuminations IX" in the Museum of Modern Art. Blue, red, yellow, white, green—the colors formed their geometric patterns. Along with double jet-lag and exhaustion from anxiety and fear, the patterns hypnotized me. I slept.

I was awakened by a high-pitched, pulsing sound—a thousand satellites holding a family reunion, maybe, or calling home. The display screen on the opposite wall came alive and was filled with racing lines of characters, and both printers chattered as paper boiled out of them.

Then the light sculpture began a crazy dance. Sheets of light formed, grids of color appeared on them, and they folded and twisted as if in a strong wind. Doughnuts and spheres, regular and irregular polyhedrons, bundles of rods and cones, spiraling helices—these figures and others climbed from floor to ceiling, then raced away down lines of vanishing perspective.

A rod of green light jumped from the sculpture and flashed to the middle of the room. From its tip a point of white light grew, and the rod disappeared, leaving the point behind, pulsating to the high-pitched sounds.

Cute high-tech tricks. I wanted to tell myself, but it didn't feel that way. What it felt like was *something was saying hello.* There seemed to be a cold wind blowing through the room.

Metal clanged in the printers, and they stopped. The display screen sagged like a Dalí watch and went out. Ruby-red tubes of laser light cartwheeled through the room, searing the walls and furniture and setting afire the paper that had spilled onto the floor.

I stood in some still corner, untouched by light and fire.

Everything ceased at once, leaving behind the yellow flicker of burning paper and the shrill whistle of the smoke alarm. I got the extinguisher from the kitchen and put out the fires, then sat down.

And I'm still sitting, still waiting. But while I'm waiting, I decided to put this story on the wire—it's addressed to

BioTron, but that doesn't matter because I know you will be sure to get it.

That's right. I'm talking to *you*, because it looks like you're there after all.

So listen.

The programs are inside you, and if I don't stop them—soon—they run. You could try to disarm them, but one mistake and the networks get hashed. Ever hear of an information sink? You put information in, and it goes . . . where the wild goose goes, where the woodbine twineth. You get my point; that's your *mind* I'm after.

Here's the way it seems to me. You used BioTron like white cells to attack a disease—sent out orders, I would imagine, that the recipients followed because you knew just how to give them.

Because you fear bio-computers. I am guessing Carol was in the wrong place at the wrong time; Bergman was the real disease carrier. Charley said they might make artificial intelligence possible. Is that it? Would they be *competition?*

You removed Carol and Bergman from the public record, I know that much. Would have complicated matters if I had gone to the police. "Carol who? Doesn't exist. It says so right here." Or did you just panic? If you're alive and intelligent, that's possible.

But I don't really know much, just this: if Carol's dead, you are, too. If you don't exist, and I'm wrong, too bad, because the information economy is about to suffer its first catastrophic collapse.

So what's it going to be? Fill your hand, stranger? Bet your life?

Don't! I love her, I need her. Just give her back.

I'm waiting.

BLOOD SISTERS

Greg Egan

*Only a few years into the decade, it's already a fairly safe bet
to predict that Australian writer Greg Egan is going to come
to be recognized (if indeed he hasn't already been so
recognized) as being one of the Big New Names to emerge in
SF in the nineties. In the last few years, he has become a
frequent contributor to* Interzone *and* Asimov's Science
Fiction, *and has made sales as well as to* Pulphouse, Analog,
Aurealis, Eidolon, *and elsewhere; many of his stories have
also appeared in various "Best of the Year" series, and he
was on the Hugo final ballot in 1995 for his story "Cocoon,"
which won the Ditmar Award and the* Asimov's Readers
Award. *His first novel,* Quarantine, *appeared in 1992, to wide
critical acclaim, and was followed by a second novel in 1994,*
Permutation City, *which won the John W. Campbell Memorial Award. His most recent book is a collection of his short
fiction,* Axiomatic. *Upcoming are two new novels,* Distress
and Diaspora.*

*Here he gives us a haunting glimpse of a crowded,
high-tech future that has become perhaps a little too fond of
that dispassionate Long View we hear so much about . . .
and suggests that one thing that may spur a hacker on to
overcome even the most formidable of obstacles is the oldest
motive of them all: revenge.*

When we were nine years old, Paula decided we should
prick our thumbs, and let our blood flow into each other's
veins.

I was scornful. "Why bother? Our blood's already exactly
the same. We're *already* blood sisters."

She was unfazed. "I know that. That's not the point. It's
the ritual that counts."

We did it in our bedroom, at midnight, by the light of a single candle. She sterilized the needle in the candle flame, then wiped it clean of soot with a tissue and saliva.

When we'd pressed the tiny, sticky wounds together, and recited some ridiculous oath from a third-rate children's novel, Paula blew out the candle. While my eyes were still adjusting to the dark, she added a whispered coda of her own: "Now we'll dream the same dreams, and share the same lovers, and die at the very same hour."

I tried to say, indignantly, "That's just not true!" but the darkness and the scent of the dead flame made the protest stick in my throat, and her words remained unchallenged.

As Dr. Packard spoke, I folded the pathology report, into halves, into quarters, obsessively aligning the edges. It was far too thick for me to make a neat job of it; from the micrographs of the misshapen lymphocytes proliferating in my bone marrow, to the print-out of portions of the RNA sequence of the virus that had triggered the disease, thirty-two pages in all.

In contrast, the prescription, still sitting on the desk in front of me, seemed ludicrously flimsy and insubstantial. No match at all. The traditional—indecipherable—polysyllabic scrawl it bore was nothing but a decoration; the drug's name was reliably encrypted in the bar code below. There was no question of receiving the wrong medication by mistake. The question was, *would the right one help me?*

"Is that clear? Ms. Rees? Is there anything you don't understand?"

I struggled to focus my thoughts, pressing hard on an intractable crease with my thumb. She'd explained the situation frankly, without resorting to jargon or euphemisms, but I still had the feeling that I was missing something crucial. It seemed like every sentence she'd spoken had started one of two ways: "The virus . . ." or "The drug . . ."

"Is there anything *I* can do? Myself? To . . . improve the odds?"

She hesitated, but not for long. "No, not really. You're in

excellent health, otherwise. Stay that way." She began to rise from her desk to dismiss me, and I began to panic.

"But, there must be *something*." I gripped the arms of my chair, as if afraid of being dislodged by force. Maybe she'd misunderstood me, maybe I hadn't made myself clear. "Should I . . . stop eating certain foods? Get more exercise? Get more sleep? I mean, there has to be *something* that will make a difference. And I'll do it, whatever it is. Please, just *tell* me—" My voice almost cracked, and I looked away, embarrassed. *Don't ever start ranting like that again. Not ever.*

"Ms. Rees, I'm sorry. I know how you must be feeling. But the Monte Carlo diseases are all like this. In fact, you're exceptionally lucky; the WHO computer found eighty thousand people, worldwide, infected with a similar strain. That's not enough of a market to support any hard-core research, but enough to have persuaded the pharmaceutical companies to rummage through their databases for something that might do the trick. A lot of people are on their own, infected with viruses that are virtually unique. Imagine how much useful information the health profession can give *them*." I finally looked up; the expression on her face was one of sympathy, tempted by impatience.

I declined the invitation to feel ashamed of my ingratitude. I'd made a fool of myself, but I still had a right to ask the question. "I understand all that. I just thought there might be something *I* could do. You say this drug might work, or it might not. If I could contribute, *myself*, to fighting this disease, I'd feel . . ."

What? More like a human being, and less like a test tube—a passive container in which the wonder drug and the wonder virus would fight it out between themselves.

". . . better."

She nodded. "I know, but trust me, nothing you can do would make the slightest difference. Just look after yourself as you normally would. Don't catch pneumonia. Don't gain or lose ten kilos. Don't do *anything* out of the ordinary. Millions of people must have been exposed to this virus, but the reason you're sick, and they're not, is *a purely genetic matter*. The cure will be just the same. The biochemistry that determines whether or not the drug will work for you isn't going to change if you start taking vitamin pills, or stop eating junk food—and I should warn you that going on one of those "miracle-cure" diets will simply make you sick; the charlatans selling them ought to be in prison."

I nodded fervent agreement to *that*, and felt myself flush with anger. Fraudulent cures had long been my *bête noire*—although now, for the first time, I could almost understand why other Monte Carlo victims paid good money for such things: crackpot diets, meditation schemes, aromatherapy, self-hypnosis tapes, you name it. The people who peddled that garbage were the worst kind of cynical parasites, and I'd always thought of their customers as being either congenitally gullible, or desperate to the point of abandoning their wits, but there was more to it than that. When your life is at stake, you want to fight for it—with every ounce of your strength, with every cent you can borrow, with every waking moment. Taking one capsule, three times a day, just isn't *hard enough*—whereas the schemes of the most perceptive con men were sufficiently arduous (or sufficiently expensive) to make the victims feel that they were engaged in the kind of struggle that the prospect of death requires.

This moment of shared anger cleared the air completely. We were on the same side, after all; I'd been acting like a child. I thanked Dr. Packard for her time, picked up the prescription, and left.

On my way to the pharmacy, though, I found myself almost wishing that she'd lied to me—that she'd told me my chances would be vastly improved if I ran ten kilometers a day and ate raw seaweed with every meal—but then I angrily recoiled, thinking: Would I really want to be deceived "for my own good"? If it's down to my DNA, it's down to my DNA, and I ought to expect to be told that simple truth, however unpalatable I find it—and I ought to be grateful that the medical profession has abandoned its old patronizing, paternalistic ways.

• • •

I was twelve years old when the world learned about the Monte Carlo project.

A team of biological warfare researchers (located just a stone's throw from Las Vegas—alas, the one in New Mexico, not the one in Nevada) had decided that *designing* viruses was just too much hard work (especially when the Star Wars boys kept hogging the supercomputers). Why waste hundreds of Ph.D.-years—why expend any intellectual effort whatsoever—when the time-honored partnership of blind mutation and natural selection was all that was required?

Speeded up substantially, of course.

They'd developed a three-part system: a bacterium, a virus, and a line of modified human lymphocytes. A stable portion of the viral genome allowed it to reproduce in the bacterium, while rapid mutation of the rest of the virus was achieved by neatly corrupting the transcription error repair enzymes. The lymphocytes had been altered to vastly amplify the reproductive success of any mutant which managed to infect them, causing it to out-breed those which were limited to using the bacterium.

The theory was, they'd set up a few trillion copies of this system, like row after row of little biological poker machines, spinning away in their underground lab, and just wait to harvest the jackpots.

The theory also included the best containment facilities in the world, and five hundred and twenty people all sticking scrupulously to official procedure, day after day, month after month, without a moment of carelessness, laziness or forgetfulness. Apparently, nobody bothered to compute the probability of *that*.

The bacterium was supposed to be unable to survive outside artificially beneficent laboratory conditions, but a mutation of the virus came to its aid, filling in for the genes that had been snipped out to make it vulnerable.

They wasted too much time using ineffectual chemicals before steeling themselves to nuke the site. By then, the winds had already made any human action—short of melting half a dozen states, not an option in an election year—irrelevant.

The first rumors proclaimed that we'd all be dead within a week. I can clearly recall the mayhem, the looting, the suicides (second-hand on the TV screen; our own neighborhood remained relatively tranquil—or numb). States of emergency were declared around the world. Planes were turned away from airports, ships (which had left their home ports months before the leak) were burned in the docks. Harsh laws were rushed in everywhere, to protect public order and public health.

Paula and I got to stay home from school for a month. I offered to teach her programming; she wasn't interested. She wanted to go swimming, but the beaches and pools were all closed. That was the summer that I finally managed to hack into a Pentagon computer—just an office supplies purchasing system, but Paula was suitably impressed (and neither of us had ever guessed that paperclips were *that* expensive).

We didn't believe we were going to die—at least, not within a week—and we were right. When the hysteria subsided, it soon became apparent that only the virus and the bacterium had escaped, and without the modified lymphocytcs to fine-tune the selection process, the virus had mutated away from the strain which had caused the initial deaths.

However, the cozy symbiotic pair is now found all over the world, endlessly churning out new mutations. Only a tiny fraction of strains produced are infectious in humans, and only a fraction of those are potentially fatal.

A mere hundred or so a year.

On the train home, the sun seemed to be in my eyes no matter which way I turned—somehow, every surface in the carriage caught its reflection. The glare made a headache which had been steadily growing all afternoon almost unbearable, so I covered my eyes with my forearm and faced the floor. With my other hand, I clutched the brown paper bag that held the small glass vial of red-and-black capsules that would or wouldn't save my life.

Cancer. Viral leukemia. I pulled the creased pathology report from my pocket, and flipped through it one more time. The last page hadn't magically changed into a happy ending—an oncovirology expert system's declaration of a sure-fire cure. The last page was just the bill for all the tests. Twenty-seven thousand dollars.

At home, I sat and stared at my work station.

Two months before, when a routine quarterly examination (required by my health insurance company, ever eager to dump the unprofitable sick) had revealed the first signs of trouble, I'd sworn to myself that I'd keep on working, keep on living exactly as if nothing had changed. The idea of indulging in a credit spree, or a world trip, or some kind of self-destructive binge, held no attraction for me at all. Any such final fling would be an admission of defeat. *I'd* go on a fucking world trip to celebrate my cure, and not before.

I had plenty of contract work stacked up, and that pathology bill was already accruing interest. Yet for all that I needed the distraction—for all that I needed *the money*—I sat there for three whole hours, and did nothing but brood about my fate. Sharing it with eighty thousand strangers scattered about the world was no great comfort.

Then it finally struck me. *Paula.* If I was vulnerable *for genetic reasons*, then *so was she*.

For identical twins, in the end we hadn't done too bad a job of pursuing separate lives. She had left home at sixteen, to tour central Africa, filming the wildlife, and—at considerably greater risk—the poachers. Then she'd gone to the Amazon, and become caught up in the land rights struggle there. After that, it was a bit of a blur; she'd always tried to keep me up to date with her exploits, but she moved too fast for my sluggish mental picture of her to follow.

I'd never left the country; I hadn't even moved house in a decade.

She came home only now and then, on her way between continents, but we'd stayed in touch electronically, circumstances permitting. (They take away your SatPhone in Bolivian prisons.)

The telecommunications multinationals all offer their own expensive services for contacting someone when you don't know in advance what country they're in. The advertising suggests that it's an immensely difficult task; the fact is, every SatPhone's location is listed in a central database, which is kept up to date by pooling information from all the regional satellites. Since I happened to have "acquired" the access codes to consult that database, I could phone Paula directly, wherever she was, without paying the ludicrous surcharge. It was more a matter of nostalgia than miserliness; this minuscule bit of hacking was a token gesture, proof that in spite of impending middle age, I wasn't yet terminally law-abiding, conservative and dull.

I'd automated the whole procedure long ago. The database said she was in Gabon; my program calculated local time, judged 10:23 P.M. to be civilized enough, and made the call. Seconds later, she was on the screen.

"Karen! How are you? You look like shit. I thought you were going to call last week—what happened?"

The image was perfectly clear, the sound clean and undistorted (fiber-optic cables might be scarce in central Africa, but geosynchronous satellites are directly overhead). As soon as I set eyes on her, I felt sure she didn't have the virus. She was right—I looked half-dead, whereas she was as animated as ever. Half a lifetime spent outdoors meant her skin had aged much faster than mine—but there was always a glow of energy, a purpose, about her that more than compensated.

She was close to the lens, so I couldn't see much of the background, but it looked like a fiberglass hut, lit by a couple of hurricane lamps; a step up from the usual tent.

"I'm sorry, I didn't get around to it. *Gabon?* Weren't you in Ecuador—?"

"Yes, but I met Mohammed. He's a botanist. From Indonesia. Actually, we met in Bogotá; he was on his way to a conference in Mexico—"

"But—"

"Why Gabon? This is where he was going next, that's all. There's a fungus here, attacking the crops, and I couldn't resist coming along . . ."

I nodded, bemused, through ten minutes of convoluted explanations, not paying too much attention; in three months' time it would all be ancient history. Paula survived as a freelance pop-science journalist, darting around the globe writing articles for magazines, and scripts for TV programs, on the latest ecological trouble spots. To be honest, I had severe doubts that this kind of predigested ecobabble did the planet any good, but it certainly made her happy. I envied her that. I could not have lived her life—in no sense was she the woman I "might have been"—but nonetheless it hurt me, at times, to see in her eyes the kind of sheer excitement that I hadn't felt, myself, for a decade.

My mind wandered while she spoke. Suddenly, she was saying, "Karen? Are you going to tell me what's wrong?"

I hesitated. I had originally planned to tell no one, not even her, and now my reason for calling her seemed absurd—*she* couldn't have leukemia, it was unthinkable. Then, without even realizing that I'd made the decision, I found myself recounting everything in a dull, flat voice. I watched with a strange feeling of detachment the changing expression on her face; shock, pity, then a burst of fear when she realized—far sooner than I would have done—exactly what my predicament meant for her.

What followed was even more awkward and painful than I could have imagined. Her concern for me was genuine—but she would not have been human if the uncertainty of her own position had not begun to prey on her at once, and knowing *that* made all her fussing seem contrived and false.

"Do you have a good doctor? Someone you can trust?"

I nodded.

"Do you have someone to look after you? Do you want me to come home?"

I shook my head, irritated. "No. I'm all right. I'm being looked after, I'm being *treated*. But *you* have to get tested as soon as possible." I glared at her, exasperated. I no longer believed that she could have the virus, but I wanted to stress the fact that I'd called her to warn her, not to fish for sympathy—and somehow, that finally struck home. She said, quietly, "I'll get tested today. I'll go straight into town. OK?"

I nodded. I felt exhausted, but relieved; for a moment, all the awkwardness between us melted away.

"You'll let me know the results?"

She rolled her eyes. "Of course I will."

I nodded again. "OK."

"Karen. Be careful. Look after yourself."

"I will. You too." I hit the ESCAPE key.

Half an hour later, I took the first of the capsules, and climbed into bed. A few minutes later, a bitter taste crept up into my throat.

Telling Paula was essential. Telling Martin was insane. I'd only known him six months, but I should have guessed exactly how he'd take it.

"Move in with me. I'll look after you."

"I don't *need* to be looked after."

He hesitated, but only slightly. "Marry me."

"*Marry* you? Why? Do you think I have some desperate need to be married before I die?"

He scowled. "Don't talk like that. I *love you*. Don't you understand that?"

I laughed. "I don't *mind* being pitied—people always say it's degrading, but I think it's a perfectly normal response—but I don't want to have to live with it twenty-four hours a day." I kissed him, but he kept on scowling. At least I'd waited until after we'd had sex before breaking the news; if not, he probably would have treated me like porcelain.

He turned to face me. "Why are you being so hard on yourself? What are you trying to prove? That you're superhuman? That you don't need anyone?"

"*Listen*. You've known from the very start that I need independence and privacy. What do you want me to say? That I'm terrified. OK. I am. But I'm still the same person. I still need the same things." I slid one hand across his chest, and said as gently as I could, "So thanks for the offer, but no thanks."

"I don't mean very much to you, do I?"

I groaned, and pulled a pillow over my face. I thought: *Wake me when you're ready to fuck me again. Does that answer your question?* I didn't say it out loud, though.

A week later, Paula phoned me. She had the virus. Her white cell count was up, her red cell count was down—the numbers she quoted sounded just like my own from the month before. They'd even put her on the very same drug. That was hardly surprising, but it gave me an unpleasant, claustrophobic feeling, when I thought about what it meant:

We would both live, or we would both die.

In the days that followed, this realization began to obsess me. It was like voodoo, like some curse out of a fairy tale—or the fulfillment of the words she'd uttered, the night we became "blood sisters." We had never dreamed the same dreams, we'd certainly never loved the same men, but now . . . it was as if we were being punished, for failing to respect the forces that bound us together.

Part of me *knew* this was bullshit. *Forces that bound us together!* It was mental static, the product of stress, nothing more. The truth, though, was just as oppressive: the biochemical machinery would grind out its identical verdict on both of us, for all the thousands of kilometers between us, for all that we had forged separate lives in defiance of our genetic unity.

I tried to bury myself in my work. To some degree, I succeeded—if the gray stupor produced by eighteen-hour days in front of a terminal could really be considered a success.

I began to avoid Martin; his puppy-dog concern was just too much to bear. Perhaps he meant well, but I didn't have the energy to justify myself to him, over and over again. Perversely, at the very same time, I missed our arguments terribly; resisting his excessive mothering had at least made me feel strong, if only in contrast to the helplessness he seemed to expect of me.

I phoned Paula every week at first, but then gradually less and less often. We ought to have been ideal confidantes; in fact, nothing could have been less true. Our conversations were redundant; we already knew what the other was thinking, far too well. There was no sense of unburdening, just a suffocating, monotonous feeling of recognition. We took to trying to outdo each other in affecting a veneer of optimism, but it was a depressingly transparent effort. Eventually, I thought: when—if—I get the good news, I'll call her, until then, what's the point? Apparently, she came to the same conclusion.

All through childhood, we were forced together. We loved each other, I suppose, but . . . we were always in the same classes at school, bought the same clothes, given the same Christmas and birthday presents—and we were always sick at the same time, with the same ailment, for the same reason. When she left home, I was envious, and horribly lonely for a while, but then I felt a surge of joy, of *liberation*, because I knew that I had no real wish to follow her, and I knew that from then on, our lives could only grow further apart.

Now, it seemed that had all been an illusion. We would live or die together, and all our efforts to break the bonds had been in vain.

About four months after the start of treatment, my blood counts began to turn around. I was more terrified than ever of my hopes being dashed, and I spent all my time battling to keep myself from premature optimism. I didn't dare ring Paula; I could think of nothing worse than leading her to think that we were cured, and then turning out to have been mistaken. Even when Dr. Packard—cautiously, almost begrudgingly—admitted that things were looking up, I told myself that she might have relented from her policy of unflinching honesty and decided to offer me some palliative lies.

One morning I woke, not yet convinced that I was cured, but sick of feeling I had to drown myself in gloom for fear of being disappointed. If I wanted absolute certainty, I'd be miserable all my life; a relapse would always be possible, or a *whole new virus* could come along.

It was a cold, dark morning, pouring with rain outside, but as I climbed, shivering, out of bed, I felt more cheerful than I had since the whole thing had begun.

There was a message in my work station mailbox, tagged CONFIDENTIAL. It took me thirty seconds to recall the password I needed, and all the while my shivering grew worse.

The message was from the Chief Administrator of the Libreville People's Hospital, offering his or her condolences on the death of my sister, and requesting instructions for the disposal of the body.

I don't know what I felt first. Disbelief. Guilt. Confusion. Fear. How could she have died, when I was so close to recovery? How could she have died without a word to me? *How could I have let her die alone?* I walked away from the terminal, and slumped against the cold brick wall.

The worst of it was, I suddenly *knew* why she'd stayed silent. She must have thought that I was dying, too, and that was the one thing we'd both feared most of all: dying together. In spite of everything, dying together, as if we were one.

How could the drug have failed her, and worked for me? *Had it worked for me?* For a moment of sheer paranoia, I wondered if the hospital had been faking my test results, if in fact I was on the verge of death, myself. That was ludicrous, though.

Why, then, had Paula died? There was only one possible answer. She should have come home—I should have *made her* come home. How could I have let her stay there, in a tropical, Third World country, with her immune system weakened, living in a fiberglass hut, without proper sanitation, probably malnourished? I should have sent her the money, I should have sent her the ticket, I should have flown out there in person and dragged her back home.

Instead, I'd kept her at a distance. Afraid of us dying together, afraid of the curse of our sameness, I'd let her die alone.

I tried to cry, but something stopped me. I sat in the kitchen, sobbing dryly. I was worthless. I'd killed her with my superstition and cowardice. I had no right to be alive.

I spent the next fortnight grappling with the legal and administrative complexities of death in a foreign land. Paula's will requested cremation, but said nothing about where it was to take place, so I arranged for her body and belongings to be flown home. The service was all but deserted; our parents had died a decade before, in a car crash, and although Paula had had friends all over the world, few were able to make the trip.

Martin came, though. When he put an arm around me, I turned and whispered to him angrily, "You didn't even know her. What the hell are you doing here?" He stared at me for a moment, hurt and baffled, then walked off without a word.

I can't pretend I wasn't grateful, when Packard announced that I was cured, but my failure to rejoice out loud must have puzzled even her. I might have told her about Paula, but I didn't want to be fed cheap clichés about how irrational it was of me to feel guilty for surviving.

She was dead. I was growing stronger by the day; often sick with guilt and depression, but more often simply numb. That might easily have been the end of it.

Following the instructions in the will, I sent most of her belongings—notebooks, disks, audio and video tapes—to her agent, to be passed on to the appropriate editors and producers, to whom some of it might be of use. All that remained was clothing, a minute quantity of jewelry and cosmetics, and a handful of odds and ends. Including a small glass vial of red-and-black capsules.

I don't know what possessed me to take one of the capsules. I had half a dozen left of my own, and Packard had shrugged when I'd asked if I should finish them, and said that it couldn't do me any harm.

There was no aftertaste. Every time I'd swallowed my own, within minutes there'd been a bitter aftertaste.

I broke open a second capsule and put some of the white powder on my tongue. It was entirely without flavor. I ran and grabbed my own supply, and sampled one the same way; it tasted so vile it made my eyes water.

I tried, very hard, not to leap to any conclusions. I knew perfectly well that pharmaceuticals were often mixed with inert substances, and perhaps not necessarily the same ones all the time—but why would something *bitter* be used for that purpose? The taste had to come from the drug itself. The two vials bore the same manufacturer's name and logo. The same brand name. The same generic name. The same formal chemical name for the active ingredient. The same product code, down to the very last digit. Only the batch numbers were different.

The first explanation that came to mind was corruption. Although I couldn't recall the details, I was sure that I'd read about dozens of cases of officials in the health-care systems of developing countries diverting pharmaceuticals for resale on the black market. What better way to cover up such a theft than to replace the stolen product with something else—something cheap, harmless, and absolutely useless? The gelatin capsules themselves bore nothing but the manufacturer's logo, and since the company probably made at least a thousand different drugs, it would not have been too hard to find something cheaper, with the same size and coloration.

I had no idea what to do with this theory. Anonymous bureaucrats in a distant country had killed my sister, but the prospects of finding out who they were, let alone seeing them brought to justice, were infinitesimally small. Even if I'd had real, damning evidence, what was the most I could hope for? A meekly phrased protest from one diplomat to another.

I had one of Paula's capsules analyzed. It cost me a fortune, but I was already so deeply in debt that I didn't much care.

It was full of a mixture of soluble inorganic compounds. There was no trace of the substance described on the label, nor of anything else with the slightest biological activity. It wasn't a cheap substitute drug, chosen at random.

It was a placebo.

I stood with the print-out in my hand for several minutes, trying to come to terms with what it meant. Simple greed I could have understood, but there was an utterly inhuman coldness here that I couldn't bring myself to swallow.

Someone must have made an honest mistake. *Nobody* could be so callous.

Then Packard's words came back to me. "Just look after yourself as you normally would. Don't do *anything* out of the ordinary."

Oh no, *Doctor*. Of course not, *Doctor*. Wouldn't want to go spoiling the experiment with any messy, extraneous, uncontrolled factors . . .

I contacted an investigative journalist, one of the best in the country. I arranged a meeting in a small café on the edge of town.

I drove out there—terrified, angry, triumphant—thinking I had the scoop of the decade, thinking I had dynamite, thinking I was Meryl Streep playing Karen Silkwood. I was dizzy with sweet thoughts of revenge. Heads were going to roll.

Nobody tried to run me off the road. The café was deserted, and the waiter barely listened to our orders, let alone our conversation.

The journalist was very kind. She calmly explained the facts of life.

In the aftermath of the Monte Carlo disaster, a lot of legislation had been passed to help deal with the emergency—and a lot of legislation had been repealed. As a matter of urgency, new drugs to treat the new diseases had to be developed and assessed, and the best way to ensure *that* was to remove the cumbersome regulations that had made clinical trials so difficult and expensive.

In the old "double-blind" trials, neither the patients nor the investigators knew who was getting the drug and who was getting a placebo; the information was kept secret by a third party (or a computer). Any improvement observed in the patients who were given the placebo could then be taken into account, and the drug's true efficacy measured.

There were two small problems with this traditional approach. Firstly, telling patients that there's only a fifty-fifty chance that they've been given a potentially life-saving drug subjects them to a lot of stress. Of course, the treatment and control groups were affected equally, but in terms of

predicting what would happen when the drug was finally
put out on the market, it introduced a lot of noise into the
data. Which side effects were real, and which were artifacts
of the patients' uncertainty?

Secondly—and more seriously—it had become increasingly difficult to find people willing to volunteer for placebo
trials. When you're dying, you don't give a shit about the
scientific method. You want the maximum possible chance
of surviving. Untested drugs will do, if there is no known,
certain cure—but why accept a further *halving* of the odds,
to satisfy some technocrat's obsession with details?

Of course, in the good old days the medical profession
could lay down the law to the unwashed masses: *Take part
in this double-blind trial, or crawl away and die.* AIDS had
changed all that, with black markets for the latest untried
cures, straight from the labs to the streets, and intense
politicization of the issues.

The solution to both flaws was obvious.

You lie to the patients.

No bill had been passed to explicitly declare that "triple-
blind" trials were legal. If it had, people might have noticed,
and made a fuss. Instead, as part of the "reforms" and
"rationalization" that came in the wake of the disaster, all
the laws that might have made them illegal had been
removed or watered down. At least, it looked that way—no
court had yet been given the opportunity to pass judgment.

"How could any doctor *do that?* Lie like that? How could
they justify it, even to themselves?"

She shrugged. "How did they ever justify double-blind
trials? A good medical researcher has to care more about the
quality of the data than about any one person's life. And if
a double-blind trial is good, a triple-blind trial is better. The
data *is* guaranteed to be better, you can see that, can't you?
And the more accurately a drug can be assessed, well,
perhaps in the long run, the more lives can be saved."

"Oh, *crap!* The placebo effect isn't *that* powerful. It just
isn't that important! Who cares if it's not precisely taken
into account? Anyway, *two* potential cures could still be
compared, one treatment against another. That would tell

you which drug would save the most lives, without any need
for placebos—"

"That *is* done sometimes, although the more prestigious
journals look down on those studies; they're less likely to be
published—"

I stared at her. "How can you know all this and do nothing?
The media could blow it wide open! If you let people know
what's going on . . ."

She smiled thinly. "I *could* publicize the observation that
these practices are now, theoretically, legal. Other people
have done that, and it doesn't exactly make headlines. But
if I printed any *specific* facts about an actual triple-blind
trial, I'd face a half-million-dollar fine, and twenty-five years
in prison, for endangering public health. Not to mention
what they'd do to my publisher. All the "emergency" laws
brought in to deal with the Monte Carlo leak are still
active."

"But that was twenty years ago!"

She drained her coffee and rose. "Don't you recall what
the experts said at the time?"

"No."

"The effects will be with us for generations."

It took me four months to penetrate the drug manufacturer's
network.

I eavesdropped on the data flow of several company
executives who chose to work from home. It didn't take
long to identify the least computer-literate. A real bumbling
fool, who used ten-thousand-dollar spreadsheet software to
do what the average five-year-old could have done without
fingers and toes. I watched his clumsy responses when the
spreadsheet package gave him error messages. He was a gift
from heaven; he simply didn't have a clue.

And, best of all, he was forever running a tediously
unimaginative pornographic video game.

If the computer said, "Jump!" he'd say, "Promise not to
tell?"

I spent a fortnight minimizing what he had to do; it

started out at seventy keystrokes, but I finally got it down to twenty-three.

I waited until his screen was at its most compromising, then I suspended his connection to the network, and took its place myself.

FATAL SYSTEM ERROR! TYPE THE FOLLOWING TO RECOVER.

He botched it the first time. I rang alarm bells, and repeated the request. The second time he got it right.

The first multi-key combination I had him strike took the work station right out of its operating system into its processor's microcode debugging routine. The hexadecimal that followed, gibberish to him, was a tiny program to dump all of the work station's memory down the communications line, right into my lap.

If he told anyone with any sense what had happened, suspicion would be aroused at once—but would he risk being asked to explain just what he was running when the "bug" occurred? I doubted it.

I already had his passwords. Included in the work station's memory was an algorithm which told me precisely how to respond to the network's security challenges.

I was in.

The rest of their defenses were trivial, at least so far as my aims were concerned. Data that might have been useful to their competitors was well shielded, but I wasn't interested in stealing the secrets of their latest hemorrhoid cure.

I could have done a lot of damage. Arranged for their backups to be filled with garbage. Arranged for the gradual deviation of their accounts from reality, until reality suddenly intruded in the form of bankruptcy—or charges of tax fraud. I considered a thousand possibilities, from the crudest annihilation of data to the slowest, most insidious forms of corruption.

In the end, though, I restrained myself. I knew the fight would soon become a political one, and any act of petty vengeance on my part would be sure to be dredged up and used to discredit me, to undermine my cause.

So I did only what was absolutely necessary.

I located the files containing the names and addresses of everyone who had been unknowingly participating in triple-blind trials of the company's products. I arranged for them all to be notified of what had been done to them. There were over two hundred thousand people, spread all around the world—but I found a swollen executive slush fund which easily covered the communications bill.

Soon, the whole world would know of our anger, would share in our outrage and grief. Half of us were sick or dying, though, and before the slightest whisper of protest was heard, my first objective had to be to save whoever I could.

I found the program that allocated medication or placebo. The program that had killed Paula, and thousands of others, for the sake of sound experimental technique.

I altered it. A very small change. I added one more lie.

All the reports it generated would continue to assert that half the patients involved in clinical trials were being given the placebo. Dozens of exhaustive, impressive files would continue to be created, containing data entirely consistent with this lie. Only one small file, never read by humans, would be different. The file controlling the assembly-line robots would instruct them to put medication in every vial of every batch.

From triple-blind to quadruple-blind. One more lie, to cancel out the others, until the time for deception was finally over.

Martin came to see me.

"I heard about what you're doing. TIM. Truth in Medicine." He pulled a newspaper clipping from his pocket. " 'A vigorous new organization dedicated to the eradication of quakery, fraud and deception in both alternative and conventional medicine.' Sounds like a great idea."

"Thanks."

He hesitated. "I heard you were looking for a few more volunteers. To help around the office."

"That's right."

"I could manage four hours a week."

I laughed. "Oh, could you really? Well, thanks very much, but I think we'll cope without you."

For a moment, I thought he was going to walk out, but then he said, not so much hurt as simply baffled, "Do you want volunteers, or not?"

"Yes, but—" *But what?* If he could swallow enough pride to offer, I could swallow enough pride to accept.

I signed him up for Wednesday afternoons.

I have nightmares about Paula, now and then. I wake smelling the ghost of a candle flame, certain that she's standing in the dark beside my pillow, a solemn-eyed nine-year-old child again, mesmerized by our strange condition.

That child can't haunt me, though. She never died. She grew up, and grew apart from me, and she fought for our separateness harder than I ever did. What if we had died "at the very same hour"? It would have signified nothing, changed nothing. Nothing could have reached back and robbed us of our separate lives, our separate achievements and failures.

I realize, now, that the blood oath that seemed so ominous to me was nothing but a joke to Paula, her way of *mocking* the very idea that our fates could be entwined. How could I have taken so long to see that?

It shouldn't surprise me, though. The truth—and the measure of her triumph—is that I never really knew her.

ROCK ON

Pat Cadigan

*There's an old adage that says, "Rock'n'roll never forgets."
And in a future where hackers are needed to create the music
in the* first *place, rock'n'roll really* never forgets . . . *even
if you* want *it to.*

   *Pat Cadigan was born in Schenectady, New York, and now
lives in Overland Park, Kansas. She made her first professional sale in 1980, and has subsequently come to be
regarded as one of the best new writers in SF. Her story
"Pretty Boy Crossover" has recently appeared on several
critic's lists as among the best science fiction stories of the
1980s, her story "Angel" was a finalist for the Hugo Award,
the Nebula Award, and the World Fantasy Award (one of the
few stories ever to earn that rather unusual distinction) and
her collection* Patterns *has been hailed as one of the
landmark collections of the decade. Her first novel,* Mind-
players, *was released in 1987 to excellent critical response,
and her second novel,* Synners, *released in 1991, won the
prestigious Arthur C. Clarke Award as the year's best
science-fiction novel, as did her third novel,* Fools, *making
her the only writer ever to win the Clarke Award twice. Her
most recent book is a new collection called* Dirty Work.
Coming up is a new novel, tentatively entitled Parasites.*

Rain woke me. I thought, shit, here I am, Lady Rain-in-the-
Face, because that's where it was hitting, right in the old
face. Sat up and saw I was still on Newbury Street. See
beautiful downtown Boston. Was Newbury Street downtown? In the middle of the night, did it matter? No, it did
not. And not a soul in sight. Like everybody said, let's get
Gina drunk and while she's passed out, we'll all move to

Vermont. Do I love New England? A great place to live, but you wouldn't want to visit here.

I smeared my hair out of my eyes and wondered if anyone was looking for me now. Hey, anybody shy a forty-year-old rock'n'roll sinner?

I scuttled into the doorway of one of those quaint old buildings where there was a shop with the entrance below ground level. A little awning kept the rain off but pissed water down in a maddening beat. Wrung the water out of my wrap pants and my hair and just sat being damp. Cold, too, I guess, but didn't feel that so much.

Sat a long time with my chin on my knees; you know, it made me feel like a kid again. When I started nodding my head, I began to pick up on something. Just primal but I tap into that amazing well. Man-O-War, if you could see me now. By the time the blueboys found me, I was rocking pretty good.

And that was the punchline. I'd never tried to get up and leave, but if I had, I'd have found I was locked into place in a sticky field. Made to catch the b&e kids in the act until the blueboys could get around to coming out and getting them. I'd been sitting in a trap and digging it. The story of my life.

They were nice to me. Led me, read me, dried me out. Fined me a hundred, sent me on my way in time for breakfast.

Awful time to see and be seen, righteous awful. For the first three hours after you get up, people can tell whether you've got a broken heart or not. The solution is, either you get up *real* early so your camouflage is in place by the time everybody else is out, or you don't go to bed. Don't go to bed ought to work all the time, but it doesn't. Sometimes when you don't go to bed, people can see whether you've got a broken heart all day long. I schlepped it, searching for an uncrowded breakfast bar and not looking at anyone who was looking at me. But I had this urge to stop random pedestrians and say, Yeah, yeah, it's true, but it was rock'n'roll broke my poor old heart, not a person, don't cry for me or I'll pop your chocks.

I went around and up and down and all over until I found

Tremont Street. It had been the pounder with that group from the Detroit Crater—the name was gone but the malady lingered on—anyway, him, he'd been the one told me Tremont had the best breakfast bars in the world, especially when you were coming off a bottle drunk you couldn't remember.

When the c'muters cleared out some, I found a space at a Greek hole-in-the-wall. We shut down 10:30 A.M. sharp, get the hell out when you're done, counter service only, take it or shake it. I like a place with Attitude. I folded a seat down and asked for coffee and a feta cheese omelet. Came with home fries from the home fries mountain in a corner of the grill (no microwave *gar-bazhe*, hoo-ray). They shot my retinas before they even brought my coffee, and while I was pouring the cream, they checked my credit. Was that badass? It was badass. Did I care? I did not. No waste, no machines when a human could do it, and real food, none of this edible polyester that slips clear through you so you can stay looking like a famine victim, my deah.

They came in when I was half finished with the omelet. Went all night by the look and sound of them, but I didn't check their faces for broken hearts. Made me nervous but I thought, well, they're tired; who's going to notice this old lady? Nobody.

Wrong again. I became visible to them right after they got their retinas shot. Seventeen-year-old boy with tattooed cheeks and a forked tongue leaned forward and hissed like a snake.

"Sssssssinner."

The other four with him perked right up. "Where?" "Whose?" "In here?"

"Rock'n'roll sssssssinner."

The lady identified me. She bore much resemblance to nobody at all, and if she had a heart it wasn't even sprained a little. With a sinner, she was probably Madame Magnifica. "Gina," she said, with all confidence.

My left eye tic'ed. Oh, please. Feta cheese on my knees. What the hell, I thought, I'll nod, they'll nod, I'll eat, I'll go. And then somebody whispered the word, *reward*.

I dropped my fork and ran.

Safe enough, I figured. Were they all going to chase me before they got their Greek breakfasts? No, they were not. They sent the lady after me.

She was much the younger, and she tackled me in the middle of a crosswalk when the light changed. A car hopped over us, its undercarriage just ruffling the top of her hard copper hair.

"Just come back and finish your omelet. Or we'll buy you another."

"No."

She yanked me up and pulled me out of the street. "Come on." People were staring but Tremont's full of theaters. You see that here, live theater; you can still get it. She put a bring-along on my wrist and brought me along, back to the breakfast bar, where they'd sold the rest of my omelet at a discount to a bum. The lady and her group made room for me among themselves and brought me another cup of coffee.

"How can you eat and drink with a forked tongue?" I asked Tatooed Cheeks. He showed me. A little appliance underneath, like a *zipper*. The Featherweight to the left of the big boy on the lady's other side leaned over and frowned at me.

"Give us one good reason why we shouldn't turn you in for Man-O-War's reward."

I shook my head. "I'm through. This sinner's been absolved."

"You're legally bound by contract," said the lady. "But we could c'noodle something. Buy Man-O-War out, sue on your behalf for nonfulfillment. We're Misbegotten. Oley." She pointed at herself. "Pidge." That was the silent type next to her. "Percy." The big boy. "The Krait." Mr. Tongue. "Gus." Featherweight. "We'll take care of you."

I shook my head again. "If you're going to turn me in, turn me in and collect. The credit ought to buy you the best sinner there ever was."

"We can be good to you."

"I don't have it anymore. It's gone. All my rock'n'roll sins have been forgiven."

"Untrue," said the big boy. Automatically, I started to picture on him and shut it down hard. "Man-O-War would have thrown you out if it were gone. You wouldn't have to run."

"I didn't want to tell him. Leave me alone. I just want to go and sin no more, see? Play with yourselves, I'm not helping." I grabbed the counter with both hands and held on. So what were they going to do, pop me one and carry me off?

As a matter of fact, they did.

In the beginning, I thought, and the echo effect was stupendous. *In the beginning . . . the beginning . . . the beginning . . .*

In the beginning, the sinner was not human. I know because I'm old enough to remember.

They were all there, little more than phantoms. Misbegotten. Where do they get those names? I'm old enough to remember. Oingo-Boingo and Bow-Wow-Wow. Forty, did I say? Oooh, just a little past, a little close to a lot. Old rockers never die, they just keep rocking on. I never saw The Who; Moon was dead before I was born. But I remember, barely old enough to stand, rocking in my mother's arms while thousands screamed and clapped and danced in their seats. *Start me up . . . if you start me up, I'll never stop . . .* 763 Strings did a rendition for elevator and dentist's office, I remember that, too. And that wasn't the worst of it.

They hung on the memories, pulling more from me, turning me inside out. *Are you experienced?* Only a record of my father's, because he'd died too, before my parents even met, and nobody else ever dared ask that question. *Are you experienced? . . . Well, I am.*

(Well, *I* am.)

Five against one and I couldn't push them away. Only, can you call it rape when you know you're going to like it? Well, if I couldn't get away, then I'd give them the ride of their lives. *Jerkin' Crocus didn't kill me but she sure came near . . .*

The big boy faded in first, big and wild and too much badass to him. I reached out, held him tight, showing him. The beat from the night in the rain, I gave it to him, fed it to his heart and made him live it. Then came the lady, putting down the bass theme. She jittered, but mostly in the right places.

Now the Krait, and he was slithering around the sound, in and out. Never mind the tattooed cheeks, he wasn't just flash for the fools. He knew; you wouldn't have thought it, but he knew.

Featherweight and the silent type, melody and first harmony. Bad. Featherweight was a disaster, didn't know where to go or what to do when he got there, but he was pitching ahead like the *S.S. Suicide*.

Christ. If they had to rape me, couldn't they have provided someone upright? The other four kept on, refusing to lose it, and I would have to make the best of it for all of us. Derivative, unoriginal—Featherweight did not rock. It was a crime, but all I could do was take them and shake them. Rock gods in the hands of an angry sinner.

They were never better. Small change getting a glimpse of what it was like to be big bucks. Hadn't been for Featherweight, they might have gotten all the way there. More groups now than ever there was, all of them sure that if they just got the right sinner with them, they'd rock the moon down out of the sky.

We maybe vibrated it a little before we were done. Poor old Featherweight.

I gave them better than they deserved, and they knew that, too. So when I begged out, they showed me respect at last and went. Their techies were gentle with me, taking the plugs from my head, my poor old throbbing abused broken-hearted sinning head, and covered up the sockets. I had to sleep and they let me. I heard the man say, "That's a take, righteously. We'll rush it into distribution. Where in *hell* did you find that sinner?"

"Synthesizeer," I muttered, already asleep. "The actual word, my boy, is synthesizer."

Crazy old dreams. I was back with Man-O-War in the big CA, leaving him again, and it was mostly as it happened, but you know dreams. His living room was half outdoors, half indoors, the walls all busted out. You know dreams; I didn't think it was strange.

Man-O-War was mostly undressed, like he'd forgotten to finish. Oh, that *never* happened. Man-O-War forget a sequin or a bead? He loved to act it out, just like the Krait.

"No more," I was saying, and he was saying, "But you don't know anything else, you shitting?" Nobody in the big CA kids, they all shit; loose juice.

"Your contract goes another two and I get the option, I always get the option. And you love it, Gina, you know that, you're no good without it."

And then it was flashback time and I was in the pod with all my sockets plugged, rocking Man-O-War through the wires, giving him the meat and bone that made him Man-O-War and the machines picking it up, sound and vision, so all the tube babies all around the world could play it on their screens whenever they wanted. Forget the road, forget the shows, too much trouble, and it wasn't like the tapes, not as exciting, even with the biggest FX, lasers, spaceships, explosions, no good. And the tapes weren't as good as the stuff in the head, rock'n'roll visions straight from the brain. No hours of setup and hours more doctoring in the lab. But you had to get everyone in the group dreaming the same way. You needed a synthesis, and for that you got a synthesizer, not the old kind, the musical instrument, but something—somebody—to channel your group through, to bump up their tube-fed little souls, to rock them and roll them the way they couldn't do themselves. And anyone could be a rock'n'roll hero then. Anyone!

In the end, they didn't have to play instruments unless they really wanted to, and why bother? Let the synthesizer take their imaginings and boost them up to Mount Olympus.

Synthesizer. Synner. Sinner.

Not just anyone can do that, sin for rock'n'roll. I can.

But it's not the same as jumping all night to some bar band nobody knows yet. . . . Man-O-War and his blown-out living room came back and he said, "You rocked the walls right out of my house. I'll never let you go."

And I said, "I'm gone."

Then I was out, going fast at first because I thought he'd be hot behind me. But I must have lost him and then somebody grabbed my ankle.

Featherweight had a tray, he was Mr. Nursie-Angel-of-Mercy. Nudged the foot of the bed with his knee, and it sat me up slow. She rises from the grave, you can't keep a good sinner down.

"Here." He set the tray over my lap, pulled up a chair. Some kind of thick soup in a bowl he'd given me, with veg wafers to break up and put in. "Thought you'd want something soft and easy." He put his left foot up on his right leg and had a good look at it. "I *never* been rocked like that before."

"You don't have it, no matter who rocks you ever in this world. Cut and run, go into management. The *big* Big Money's in management."

He snaked on his thumbnail. "Can you always tell?"

"If the Stones came back tomorrow, you couldn't even tap your toes."

"What if you took my place?"

"I'm a sinner, not a clown. You can't sin and do the dance. It's been tried."

"*You* could do it. If anyone could."

"No."

His stringy cornsilk fell over his face and he tossed it back. "Eat your soup. They want to go again shortly."

"No." I touched my lower lip, thickened to sausage-size. "I won't sin for Man-O-War and I won't sin for you. You want to pop me one again, go to. Shake a socket loose, most likely, give me aphasia."

So he left and came back with a whole bunch of them, techies and do-kids, and they poured the soup down my throat and gave me a poke and carried me out to the pod so I could make Misbegotten this year's firestorm.

I knew as soon as the first tape got out, Man-O-War would pick up the scent. They were already starting the machine to get me away from him. And they kept me good in the room—where their old sinner had done penance, the lady told me. Their sinner came to see me, too. I thought, poison dripping from his fangs, death threats. But he was just a guy about my age with a lot of hair to hide his sockets (I never bothered, didn't care if they showed). Just came to pay his respects, how'd I ever learn to rock the way I did?

Fool.

They kept me good in the room. Drinks when I wanted them and a poke to get sober again, a poke for vitamins, a poke to lose the bad dreams. Poke, poke, pig in a poke. I had tracks like the old B&O, and they didn't even know what I meant by that. They lost Featherweight, got themselves someone a little more righteous, sixteen-year-old snipe girl with a face like a praying mantis. But she rocked and they rocked and we all rocked until Man-O-War came to take me home.

Strutted into my room in full plumage with his hair all fanned out (hiding his sockets) and said, "Did you want to press charges, Gina, darling?"

Well, they fought it out over my bed. Misbegotten said I was theirs now; Man-O-War smiled and said, "Yeah, and I bought *you*. You're *all* mine now, you *and* your sinner. *My* sinner." That was truth. Man-O-War had his conglomerate start to buy Misbegotten right after the first tape came out. Deal all done by the time we'd finished the third one, and they never knew. Conglomerates buy and sell all the time. Everybody was in trouble but Man-O-War. And me, he said. He made them all leave and sat down on my bed to re-lay claim to me.

"Gina." Ever see honey poured over the edge of a sawtooth blade? Ever hear it? He couldn't sing without hurting someone bad and he couldn't dance, but inside, he rocked. If I rocked him.

"I don't want to be a sinner, not for you or anyone."

"It'll all look different when I get you back to Cee-Ay."

"I want to go to a cheesy bar and boogie my brains till they leak out the sockets."

"No more, darling. That was why you came here, wasn't it? But all the bars are gone and all the bands. Last call was years ago; it's all up here now. All up here." He tapped his temple. "You're an old lady, no matter how much I spend keeping your body young. And don't I give you everything? And didn't you say I had it?"

"It's not the same. It wasn't meant to be put on a tube for people to *watch*."

"But it's not as though rock'n'roll is dead, lover."

"You're killing it."

"Not me. You're trying to bury it alive. But I'll keep you going for a long, long time."

"I'll get away again. You'll either rock'n'roll on your own or you'll give it up, but you won't be taking it out of me any more. This ain't my way, it ain't my time. Like the man said, 'I don't live today.'"

Man-O-War grinned. "And like the other man said. 'Rock'n'roll never forgets.'"

He called in his do-kids and took me home.

THE PARDONER'S TALE

Robert Silverberg

Robert Silverberg is one of the most famous SF writers of modern times, with dozens of novels, anthologies, and collections to his credit. Silverberg has won five Nebula Awards and four Hugo Awards. His novels include, Dying Inside, Lord Valentine's Castle, The Book of Skulls, Downward to the Earth, Tower of Glass, The World Inside, Born With the Dead, Shadrach in the Furnace, Tom O'Bedlam, Star of Gypsies, At Winter's End, *and two novel-length expansions of famous Isaac Asimov stories,* Nightfall, *and* The Ugly Little Boy. *His collections include* Unfamiliar Territory, Capricorn Games, The Majipoor Chronicles, The Best of Robert Silverberg, At the Conglomeroid Cocktail Party, Beyond the Safe Zone, *and a massive retrospective collection,* The Collected Stories of Robert Silverberg, Volume One: Secret Sharers. *His most recent books are the novels* The Face of the Waters, Kingdoms of the Wall, Hot Sky at Morning, *and* Mountains of Majipoor. *He lives with his wife, writer Karen Haber, in Oakland, California.*

Here he takes us to a strange and forbidding future where humans no longer control the Earth, but there is still a place for hackers in the interstices of the conquering alien society . . . a marginal and dangerous place, based on the understanding that although to forgive may be divine, to pardon may be very costly indeed.

"Key sixteen, Housing Omicron Kappa, aleph sub-one," I said to the software on duty at the Alhambra gate of the Los Angeles Wall.

Software isn't generally suspicious. This wasn't even very smart software. It was working off some great biochips—I could feel them jigging and pulsing as the electron stream flowed through them—but the software itself was just a kludge. Typical gatekeeper stuff.

I stood waiting as the picoseconds went ticking away by the millions.

"Name, please," the gatekeeper said finally.

"John Doe. Beta Pi Upsilon 104324x."

The gate opened. I walked into Los Angeles.

As easy as Beta Pi.

The wall that encircles L.A. is a hundred, a hundred fifty feet thick. Its gates are more like tunnels. When you consider that the wall runs completely around the L.A. basin from the San Gabriel Valley to the San Fernando Valley and then over the mountains and down the coast and back the far side past Long Beach, and that it's at least sixty feet high and all that distance deep, you can begin to appreciate the mass of it. Think of the phenomenal expenditure of human energy that went into building it—muscle and sweat, sweat and muscle. I think about that a lot.

I suppose the walls around our cities were put there mostly as symbols. They highlight the distinction between city and countryside, between citizen and uncitizen, between control and chaos, just as city walls did five thousand years ago. But mainly they serve to remind us that we are all slaves nowadays. You can't ignore the walls. You can't pretend they aren't there. *We made you build them*, is what they say, and *don't you ever forget that*. All the same, Chicago doesn't have a wall sixty feet high and a hundred fifty feet deep. Houston doesn't. Phoenix doesn't. They make do with less. But L.A. is the main city. I suppose the Los Angeles wall is a statement: *I am the Big Cheese. I am the Ham What Am.*

The walls aren't there because the Entities are afraid of attack. They know how invulnerable they are. We know it, too. They just wanted to decorate their capital with something a little special. What the hell, it isn't *their* sweat that goes into building the walls. It's ours. Not mine personally, of course. But ours.

I saw a few Entities walking around just inside the wall,

preoccupied as usual with God knows what and paying no attention to the humans in the vicinity. These were low-caste ones, the kind with the luminous orange spots along their sides. I gave them plenty of room. They have a way sometimes of picking a human up with those long elastic tongues, like a frog snapping up a fly, and letting him dangle in midair while they study him with those saucer-sized yellow eyes. I don't care for that. You don't get hurt, but it isn't agreeable to be dangled in midair by something that looks like a fifteen-foot-high purple squid standing on the tips of its tentacles. Happened to me once in St. Louis, long ago, and I'm in no hurry to have it happen again.

The first thing I did when I was inside L.A. was find me a car. On Valley Boulevard about two blocks in from the wall I saw a '31 Toshiba El Dorado that looked good to me, and I matched frequencies with its lock and slipped inside and took about ninety seconds to reprogram its drive control to my personal metabolic cues. The previous owner must have been fat as a hippo and probably diabetic: her glycogen index was absurd and her phosphenes were wild.

Not a bad car, a little slow in the shift but what can you expect, considering the last time any cars were manufactured on this planet was the year 2034.

"Pershing Square," I told it.

It had nice capacity, maybe sixty megabytes. It turned south right away and found the old freeway and drove off toward downtown. I figured I'd set up shop in the middle of things, work two or three pardons to keep my edge sharp, get myself a hotel room, a meal, maybe hire some companionship. And then think about the next move. It was winter, a nice time to be in L.A. That golden sun, those warm breezes coming down the canyons.

I hadn't been out on the Coast in years. Working Florida mainly, Texas, sometimes Arizona. I hate the cold. I hadn't been in L.A. since '36. A long time to stay away, but maybe I'd been staying away deliberately. I wasn't sure. That last L.A. trip had left bad-tasting memories. There had been a woman who wanted a pardon, and I sold her a stiff. You have to stiff the customers now and then or else you start looking too good, which can be dangerous; but she was young and pretty and full of hope and I could have stiffed the next one instead of her, only I didn't. Sometimes I've felt bad, thinking back over that. Maybe that's what had kept me away from L.A all this time.

A couple of miles east of the big downtown interchange, traffic began backing up. Maybe an accident ahead, maybe a roadblock. I told the Toshiba to get off the freeway.

Slipping through roadblocks is scary and calls for a lot of hard work. I knew that I probably could fool any kind of software at a roadblock and certainly any human cop, but why bother if you don't have to?

I asked the car where I was.

The screen lit up. Alameda near Banning, it said. A long walk to Pershing Square, looked like. I had the car drop me at Spring Street and went the rest of the way on foot. "Pick me up at 1830 hours," I told it. "Corner of—umm—Sixth and Hill." It went away to park itself and I headed for the Square to peddle some pardons.

It isn't hard for a good pardoner to find buyers. You can see it in their eyes: the tightly controlled anger, the smoldering resentment. And something else, something intangible, a certain sense of having a shred or two of inner integrity left, that tells you right away, Here's somebody willing to risk a lot to regain some measure of freedom. I was in business within fifteen minutes.

The first one was an aging surfer sort, barrel chest and that sun-bleached look. The Entities haven't allowed surfing for ten, fifteen years—they've got their plankton seines just offshore from Santa Barbara to San Diego, gulping in the marine nutrients they have to have, and any beach boy who tried to take a whack at the waves out there would be chewed right up. But this guy must have been one hell of a performer in his day. The way he moved through the park, making little balancing moves as if he needed to compensate for the regularities of the earth's rotation, you could see how he would have been in the water. Sat down next to me, began working on his lunch. Thick forearms, gnarled hands.

A wall laborer. Muscles knotting in his cheeks: the anger, forever simmering just below boil.

I got him talking after a while. A surfer, yes. Lost in the faraway and gone. He began sighing to me about legendary beaches where the waves were tubes and they came pumping end to end. "Trestle Beach," he murmured. "That's north of San Onofre. You had to sneak through Camp Pendleton. Sometimes the Marines would open fire, just warning shots. Or Hollister Ranch, up by Santa Barbara." His blue eyes got misty. "Huntington Beach. Oxnard. I got everywhere, man." He flexed his huge fingers. "Now these fucking Entity hodads own the shore. Can you believe it? They *own* it. And I'm pulling wall, my second time around, seven days a week next ten years."

"Ten?" I said. "That's a shitty deal."

"You know anyone who doesn't have a shitty deal?"

"Some," I said. "They buy out."

"Yeah."

"It can be done."

A careful look. You never know who might be a borgmann. Those stinking collaborators are everywhere.

"Can it?"

"All it takes is money," I said.

"And a pardoner."

"That's right."

"One you can trust."

I shrugged. "You've got to go on faith, man."

"Yeah," he said. Then, after a while: "I heard of a guy, he bought a three-year pardon and wall passage thrown in. Went up north, caught a krill trawler, wound up in Australia, on the Reef. Nobody's ever going to find him there. He's out of the system. Right out of the fucking system. What do you think that cost?"

"About twenty grand," I said.

"Hey, that's a sharp guess!"

"No guess."

"Oh?" Another careful look. "You don't sound local."

"I'm not. Just visiting."

"That's still the price? Twenty grand?"

"I can't do anything about supplying krill trawlers. You'd be on your own once you were outside the wall."

"Twenty grand just to get through the wall?"

"And a seven-year labor exemption."

"I pulled ten," he said.

"I can't get you ten. It's not in the configuration, you follow? But seven would work. You could get so far, in seven, that they'd lose you. You could goddamned *swim* to Australia. Come in low, below Sydney, no seines there."

"You know a hell of a lot."

"My business to know," I said. "You want me to run an asset check on you?"

"I'm worth seventeen five. Fifteen hundred real, the rest collat. What can I get for seventeen five?"

"Just what I said. Through the wall, and seven years' exemption."

"A bargain rate, hey?"

"I take what I can get," I said. "Give me your wrist. And don't worry. This part is read-only."

I keyed his data implant and patched mine in. He had fifteen hundred in the bank and a collateral rating of sixteen thou, exactly as he claimed. We eyed each other very carefully now. As I said, you never know who the borgmanns are.

"You can do it right here in the park?" he asked.

"You bet. Lean back, close your eyes, make like you're snoozing in the sun. The deal is that I take a thousand of the cash now and you transfer five thou of the collateral bucks to me, straight labor-debenture deal. When you get through the wall I get the other five hundred cash and five thou more on sweat security. The rest you pay off at three thou a year plus interest, wherever you are, quarterly key-ins. I'll program the whole thing, including beep reminders on payment dates. It's up to you to make your travel arrangements, remember. I can do pardons and wall transits, but I'm not a goddamned travel agent. Are we on?"

He put his head back and closed his eyes.

"Go ahead," he said.

It was fingertip stuff, straight circuit emulation, my

standard hack. I picked up all his identification codes, carried them into central, found his records. He seemed real, nothing more or less than he had claimed. Sure enough, he had drawn a lulu of a labor tax, ten years on the wall. I wrote him a pardon good for the first seven of that. Had to leave the final three on the books, purely technical reasons, but the computers weren't going to be able to find him by then. I gave him a wall-transit pass, too, which meant writing in a new skills class for him, programmer third grade. He didn't think like a programmer and he didn't look like a programmer, but the wall software wasn't going to figure that out. Now I had made him a member of the human elite, the relative handful of us who are free to go in and out of the walled cities as we wish. In return for these little favors I signed over his entire life savings to various accounts of mine, payable as arranged, part now, part later. He wasn't worth a nickel any more, but he was a free man. That's not such a terrible trade-off.

Oh, and the pardon was a valid one. I had decided not to write any stiffs while I was in Los Angeles. A kind of sentimental atonement, you might say, for the job I had done on that woman all those years back.

You absolutely have to write stiffs once in a while, you understand. So that you don't look too good, so that you don't give the Entities reason to hunt you down. Just as you have to ration the number of pardons you do. I didn't have to be writing pardons at all, of course. I could have just authorized the system to pay me so much a year, fifty thou, a hundred, and taken it easy forever. But where's the challenge in that?

So I write pardons, but no more than I need to cover my expenses, and I deliberately fudge some of them up, making myself look as incompetent as the rest so the Entities don't have a reason to begin trying to track the identifying marks of my work. My conscience hasn't been too sore about that. It's a matter of survival, after all. And most other pardoners are out-and-out frauds, you know. At least with me you stand a better-than-even chance of getting what you're paying for.

• • •

The next one was a tiny Japanese woman, the classic style, sleek, fragile, doll-like. Crying in big wild gulps that I thought might break her in half, while a gray-haired older man in a shabby business suit—her grandfather, you'd guess—was trying to comfort her. Public crying is a good indicator of Entity trouble. "Maybe I can help," I said, and they were both so distraught that they didn't even bother to be suspicious.

He was her father-in-law, not her grandfather. The husband was dead, killed by burglars the year before. There were two small kids. Now she had received her new labor-tax ticket. She had been afraid they were going to send her out to work on the wall, which of course wasn't likely to happen: the assignments are pretty random, but they usually aren't crazy, and what use would a ninety-pound girl be in hauling stone blocks around? The father-in-law had some friends who were in the know, and they managed to bring up the hidden encoding on her ticket. The computers hadn't sent her to the wall, no. They had sent her to Area Five. And they had given her a TTD classification.

"The wall would have been better," the old man said. "They'd see, right away, she wasn't strong enough for heavy work, and they'd find something else, something she could do. But Area Five? Who ever comes back from that?"

"You know what Area Five is?" I said.

"The medical experiment place. And this mark here, TTD. I know what that stands for, too."

She began to moan again. I couldn't blame her. TTD means Test To Destruction. The Entities want to find out how much work we can really do, and they feel that the only reliable way to discover that is to put us through tests that show where the physical limits are.

"I will die," she wailed. "My babies! My babies!"

"Do you know what a pardoner is?" I asked the father-in-law.

A quick excited response: sharp intake of breath, eyes going bright, head nodding vehemently. Just as quickly the excitement faded, giving way to bleakness, helplessness, despair.

"They all cheat you," he said.

"Not all."

"Who can say? They take your money, they give you nothing."

"You know that isn't true. Everybody can tell you stories of pardons that came through."

"Maybe. Maybe," the old man said. The woman sobbed quietly. "You know of such a person?"

"For three thousand dollars," I said, "I can take the TTD off her ticket. For five I can write an exemption from service good until her children are in high school."

Sentimental me. A fifty-percent discount, and I hadn't even run an asset check. For all I knew, the father-in-law was a millionaire. But no, he'd have been off cutting a pardon for her, then, and not sitting around like this in Pershing Square.

He gave me a long, deep, appraising look. Peasant shrewdness coming to the surface.

"How can we be sure of that?" he asked.

I might have told him that I was the king of my profession, the best of all pardoners, a genius hacker with the truly magic touch, who could slip into any computer ever designed and make it dance to my tune. Which would have been nothing more than the truth. But all I said was that he'd have to make up his own mind, that I couldn't offer any affidavits or guarantees, that I was available if he wanted me and otherwise it was all the same to me if she preferred to stick with her TTD ticket. They went off and conferred for a couple of minutes. When they came back, he silently rolled up his sleeve and presented his implant to me. I keyed his credit balance: thirty thou or so, not bad. I transferred eight of it to my accounts, half to Seattle, the rest to Los Angeles. Then I took her wrist, which was about two of my fingers thick, and got into her implant and wrote her the pardon that would save her life. Just to be certain, I ran a double validation check on it. It's always possible to stiff a customer unintentionally, though I've never done it. But I didn't want this particular one to be my first.

"Go on," I said. "Home. Your kids are waiting for their lunch."

Her eyes glowed. "If I could only thank you some-how—"

"I've already banked my fee. Go. If you ever see me again, don't say hello."

"This will work?" the old man asked.

"You say you have friends who know things. Wait seven days, then tell the data bank that she's lost her ticket. When you get the new one, ask your pals to decode it for you. You'll see. It'll be all right."

I don't think he believed me. I think he was more than half sure I had swindled him out of one-fourth of his life's savings, and I could see the hatred in his eyes. But that was his problem. In a week he'd find out that I really had saved his daughter-in-law's life, and then he'd rush down to the Square to tell me how sorry he was that he had had such terrible feelings toward me. Only by then I'd be somewhere else, far away.

They shuffled out the east side of the park, pausing a couple of times to peer over their shoulders at me as if they thought I was going to transform them into pillars of salt the moment their backs were turned. Then they were gone.

I'd earned enough now to get me through the week I planned to spend in L.A. But I stuck around anyway, hoping for a little more. My mistake.

This one was Mr. Invisible, the sort of man you'd never notice in a crowd, gray on gray, thinning hair, mild bland apologetic smile. But his eyes had a shine. I forget whether he started talking first to me, or me to him, but pretty soon we were jockeying around trying to find out things about each other. He told me he was from Silver Lake. I gave him a blank look. How in hell am I supposed to know all the zillion L.A. neighborhoods? Said that he had come down here to see someone at the big government HQ on Figueroa Street. All right: probably an appeals case. I sensed a customer.

Then he wanted to know where I was from. Santa Monica? West L.A.? Something in my accent, I guess. "I'm a traveling man," I said. "Hate to stay in one place." True enough. I need to hack or I go crazy; if I did all my hacking in just one city I'd be virtually begging them to slap a trace on me sooner or later, and that would be the end. I didn't tell him any of that. "Came in from Utah last night. Wyoming before that." Not true, either one. "Maybe on to New York, next." He looked at me as if I'd said I was planning a voyage to the moon. People out here, they don't go east a lot. These days most people don't go anywhere.

Now he knew that I had wall-transit clearance, or else that I had some way of getting it when I wanted it. That was what he was looking to find out. In no time at all we were down to basics.

He said he had drawn a new ticket, six years at the salt-field reclamation site out back of Mono Lake. People die like mayflies out there. What he wanted was a transfer to something softer, like Operations & Maintenance, and it had to be within the walls, preferably in one of the districts out by the ocean where the air is cool and clear. I quoted him a price and he accepted without a quiver.

"Let's have your wrist," I said.

He held out his right hand, palm upward. His implant access was a pale-yellow plaque, mounted in the usual place but rounder than the standard kind and of a slightly smoother texture. I didn't see any great significance in that. As I had done maybe a thousand times before, I put my own arm over his, wrist to wrist, access to access. Our biocomputers made contact, and instantly I knew that I was in trouble.

Human beings have been carrying biochip-based computers in their bodies for the last forty or fifty years or so—long before the Entity invasion, anyway—but for most people it's just something they take for granted, like the vaccination mark on their thighs. They use them for the things they're meant to be used for, and don't give them a thought beyond that. The biocomputer's just a commonplace tool for them, like a fork, like a shovel. You have to have the hacker sort of mentality to be willing to turn your biocomputer into something more. That's why, when the Entities came and took us over and made us build walls around our cities, most people reacted just like sheep, letting themselves be herded inside and politely staying there. The only ones who can move around freely now—because we know how to manipulate the mainframes through which the Entities rule us—are the hackers. And there aren't many of us. I could tell right away that I had hooked myself onto one now.

The moment we were in contact, he came at me like a storm.

The strength of his signal let me know I was up against something special, and that I'd been hustled. He hadn't been trying to buy a pardon at all. What he was looking for was a duel. Mr. Macho behind the bland smile, out to show the new boy in town a few of his tricks.

No hacker had ever mastered me in a one-on-one anywhere. Not ever. I felt sorry for him, but not much.

He shot me a bunch of stuff, cryptic but easy, just by way of finding out my parameters. I caught it and stored it and laid an interrupt on him and took over the dialog. My turn to test him. I wanted him to begin to see who he was fooling around with. But just as I began to execute, he put an interrupt on *me*. That was a new experience. I stared at him with some respect.

Usually any hacker anywhere will recognize my signal in the first thirty seconds, and that'll be enough to finish the interchange. He'll know that there's no point in continuing. But this guy either wasn't able to identify me or just didn't care, and he came right back with his interrupt. Amazing. So was the stuff he began laying on me next.

He went right to work, really trying to scramble my architecture. Reams of stuff came flying at me up in the heavy-megabyte zone.

—*jspike. dbltag. nslice. dzcnt.*

I gave it right back to him, twice as hard.

—*maxfrq. minpau. spktot. jspike.*

He didn't mind at all.

—*maxdz. spktim. falter. nslice.*

—frqsum. eburst.
—iburst.
—prebst.
—nobrst.

Mexican standoff. He was still smiling. Not even a trace of sweat on his forehead. Something eerie about him, something new and strange. This is some kind of borgmann hacker, I realized suddenly. He must be working for the Entities, roving the city, looking to make trouble for free-lancers like me. Good as he was, and he was plenty good, I despised him. A hacker who had become a borgmann— now, that was truly disgusting. I wanted to short him. I wanted to burn him out, now. I had never hated anyone so much in my life.

I couldn't do a thing with him.

I was baffled. I was the Data King, I was the Megabyte Monster. All my life I had floated back and forth across a world in chains, picking every lock I came across. And now this nobody was tying me in knots. Whatever I gave him, he parried; and what came back from him was getting increasingly bizarre. He was working with an algorithm I had never seen before and was having serious trouble solving. After a little while I couldn't even figure out what he was doing to me, let alone what I was going to do to cancel it. It was getting so I could barely execute. He was forcing me inexorably toward a wetware crash.

"Who are you?" I yelled.

He laughed in my face.

And kept pouring it on. He was threatening the integrity of my implant, going at me down on the microcosmic level, attacking the molecules themselves. Fiddling around with electron shells, reversing charges and mucking up valences, clogging my gates, turning my circuits to soup. The computer that is implanted in my brain is nothing but a lot of organic chemistry, after all. So is my brain. If he kept this up the computer would go and the brain would follow, and I'd spend the rest of my life in the bibble-bibble academy.

This wasn't a sporting contest. This was murder.

I reached for the reserves, throwing up all the defensive

blockages I could invent. Things I had never had to use in my life, but they were there when I needed them, and they did slow him down. For a moment I was able to halt his ballbreaking onslaught and even push him back. And give myself the breathing space to set up a few offensive combinations of my own. But before I could get them running, he shut me down once more and started to drive me toward crashville all over again. He was unbelievable.

I blocked him. He came back again. I hit him hard and he threw the punch into some other neural channel altogether and it went fizzling away.

I hit him again. Again he blocked it.

Then he hit me and I went reeling and staggering, and managed to get myself together when I was about three nanoseconds from the edge of the abyss.

I began to set up a new combination. But even as I did it, I was reading the tone of his data, and what I was getting was absolute cool confidence. He was waiting for me. He was ready for anything I could throw. He was in that realm beyond mere self-confidence into utter certainty.

What it was coming down to was this. I was able to keep him from ruining me, but only just barely, and I wasn't able to lay a glove on him at all. And he seemed to have infinite resources behind him. I didn't worry him. He was tireless. He didn't appear to degrade at all. He just took all I could give and kept throwing new stuff at me, coming at me from six sides at once.

Now I understood for the first time what it must have felt like for all the hackers I had beaten. Some of them must have felt pretty cocky, I suppose, until they ran into me. It costs more to lose when you think you're good. When you *know* you're good. People like that, when they lose, they have to reprogram their whole sense of their relation to the universe.

I had two choices. I could go on fighting until he wore me down and crashed me. Or I could give up right now. In the end everything comes down to yes or no, on or off, one or zero, doesn't it?

I took a deep breath. I was staring straight into chaos.

"All right," I said. "I'm beaten. I quit."

I wrenched my wrist free of his, trembled, swayed, went toppling down on the ground.

A minute later five cops jumped me and trussed me up like a turkey and hauled me away, with my implant arm sticking out of the package and a security lock wrapped around my wrist, as if they were afraid I was going to start pulling data right out of the air.

Where they took me was Figueroa Street, the big black marble ninety-story job that is the home of the puppet city government. I didn't give a damn. I was numb. They could have put me in the sewer and I wouldn't have cared. I wasn't damaged—the automatic circuit check was still running and it came up green—but the humiliation was so intense that I felt crashed. I felt destroyed. The only thing I wanted to know was the name of the hacker who had done it to me.

The Figueroa Street building has ceilings about twenty feet high everywhere, so that there'll be room for Entities to move around. Voices reverberate in those vast open spaces like echoes in a cavern. The cops sat me down in a hallway, still all wrapped up, and kept me there for a long time. Blurred sounds went lalloping up and down the passage. I wanted to hide from them. My brain felt raw. I had taken one hell of a pounding.

Now and then a couple of towering Entities would come rumbling through the hall, tiptoeing on their tentacles in that weirdly dainty way of theirs. With them came a little entourage of humans whom they ignored entirely, as they always do. They know that we're intelligent, but they just don't care to talk to us. They let their computers do that, via the Borgmann interface, and may his signal degrade forever for having sold us out. Not that they wouldn't have conquered us anyway, but Borgmann made it ever so much easier for them to push us around by showing them how to connect our little biocomputers to their huge mainframes. I bet he was very proud of himself, too: just wanted to see if his gadget would work, and to hell with the fact that he was selling us into eternal bondage.

Nobody has ever figured out why the Entities are here or what they want from us. They simply came, that's all. Saw. Conquered. Rearranged us. Put us to work doing god-awful unfathomable tasks. Like a bad dream.

And there wasn't any way we could defend ourselves against them. Didn't seem that way to us at first—we were cocky, we were going to wage guerrilla war and wipe them out—but we learned fast how wrong we were, and we are theirs for keeps. There's nobody left with anything close to freedom except the handful of hackers like me; and, as I've explained, we're not dopey enough to try any serious sort of counterattack. It's a big enough triumph for us just to be able to dodge around from one city to another without having to get authorization.

Looked like all that was finished for me now. Right then I didn't give a damn. I was still trying to integrate the notion that I had been beaten; I didn't have capacity left over to work on a program for the new life I would be leading now.

"Is this the pardoner, over here?" someone said.

"That one, yeah."

"She wants to see him now."

"You think we should fix him up a little first?"

"She said now."

A hand at my shoulder, rocking me gently. "Up, fellow. It's interview time. Don't make a mess or you'll get hurt."

I let them shuffle me down the hall and through a gigantic doorway and into an immense office with a ceiling high enough to give an Entity all the room it would want. I didn't say a word. There weren't any Entities in the office, just a woman in a black robe, sitting behind a wide desk at the far end. It looked like a toy desk in that colossal room. She looked like a toy woman. The cops left me alone with her. Trussed up like that, I wasn't any risk.

"Are you John Doe?" she asked.

I was halfway across the room, studying my shoes. "What do you think?" I said.

"That's the name you gave upon entry to the city."

"I give lots of names. John Smith, Richard Roe, Joe

Blow. It doesn't matter much to the gate software what name I give."

"Because you've gimmicked the gate?" She paused. "I should tell you, this is a court of inquiry."

"You already know everything I could tell you. Your borgmann hacker's been swimming around in my brain."

"Please," she said. "This'll be easier if you cooperate. The accusation is illegal entry, illegal seizure of a vehicle, and illegal interfacing activity, specifically, selling pardons. Do you have a statement?"

"No."

"You deny that you're a pardoner?"

"I don't deny, I don't affirm. What's the goddamned use."

"Look up at me," she said.

"That's a lot of effort."

"Look up," she said. There was an odd edge on her voice. "Whether you're a pardoner or not isn't the issue. We know you're a pardoner. *I* know you're a pardoner." And she called me by a name I hadn't used in a very long time. Not since '36, as a matter of fact.

I looked at her. Stared. Had trouble believing I was seeing what I saw. Felt a rush of memories come flooding up. Did some mental editing work on her face, taking out some lines here, subtracting a little flesh in a few places, adding some in others. Stripping away the years.

"Yes," she said. "I'm who you think I am."

I gaped. This was worse than what the hacker had done to me. But there was no way to run from it.

"You work for them?" I asked.

"The pardon you sold me wasn't any good. You knew that, didn't you? I had someone waiting for me in San Diego, but when I tried to get through the wall they stopped me just like that, and dragged me away screaming. I could have killed you. I would have gone to San Diego and then we would have tried to make it to Hawaii in his boat."

"I didn't know about the guy in San Diego," I said.

"Why should you? It wasn't your business. You took my money, you were supposed to get me my pardon. That was the deal."

Her eyes were gray with golden sparkles in them. I had trouble looking into them.

"You still want to kill me?" I asked. "Are you planning to kill me now?"

"No and no." She used my old name again. "I can't tell you how astounded I was, when they brought you in here. A pardoner, they said. John Doe. Pardoners, that's my department. They bring all of them to me. I used to wonder years ago if they'd ever bring *you* in, but after a while I figured, no, not a chance, he's probably a million miles away, he'll never come back this way again. And then they brought in this John Doe, and I saw your face."

"Do you think you could manage to believe," I said, "that I've felt guilty for what I did to you ever since? You don't have to believe it. But it's the truth."

"I'm sure it's been unending agony for you."

"I mean it. Please. I've stiffed a lot of people, yes, and sometimes I've regretted it and sometimes I haven't, but you were one that I regretted. You're the one I've regretted most. This is the absolute truth."

She considered that. I couldn't tell whether she believed it even for a fraction of a second, but I could see that she was considering it.

"Why did you do it?" she asked after a bit.

"I stiff people because I don't want to seem too perfect," I told her. "You deliver a pardon every single time, word gets around, people start talking, you start to become legendary. And then you're known everywhere and sooner or later the Entities get hold of you, and that's that. So I always make sure to write a lot of stiffs. I tell people I'll do my best, but there aren't any guarantees, and sometimes it doesn't work."

"You deliberately cheated me."

"Yes."

"I thought you did. You seemed so cool, so professional. So perfect. I was sure the pardon would be valid. I couldn't see how it would miss. And then I got to the wall and they grabbed me. So I thought, That bastard sold me out. He was too good just to have flubbed it up." Her tone was calm, but the anger was still in her eyes. "Couldn't you have stiffed the next one? Why did it have to be me?"

I looked at her for a long time.

"Because I loved you," I said.

"Shit," she said. "You didn't even know me. I was just some stranger who had hired you."

"That's just it. There I was full of all kinds of crazy instant lunatic fantasies about you, all of a sudden ready to turn my nice orderly life upside down for you, and all you could see was somebody you had hired to do a job. I didn't know about the guy from San Diego. All I knew was I saw you and I wanted you. You don't think that's love? Well, call it something else, then, whatever you want. I never let myself feel it before. It isn't smart, I thought, it ties you down, the risks are too big. And then I saw you and I talked to you a little and I thought something could be happening between us and things started to change inside me, and I thought, Yeah, yeah, go with it this time, let it happen, this may make everything different. And you stood there not seeing it, not even beginning to notice, just jabbering on and on about how important the pardon was for you. So I stiffed you. And afterwards I thought, Jesus, I ruined that girl's life and it was just because I got myself into a snit, and that was a fucking petty thing to have done. So I've been sorry ever since. You don't have to believe that. I didn't know about San Diego. That makes it even worse for me." She didn't say anything all this time, and the silence felt enormous. So after a moment I said, "Tell me one thing, at least. That guy who wrecked me in Pershing Square: who was he?"

"He wasn't anybody," she said.

"What does that mean?"

"He isn't a who. He's a *what*. It's an android, a mobile antipardoner unit, plugged right into the big Entity mainframe in Culver City. Something new that we have going around town."

"Oh," I said. "Oh."

"The report is that you gave it one hell of a workout."

"It gave me one, too. Turned my brain half to mush."

"You were trying to drink the sea through a straw. For a

while it looked like you were really going to do it, too. You're one goddamned hacker, you know that?"

"Why did you go to work for them?" I said.

She shrugged. "Everybody works for them. Except people like you. You took everything I had and didn't give me my pardon. So what was I supposed to do?"

"I see."

"It's not such a bad job. At least I'm not out there on the wall. Or being sent off for TTD."

"No," I said. "It's probably not so bad. If you don't mind working in a room with such a high ceiling. Is that what's going to happen to me? Sent off for TTD?"

"Don't be stupid. You're too valuable."

"To whom?"

"The system always needs upgrading. You know it better than anyone alive. You'll work for us."

"You think I'm going to turn borgmann?" I said, amazed.

"It beats TTD," she said.

I fell silent again. I was thinking that she couldn't possibly be serious, that they'd be fools to trust me in any kind of responsible position. And even bigger fools to let me near their computer.

"All right," I said. "I'll do it. On one condition."

"You really have balls, don't you?"

"Let me have a rematch with that android of yours. I need to check something out. And afterward we can discuss what kind of work I'd be best suited for here. Okay?"

"You know you aren't in any position to lay down conditions."

"Sure I am. What I do with computers is a unique art. You can't make me do it against my will. You can't make me do anything against my will."

She thought about that. "What good is a rematch?"

"Nobody ever beat me before. I want a second try."

"You know it'll be worse for you than before."

"Let me find that out."

"But what's the point?"

"Get me your android and I'll show you the point," I said.

• • •

She went along with it. Maybe it was curiosity, maybe it was something else, but she patched herself into the computer net and pretty soon they brought in the android I had encountered in the park, or maybe another one with the same face. It looked me over pleasantly, without the slightest sign of interest.

Someone came in and took the security lock off my wrist and left again. She gave the android its instructions and it held out its wrist to me and we made contact. And I jumped right in.

I was raw and wobbly and pretty damned battered, still, but I knew what I needed to do and I knew I had to do it fast. The thing was to ignore the android completely—it was just a terminal, it was just a unit—and go for what lay behind it. So I bypassed the android's own identity program, which was clever but shallow. I went right around it while the android was still setting up its combinations, dived underneath, got myself instantly from the unit level to the mainframe level and gave the master Culver City computer a hearty handshake.

Jesus, that felt good!

All that power, all those millions of megabytes squatting there, and I was plugged right into it. Of course, I felt like a mouse hitchhiking on the back of an elephant. That was all right. I might be a mouse, but that mouse was getting a tremendous ride. I hung on tight and went soaring along on the hurricane winds of that colossal machine.

And as I soared, I ripped out chunks of it by the double handful and tossed them to the breeze.

It didn't even notice for a good tenth of a second. That's how big it was. There I was, tearing great blocks of data out of its gut, joyously ripping and rending. And it didn't even know it, because even the most magnificent computer ever assembled is still stuck with operating at the speed of light, and when the best you can do is 186,000 miles a second it can take quite a while for the alarm to travel the full distance down all your neural channels. That thing was *huge*. Mouse riding on elephant, did I say? Amoeba piggybacking on brontosaurus, was more like it.

God knows how much damage I was able to do. But of

course the alarm circuitry did cut in eventually. Internal gates came clanging down and all sensitive areas were sealed away and I was shrugged off with the greatest of ease. There was no sense staying around waiting to get trapped, so I pulled myself free.

I had found out what I needed to know. Where the defenses were, how they worked. This time the computer had kicked me out, but it wouldn't be able to, the next. Whenever I wanted, I could go in there and smash whatever I felt like.

The android crumpled to the carpet. It was nothing but an empty husk now.

Lights were flashing on the office wall.

She looked at me, appalled. "What did you do?"

"I beat your android," I said. "It wasn't all that hard, once I knew the scoop."

"You damaged the main computer."

"Not really. Not much. I just gave it a little tickle. It was surprised, seeing me get access in there, that's all."

"I think you really damaged it."

"Why would I want to do that?"

"The question ought to be why you haven't done it already. Why you haven't gone in there and crashed the hell out of their programs."

"You think I could do something like that?"

She studied me. "I think maybe you could, yes."

"Well, maybe so. Or maybe not. But I'm not a crusader, you know. I like my life the way it is. I move around, I do as I please. It's a quiet life. I don't start revolutions. When I need to gimmick things, I gimmick them just enough, and no more. And the Entities don't even know I exist. If I stick my finger in their eye, they'll cut my finger off. So I haven't done it."

"But now you might," she said.

I began to get uncomfortable. "I don't follow you," I said, although I was beginning to think that I did.

"You don't like risk. You don't like being conspicuous. But if we take your freedom away, if we tie you down in L.A. and put you to work, what the hell would you have to

lose? You'd go right in there. You'd gimmick things but
good." She was silent for a time. "Yes," she said. "You
really would. I see it now, that you have the capability and
that you could be put in a position where you'd be willing
to use it. And then you'd screw everything up for all of us,
wouldn't you?"

"What?"

"You'd fix the Entities, sure. You'd do such a job on their
computer that they'd have to scrap it and start all over again.
Isn't that so?"

She was onto me, all right.

"But I'm not going to give you the chance. I'm not crazy.
There isn't going to be any revolution and I'm not going to
be its heroine and you aren't the type to be a hero. I
understand you now. It isn't safe to fool around with you.
Because if anybody did, you'd take your little revenge, and
you wouldn't care what you brought down on everybody
else's head. You could ruin their computer, but then they'd
come down on us and they'd make things twice as hard for
us as they already are, and you wouldn't care. We'd all
suffer, but you wouldn't care. No. My life isn't so terrible
that I need you to turn it upside down for me. You've
already done it to me once. I don't need it again."

She looked at me steadily and all the anger seemed to be
gone from her and there was only contempt left.

After a little she said, "Can you go in there again and
gimmick things so that there's no record of your arrest
today?"

"Yeah. Yeah, I could do that."

"Do it, then. And then get going. Get the hell out of here,
fast."

"Are you serious?"

"You think I'm not?"

I shook my head. I understood. And I knew that I had won
and I had lost, both at the same time.

She made an impatient gesture, a shoofly gesture.

I nodded. I felt very very small.

"I just want to say—all that stuff about how much I

regretted the thing I did to you back then—it was true. Every word of it."

"It probably was," she said. "Look, do your gimmicking and edit yourself out and then I want you to start moving. Out of the building. Out of the city. Okay? Do it real fast."

I hunted around for something else to say and couldn't find it. Quit while you're ahead, I thought. She gave me her wrist and I did the interface with her. As my implant access touched hers, she shuddered a little. It wasn't much of a shudder, but I noticed it. I felt it, all right. I think I'm going to feel it every time I stiff anyone, ever again. Any time I even think of stiffing anyone.

I went in and found the John Doe arrest entry and got rid of it, and then I searched out her civil service file and promoted her up two grades and doubled her pay. Not much of an atonement. But what the hell, there wasn't much I could do. Then I cleaned up my traces behind me and exited the program.

"All right," I said. "It's done."

"Fine," she said, and rang for her cops.

They apologized for the case of mistaken identity and let me out of the building and turned me loose on Figueroa Street. It was late afternoon and the street was getting dark and the air was cool. Even in Los Angeles winter is winter, of a sort. I went to a street access and summoned the Toshiba from wherever it had parked itself and it came driving up, five or ten minutes later, and I told it to take me north. The going was slow, rush-hour stuff, but that was okay. We came to the wall at the Sylmar gate, fifty miles or so out of town. The gate asked me my name. "Richard Roe," I said. "Beta Pi Upsilon 104324x. Destination San Francisco."

It rains a lot in San Francisco in the winter. Still, it's a pretty town. I would have preferred Los Angeles that time of year, but what the hell. Nobody gets all his first choices all the time. The gate opened and the Toshiba went through. Easy as Beta Pi.

LIVING WILL

Alexander Jablokov

With only a handful of elegant, coolly pyrotechnic stories, like the one that follows, and a few well-received novels, Alexander Jablokov has established himself as one of the most highly regarded and promising new writers in SF. He is a frequent contributor to Asimov's Science Fiction, Amazing, *and other markets. His first novel,* Carve the Sky, *was released in 1991 to wide critical acclaim, and was followed by other successful novels such as* A Deeper Sea *and* Nimbus. *His most recent books are a collection of his short fiction,* The Breath of Suspension, *and a new novel,* Red Dust. *He lives in Cambridge, Massachusetts.*

Here he relates the powerful story of a far-sighted man who makes all the necessary preparations for his eventual death—including a few that most *people would not think of. . . .*

The *computer screen* lay on the desk like a piece of paper. Like fine calfskin parchment, actually—the software had that as a standard option. At the top, in block capitals, were the words **COMMENCE ENTRY.**

"Boy, you have a lot to learn." Roman Maitland leaned back in his chair. "That's something I would *never* say. Let that be your first datum."

PREFERRED PROMPT?

"Surprise me." Roman turned away to pour himself a cup of coffee from the thermos next to a stone bust of Archimedes. The bust had been given to him by his friend Gerald "to help you remember your roots," as Gerald had put it. Archimedes desperately shouldered the disorganized stack of optical disks that threatened to sweep him from his shelf.

Roman turned back to the screen. **TELL ME A STORY**, it said. He barked a laugh. "Fair enough." He stood up and slouched around his office. The afternoon sun slanted through the high windows. Through the concealing shrubs he could just hear the road in front of the house, a persistent annoyance. What had been a minor street when he built the house had turned into a major thoroughfare.

"My earliest memory is of my sister." Roman Maitland was a stocky white-haired man with high-arched dark eyebrows. His wife Abigail claimed that with each passing year he looked more and more like Warren G. Harding. Roman had looked at the picture in the encyclopedia and failed to see the resemblance. He was much better looking than Harding.

"The hallway leading to the kitchen had red-and-green linoleum in a kind of linked circle pattern. You can cross-reference linoleum if you want." The antique parchment remained blank. "My sister's name is Elizabeth—Liza. I can see her. She has her hair in two tiny pink bows and is wearing a pale blue dress and black shoes. She's sitting on the linoleum, playing with one of my trucks. One of my *new* trucks. I grab it away from her. She doesn't cry. She just looks up at me with serious eyes. She has a pointy little chin. I don't remember what happened after that. Liza lives in Seattle now. Her chin is pointy again."

The wall under the windows was taken up with the black boxes of field memories. They linked into the processor inside the desk. The screen swirled and settled into a pattern of interlocking green-and-pink circles. "That's not quite it. The diamond parts were a little more—" Another pattern appeared, subtly different. Roman stared at it in wonder. "Yes. Yes! That's it. How did you know?" The computer, having linked to some obscure linoleum-pattern database on the network, blanked the screen. Roman wondered how many more of his private memories would prove to be publicly accessible. **TELL ME A STORY.**

He pulled a book from the metal bookshelf. "My favorite

book by Raymond Chandler is *The Little Sister*. I think
Orfamay Quest is one of the great characters of literature.
Have you read Chandler?"

**I HAVE ACCESS TO THE ENTIRE LIBRARY OF
CONGRESS HOLDINGS.**

"Boy, you're getting gabby. But that's not what I asked."

I HAVE NEVER READ ANYTHING.

"Give it a try. Though in some ways Elmore Leonard is
even better." He slipped Chandler back on the shelf, almost
dumping the unwieldy mass of books piled on top of the
neatly shelved ones. "There are books here I've read a
dozen times. Some *I've tried* reading a dozen times. Some
I will someday read and some I suppose I'll never read." He
squatted down next to a tall stack of magazines and
technical offprints and started sorting them desultorily.

WHY READ SOMETHING MORE THAN ONCE?

"Why see a friend more than once? I've often thought
that I would like to completely forget a favorite book."
From where he squatted, the bookshelves loomed threaten-
ingly. He'd built his study with a high ceiling, knowing how
the stuff would pile up. There was a dead plant at the top of
the shelf nearest the desk. He frowned. How long had that
been there? "Then I could read it again for the first time.
The thought's a little frightening. What if I didn't *like* it? I'm
not the person who read it for the first time, after all. Just as
well, I guess, that it's an experiment I can't try. Abigail likes
to reread Jane Austen. Particularly *Emma*." He snorted.
"But that's not what you're interested in, is it?" His stomach
rumbled. "I'm hungry. It's time for lunch."

BON APPETIT.

"Thank you."

Roman had built his house with exposed posts and beams
and protected it outside with dark brick and granite. Abigail
had filled it with elegant clean-lined furniture, which was
much less obtrusive about showing its strength. Roman had
only reluctantly ceded control of everything but his study
and his garage workshop. He'd grown to like it. He could
never have remembered to water so many plants, and the
cunning arrangement of bright yellow porcelain vases and

darkly rain-swept watercolors was right in a way he couldn't have achieved.

At the end of the hallway, past the kitchen's clean flare, glowed the rectangle of the rear screen door. Abigail bent over her flowers, fuzzy through its mesh like a romantic memory, a sun hat hiding her face. Her sun-dappled dress gleamed against the dark garden.

Roman pressed his nose against the screen, smelling its forgotten rust. Work gloves protecting her hands, his wife snipped flowers with a pruner and placed them in a basket on her arm. A blue ribbon accented the sun hat. Beyond her stretched the perennial bed, warmed by its reflecting stone wall, and the crazy-paving walk that led to the carp pond. White anemones and lilies glowed amid the ferns, Abigail's emulation of Vita Sackville-West's white garden. A few premature leaves, anxious for the arrival of autumn, flickered through the sun and settled in the grass.

"I'll have lunch ready in a minute." She didn't look up at him, so what spoke was the bobbing and amused sun hat. "I could hear your stomach all the way from the white garden." She stripped off the gardening gloves.

"I'll make lunch." Roman felt nettled. Why should she assume he was staring at her just because he was hungry?

As he regarded the white kitchen cabinets, collecting his mind and remembering where the plates, tableware, and napkins were, Abigail swept past him and set the table in a quick flurry of activity. Finding a vase and putting flowers into it would have been a contemplative activity of some minutes for Roman. She performed the task in one motion.

She was a sharp-featured woman. Her hair was completely white, and she usually kept it tied up in a variety of braids. Her eyes were large and blue. She looked at her husband.

"What are you doing up there in your office? Did you invent a robot confessor or something?"

"You haven't been—"

"No, Roman, I haven't been eavesdropping." She was indulgent. "But you do have a piercing voice, particularly when you get excited. Usually you talk to your computer only when you're swearing at it."

"It's my new project." Roman hadn't told Abigail a thing about it, and he knew that bothered her. She hated big-secret little-boy projects. She was the kind of girl who'd always tried to break into the boys' clubhouse and beat them at their games. He really should have told her. But the thought made him uncomfortable.

"It's kind of egomaniacal, actually. You know that computer I'm beta-testing for Hyperneuron?"

"That thing it took them a week to move in! Yes, I know it. They scratched the floor in two places. You should hire a better class of movers."

"We'd like to. It's a union problem, I've told you that. Anyway, it's a wide-aspect parallel processor with a gargantuan set of field memories. Terabytes worth."

She placidly spread jam on a piece of bread. "I'll assume all that jargon actually means something. Even if it does, it doesn't tell me why you're off chatting with that box instead of with me."

He covered her hand with his. "I'm sorry, Abigail. You know how it is."

"I know, I know." She sounded irritated but turned her hand over and curled her fingers around his.

"I'm programming the computer with a model of a human personality. People have spent a lot of time and energy analyzing what they call 'computability': how easily problems can be solved. But there's another side to it: what problems *should* be solved. Personality can be defined by the way problems are chosen. It's an interesting project."

"And whose personality are you using?" She raised an eyebrow, ready to be amused at the answer.

He grimaced, embarrassed. "The most easily accessible one: my own."

She laughed. Her voice was still-untarnished silver. "Can the computer improve over the original?"

"Improve *how*, I would like to know."

"Oh, just as a random example, could it put clothes, books, and magazines *away* when it's done with them? Just a basic sense of neatness. No major psychological surgery."

"I tried that. It turned into a psychotic killer. Seems that messiness is an essential part of a healthy personality. Kind of an interesting result, really . . ."

She laughed again, and he felt embarrassed that he hadn't told her before. After all, they had been married over thirty years. But he couldn't tell her all of it. He couldn't tell her how afraid he was.

"So what's the problem with it?" Roman, irritated, held the phone receiver against his ear with his shoulder and leafed through the papers in his file drawer. His secretary had redone it all with multicolored tabs, and he had no idea what they meant. "Isn't the paperwork in order?"

"The paperwork's in order." The anonymous female voice from Financial was matter-of-fact. "It just doesn't look at all like your signature, Dr. Maitland. And this is an expensive contract. Did you sign it yourself?"

"Of course I signed it." He had no memory of it. Why not? It sounded important.

"But this signature—"

"I injured my arm playing tennis a few weeks ago." He laughed nervously, certain she would catch the lie. "It must have affected my handwriting." But was it a lie? He swung his arm. The muscles weren't right. He had strained his forearm, trying to change his serve. Old muscles are hard to retrain. The more he thought about it, the more sense it made. If only he could figure out what she was talking about.

"All right then, Dr. Maitland. Sorry to bother you."

"That's quite all right." He desperately wanted to ask her the subject of the requisition, but it was too late.

After fifteen minutes he found it, a distributed-network operating-system software package. Extremely expensive. Of course, of course. He read over it. It made sense now. But was that palsied scrawl at the bottom really his signature?

Roman stared at the multiple rolling porcelain boards on the wall, all of them covered with diagrams and equations in many colors of Magic Marker. There were six projects up there, all of which he was juggling simultaneously. He felt a sudden cold, sticky sweat in his armpits. He was juggling them, but had absolutely no *understanding* of them. It was all meaningless nonsense.

The previous week he had lost it in the middle of briefing. Hed been explaining the operation of some cognitive algorithms when he blanked, forgetting everything about them. A young member of his staff had helped him out. "It's all this damn management," Roman had groused. "It fills up all available space, leaving room for nothing important. I've overwritten everything." The room had chuckled while Roman stood there feeling a primitive terror. He'd worked those algorithms out himself. He remembered the months of skull sweat, the constant dead ends, the modifications. He remembered all that, but still the innards of those procedures would not come clear.

The fluorescent light hummed insolently over his head. He glanced up. It was dark outside, most of the cars gone from the lot. A distant line of red-and-white lights marked the highway. How long had he been in this room? What time was it? For an instant he wasn't even sure where he was. He poked his head out of his office. The desks were empty. He could hear the vacuum cleaners of the night cleaning crew. He put on his coat and went home.

"She seemed a lovely woman, from what I saw of her." Roman peered into the insulated take-out container. All of the oyster beef was gone. He picked up the last few rice grains from the china plate Abigail had insisted they use, concentrating with his chopsticks. Abigail herself was out with one of her own friends, Helen Tourmin. He glanced at the other container. Maybe there was some chicken left.

Gerald Parks grimaced slightly, as if Roman had picked a flaw in his latest lady friend. "She *is* lovely. Roman, leave the Szechuan chicken alone. You've had your share. That's mine." Despite his normal irritation, he seemed depressed.

Roman put the half-full container down. His friend always ate too slowly, as if teasing him. Gerald leaned back, contemplative. He was an ancient and professional bachelor, dressed and groomed with razor sharpness. His severely brushed hair was steel gray. For him, eating Chinese takeout off Abigail's Limoges china made sense, which was why she had offered it.

"Anna's a law professor at Harvard." Gerald took on the tone of a man about to state a self-created aphorism. "Women at Harvard think that they're sensible because they get their romantic pretensions from Jane Austen and the Brontë sisters rather than from Barbara Cartland and Danielle Steel."

"Better than getting your romantic pretensions from Jerzy Kosinski and Vladimir Nabokov."

Sometimes the only way to cheer Gerald up was to insult him cleverly. He snorted in amusement. "Touché, I suppose. It takes Slavs to come up with that particular kind of overintellectualized sexual perversity. With a last name like Parks, I've always been jealous of it. So don't make fun of my romantic pretensions." He scooped out the last of the Szechuan chicken and ate it. Leaving the dishwasher humming in the kitchen they adjourned to Roman's crowded study.

Gerald Parks was a consulting ethnomusicologist who made a lot of money translating popular music into other idioms. His bachelor condo on Commonwealth Avenue in Boston had gotten neater and neater over the years. To Roman, Gerald's apartment felt like a cabin on an ocean liner. Various emotions had been packed away somewhere in the hold with the old Cunard notice NOT WANTED ON THE VOYAGE.

Gerald regarded the black field memories, each with its glowing indicator light. "This place seems more like an industrial concern every time I'm in here." His own study was filled with glass-fronted wood bookcases and had a chaise longue covered with yellow-and-white striped silk. It also had a computer. Gerald was no fool.

"Maybe it looks that way to you because I get so much work done here." Roman refused to be irritated.

But Gerald was in an irritating mood. He took a sip of his

Calvados and listened to the music, a CD of Christopher Hogwood's performance of Mozart's great G Minor Symphony. "All original instrumentation. Seventeenth-century Cremona viols, natural horns, Grenser oboes. Bah."

"What's wrong with that?" Roman loved the clean precision of Mozart in the original eighteenth-century style.

"Because we're not *hearing* any of those things, only a computer generating electronic frequencies. A CD player is just a high-tech player piano, those little laser spots on the disk an exact analog of the holes in a player piano roll. Do you think Mozart composed for gadgets like that? And meant to have his symphonies sound *exactly the same* every time they're heard? These original music fanatics have the whole thing bass-ackwards."

Roman listened to an oboe. And it *was* distinguishable as an oboe, Grenser or otherwise, not a clarinet or bass horn. The speakers, purchased on Gerald's recommendation, were transparent. "This performance will continue to exist after every performer on it is dead. Wouldn't it be wonderful to have a recording of Mozart's original version?"

"You wouldn't like it. Those gut-stringed instruments went out of tune before a movement was over." Gerald looked gloomy. "But you don't have to wait until the performers are dead. I recently listened to a recording I made of myself when I was young, playing Szymanowski's *Masques*. Not bad technically, but I sound so young. So *young*. Naïve and energetic. I couldn't duplicate that now, not with these old fingers. The man who made that recording is gone forever. He lived in a couple of little rooms on the third floor in a bad neighborhood on the northwest side of Chicago. He had a crummy upright piano he'd spent his last dime on. Played the thing constantly. Drove the neighbors absolutely nuts." Gerald looked at his fingers. He played superbly, at least to Roman's layman's ear, but it had never been good enough for a concert career.

"Did you erase the tape?"

Gerald shook his head. "What good would that do?"

They sat for a long moment in companionable silence. At last Gerald bestirred himself. "How is your little electronic brain doing? Does it have your personality down pat yet?"

"Test it out."

"How? Do you want me to have an argument with it?"

Roman smiled. "That's probably the best way. It can talk now. It's not my voice, not quite yet."

Gerald looked at the speakers. "If it's not sitting in a chair with a snifter of Calvados, how is it supposed to be you?"

"It's *not* me. It just thinks and feels like me."

"The way you would if you were imprisoned in a metal box?"

"Don't be absurd." Roman patted one of the field memories. "There's a universe in these things. A conceptual universe. The way I used to feel on our vacations in Truro is in here, including the time I cut my foot on a fishhook and the time I was stung by a jellyfish. That annoyed me, being molested by a jellyfish. My differential equations prof, Dr. Yang, is in here. He said 'theta' as 'teeta' and 'minus one' as 'mice wa.' And 'physical meaning' as 'fiscal meaning.' For half a semester I thought I was learning economics. The difference in the way my toy car rolled on the linoleum and on the old rug. The time I got enough nerve to ask Mary Tomkins on a date, and she told me to ask Helga Pilchard from the Special Needs class instead. The clouds over the Cotswolds when I was there with Abigail on our honeymoon. It's all there."

"How the hell does it know what cloud formations over the Cotswolds look like?"

Roman shrugged. "I described them. It went through meteorological databases until it found good cumulus formations for central England at that season."

"Including the cloud you thought looked like a power amplifier and Abigail thought looked like a springer spaniel?" Gerald smiled maliciously. He'd made up the incident, but it characterized many of Roman and Abigial's arguments.

"Quit bugging me. Bug the computer instead."

"Easier said than done." Roman could see that his friend was nervous. "How did we meet?" Gerald's voice was shaky.

"The day of registration." The computer's voice was smoothly modulated, generic male, without Roman's inflections or his trace of a Boston accent. "You were standing against a pillar reading a copy of *The Importance of Being Earnest*. Classes hadn't started yet, so I knew you were reading it because you wanted to. I came up and told you that if Lady Bracknell knew who you were pretending to be *this* time, you'd really be in trouble."

"Quite a pickup line," Gerald muttered. "I never did believe that an engineering student had read Wilde. What was I wearing?"

"Come on." The computer voice actually managed to sound exasperated. "How am I supposed to remember that? It was forty-five years ago. If I had to guess I'd say it was that ridiculous shirt you like, with the weave falling apart, full of holes. You wore it until it barely existed."

"I'm still wearing it." Gerald looked at Roman. "This is scary." He took a gulp of his Calvados. "Why are you doing this, Roman?"

"It's just a test, a project. A proof of concept."

"You're lying." Gerald shook his head. "You're not much good at it. Did your gadget pick up that characteristic, I wonder?" He raised his voice. "Computer Roman, why do you exist?"

"I'm afraid I'm losing my mind," the computer replied. "My memory is going, my personality fractionating. I don't know if it's the early stages of Alzheimer's or something else. *I*, here, this device, is intended to serve as a marker personality so that I can trace—"

"Silence!" Roman shouted. The computer ceased speaking. He stood, shaking. "Damn you, Gerald. How dare you?"

"This device is more honest than you are." If Gerald was afraid of his friend's anger he showed no sign of it. "There must be some flaw in your programming."

Roman went white. He sat back down. "That's because I've already lost some of the personality I've given it. It remembers things I've forgotten, prompting me the way

Abigail does." He put his face in his hands. "Oh, my God, Gerald, what am I going to do?"

Gerald set his drink down carefully and put his arm around his friend's shoulders, something he rarely did. And they sat there in the silent study, two old friends stuck at the wrong end of time.

The pursuing, choking darkness had almost gotten him. Roman sat bolt upright in bed, trying desperately to drag air in through his clogged throat.

The room was dark. He had no idea of where he was or even who he was. All he felt was stark terror. The bedclothes seemed to be grabbing for him, trying to pull him back into that all-consuming darkness. Whimpering, he tried to drag them away from his legs.

The lights came on. "What's wrong, Roman?" Abigail looked at him in consternation.

"Who are you?" Roman shouted at this ancient white-haired woman who had somehow come to be in his bed. "Where's Abigail? What have you done with her?" He took the old woman by her shoulders and shook her.

"Stop it, Roman. Stop it!" Her eyes filled with tears. "You're having a nightmare. You're here in bed. With me. I'm Abigail, your wife. Roman!"

Roman stared at her. Her long hair had once been raven black and was now pure white.

"Oh, Abigail." The bedroom fell into place around him, the spindle bed, the nightstands, the lamps—his green-glass shaded, hers crystal. "Oh, Pookie, I'm sorry." He hadn't used that ridiculous endearment in years. He hugged her, feeling how frail she had become. She kept herself in shape, but she was old, her once-full muscles now like taut cords, pulling her bones as if she was a marionette. "I'm sorry."

She sobbed against him, then withdrew, wiping at her eyes. "What a pair of hysterical old people we've become." Her vivid blue eyes glittered with tears. "One nightmare and we go all to pieces."

It wasn't just one nightmare, not at all. What was he supposed to say to her? Roman freed himself from the down comforter, carefully fitted his feet into his leather slippers, and shuffled into the bathroom.

He looked at himself in the mirror. He was an old man, hair standing on end. He wore a nice pair of flannel pajamas and leather slippers his wife had given him for Christmas. His mind was dissolving like a lump of sugar in hot coffee.

The bathroom was clean tile with a wonderful claw-footed bathtub. The floor was tiled in a colored parquet-deformation pattern that started with ordinary bathroom-floor hexagons near the toilet, slowly modified itself into complex knotted shapes in the middle, and then, by another deformation, returned to hexagons under the sink. It had cost him a small fortune and months of work to create this complex mathematical tessellation. It was a dizzying thing to contemplate from the throne, and it now turned the ordinarily safe bathroom into a place of nightmare. Why couldn't he have picked something more comforting?

He stared at his image with some bemusement. He normally combed his thin hair down to hide his bald spot. Whom did he think he was fooling? Woken from sleep, he was red-eyed. The bathroom mirror had turned into a magic one and revealed all his flaws. He was wrinkled, had bags under his eyes, broken veins. He liked to think that he was a lovable curmudgeon. Curmudgeon, hell. He looked like a nasty old man.

"Are you all right in there?" Abigail's voice was concerned.

"I'm fine. Be right there." With one last glance at his mirror image, Roman turned the light off and went back to bed.

Roman sat in his study chair and fumed. Something had happened to the medical profession while he wasn't looking. That was what he got for being so healthy. He obviously hadn't been keeping track of things.

"What did he say?" The computer's voice was interested. Roman was impressed by the inflection. He was also impressed by how easy it was to tell that the computer desperately wanted to know. Was *he* always that obvious?

"He's an idiot." Roman was pleased to vent his spleen. "Dr. Weisner's a country-club doctor, making diagnoses between the green and the clubhouse. His office is in a building near a shopping mall. What ever happened to leather armchairs, wood paneling, and pictures of the College of Surgeons? You could trust a man with an office decorated like that, even if he was a drunken butcher."

"You're picking up Abigail's perception of style."

Roman, who'd just been making that same observation to himself, felt caught red-handed. "True. Weisner's a specialist in the diseases of aging. Jesus. He'll make a terrible old man, though, slumped in front of a TV set watching game shows." Roman sighed. "He does seem to know what he's talking about."

There was no known way to diagnose Alzheimer's disease, for example. Roman hadn't known that. There was only posthumous detection of senile plaques and argyrophilic neurofibrillary tangles in addition to cortical atrophy. Getting that information out of Weisner had been like pulling teeth. The man wasn't used to giving patients information. Roman had even browbeaten him into showing him slides of typical damage and pointing out the details. Now that he sat and imagined what was going on in his own brain he wasn't sure he should have been so adamant.

"Could you play that again?" the computer asked.

Roman was yanked from his brown study. "What?"

"The music you just had on. The Zelenka."

"Sure, sure." Roman loved Jan Dismas Zelenka's Trio Sonatas, and his computer did too. He got a snifter of Metaxa and put the music on again. The elaborate architecture of two oboes and a bassoon filled the study.

Roman sipped the rough brandy. "Sorry you can't share this."

"So am I."

Roman reached under and pulled out a game box. "You know, the biggest disappointment I have is that Gerald hates playing games of any sort. I love them: chess, backgammon, Go, cards. So I have to play with people who are a lot less interesting than he is." He opened a box and looked at the letters. "You'd think he'd at least like Scrabble."

"Care for a game?"

"What, are you kidding?" Roman looked at the computer in dismay. "That won't be any fun. You know all the words."

"Now, Roman. It's getting increasingly difficult calling you that, you know. That's *my* name. A game of Scrabble with you might not be fun, but not for that reason. My vocabulary is exactly yours, complete down to vaguenesses and mistakes. Neither of us can remember the meaning of the word 'jejune.' We will each always type 'anamoly' before correcting it to 'anomaly.' It won't be fun precisely *because* I won't know any more words than you do."

"That's probably no longer true." Roman felt like crying. "You're already smarter than I am. Or, I suppose, I'm already dumber. I should have thought of that."

"Don't be so hard on yourself—"

"No!" Roman stood up, dumping Scrabble letters to the floor. "I'm losing everything that makes me *me!* That's why you're here."

"Yes, Roman." The computer's voice was soft.

"Together we can still make a decision, a final disposition. You're me, you know what *that* is. This can all have only one conclusion. There is only one action you and I can finally take. You know that. You know!"

"That's true. You know, Roman, you are a very intelligent man. Your conclusions agree entirely with my own."

Roman laughed. "God, it's tough when you find yourself laughing at your own jokes."

When he opened the door, Roman found Gerald in the darkness of the front stoop, dressed in a trench coat, fedora pulled down low over his eyes.

"I got the gat," Gerald muttered.

Roman pulled him through the front door, annoyed. "Quit fooling around. This is serious."

"Sure, sure." Gerald slung his trench coat on a hook by

the door and handed his fedora to Roman. "Careful of the chapeau. It's a classic."

Roman spun it off onto the couch. When he turned back Gerald had the gun out. It was a smooth, deadly blue-black pistol.

"A Beretta model 92." Gerald held it nervously in his hand, obviously unused to weapons. "Fashionable. The Italians have always been leaders in style." He walked into the study and set it down on a pile of books, unwilling to hold it longer than necessary. "It took me an hour to find. It was in a trunk in the bottom of a closet, under some clothes I should have taken to Goodwill years ago."

"Where did you get it?" Roman himself wasn't yet willing to pick it up.

"An old lover. A police officer. She was worried about me. A man living all alone, that sort of thing. It had been confiscated in some raid or other. By the way, it's unregistered and thus completely illegal. You could spend a year in jail for just having it. I should have dumped it years ago."

Roman finally picked it up and checked it out, hand shaking just slightly. The double magazine was full of cartridges. "You could have fought off an entire platoon of housebreakers with this thing."

"I reloaded before I brought it over here. I broke up with Lieutenant Carpozo years ago. The bullets were probably stale . . . or whatever happens to old bullets." He stared at Roman for a long moment. "You're a crazy bastard, you know that, Roman?"

Roman didn't answer. The computer did. "It would be crazy for you, Gerald. For me, it's the only thing that makes sense."

"Great." Gerald was suddenly viciously annoyed. "Quite an achievement, programming self-importance into a computer. I congratulate you. Well, I'm getting out of here. This whole business scares the shit out of me."

"My love to Anna. You are still seeing her, aren't you?"

Gerald eyed him. "Yes, I am." He stopped and took Roman's shoulders. "Are you going to be all right, old man?"

"I'll be fine. Good night, Gerald."

Once his friend was gone, Roman calmly and methodically locked the pistol into an inaccessible computer-controlled cabinet to one side of the desk. Its basis was a steel firebox. Powerful electromagnets pulled chrome-moly steel bars through their locks and clicked shut. It would make a well-equipped machine shop a week to get into the box if the computer didn't wish it. But at the computer's decision, the thing would slide open as easily as an oiled desk drawer.

He walked into the bedroom and sat on the edge of the bed. Abigail woke up and looked at him nervously, worried that he was having another night terror attack. He leaned over and kissed her.

"Can I talk with you?"

"Of course, Roman. Just a second." She sat up and turned on her reading light. Then she ran a brush through her hair, checking its arrangement with a hand mirror. That done, she looked attentive.

"We got the Humana research contract today."

"Why, Roman, that's wonderful. Why didn't you tell me?" She pouted. "We ate dinner together and you let me babble on about the garden and Mrs. Peasley's orchids and you never said anything about it."

"That's because it has nothing to do with me. My team got the contract with their work."

"Roman—"

"Wait."

He looked around the bedroom. It had delicately patterned wallpaper and rugs on the floor. It was a graceful and relaxing room, all of it Abigail's doing. His night table was much larger than hers because he always piled six months' worth of reading into it.

"Everyone's covering for me. They know what I've done in the past, and they try to make me look good. But I'm useless. *You're* covering for me. Aren't you, Abigail? If you really think about it, you know something's happening to me. Something that can only end one way. I'm sure that in your nightstand somewhere there's a book on senile dementia. I don't have to explain anything to you."

She looked away. "I wouldn't keep it somewhere so easy for you to find."

The beautiful room suddenly looked threatening. The shadows on the wall cast by Abigail's crystal-shaded lamp were ominous looming monsters. This wasn't his room. He no longer had anything to do with it. The books in the night table would remain forever unread or, if read, would be soon forgotten. He fell forward and she held him.

"I can't make you responsible for me," he said. "I can't do that to you. I can't ruin your life."

"No, Roman. I'll always take care of you, no matter what happens." Her voice was fierce. "I love you."

"I know. But it won't be *me* you're caring for. It will be a hysterical beast with no memory and no sense. I won't even be able to appreciate what you are doing for me. I'll scream at you, run away and get lost, shit in my pants."

She drew in a long breath.

"And you know what? Right now I could make the decision to kill myself—"

"No! God, Roman, you're *fine*. You're having a few memory lapses. I hate to tell you, but that comes with age. I have them. We all do. You can live a full life along with the rest of us. Don't be such a perfectionist."

"Yes. *Now* I have the capacity to make a decision to end it, if I choose. But now I don't *need* to make a decision like that. My personality is still whole. Battered, but still there. But when enough of my mind is gone that I am a useless burden, I won't be able to make the decision. It's damnable. When I'm a drooling idiot who shits in his pants and makes your life a living, daily hell, I won't have the *sense* to end it. I'll be miserable, terrified, hysterical. And I'll keep on *living*. And none of these living wills can arrange it. They can avoid heroic measures, take someone off life support, but they can't actually *kill* anyone."

"But what about me?" Her voice was sharp. "Is that it, then? You have a problem, *you* make the decision, and I'm left to pick up whatever pieces are left? I'm supposed to abide by whatever decision *you* make?"

"That's not fair." He hadn't expected an argument. But what, then? Simple acquiescence? This was Abigail.

"Who's being unfair?" She gasped. "When you think there's not enough of you left to love, you'll just end yourself."

"Abigail, I love and care for you. I won't always be able to say that. Someday that love will vanish along with my mind. Allow me the right to live as the kind of human being I want to be. You don't want a paltry sick thing to take care of as a reminder of the man I once was. I think that after several years of that you will forget what it was about me that you once loved."

So they cried together, the way they had in their earliest days with each other, when it seemed that it would never work and they would have to spend their whole lives apart.

Roman stood in the living room in confusion. It was night outside. He remembered it being morning not more than a couple of minutes before. He had been getting ready to go to the office. There were important things to do there.

But no. He had retired from Hyperneuron. People from the office sometimes came to visit, but they never stayed long. Roman didn't notice because he couldn't pay that much attention. He offered them glasses of lemonade, sometimes bringing in second and third ones while their first was yet unfinished. Elaine had left in tears once. Roman didn't know why.

Gerald came every week. Often Roman didn't recognize him.

But Roman wanted something. He was out here for some reason. "Abigail!" he screamed. "Where's my . . . my . . . tool?"

His hair was neatly combed, he was dressed, clean. He didn't know that.

Abigail appeared at the door. "What is it, honey?"

"My tool, dammit, my tool. My . . . cutting . . ." He waved his hands.

"Your scissors?"

"Yes, yes, yes! You stole them. You threw them away."

"I haven't even seen them, Roman."

"You always say that. Why are they gone, then?" He grinned at her, pleased at having caught her in her lie.

"Please, Roman." She was near tears. "You do this every time you lose something."

"I didn't lose them!" He screamed until his throat hurt. "You threw them out!" He stalked off, leaving her at the door.

He wandered into his study. It was neat now. It had been so long since he'd worked in there that Abigail had stacked everything neatly and kept it dusted.

"Tell Abigail that you would like some spinach pies from the Greek bakery." The computer's voice was calm.

"Wha—?"

"Some spinach pies. They carry them at the all-night convenience store over on River Street. One of the small benefits of yuppification. Spanakopita at midnight. You haven't had them for a while, and you used to like them a lot. Be polite, Roman. Please. You are being cruel to Abigail."

Roman ran back out into the living room. He cried. "I'm sorry, Pookie, I'm sorry." He grabbed her and held her in a death grip. "I want, I want . . ."

"What, Roman?" She looked into his eyes.

"I want a spinach pie," he finally said triumphantly. "They have them on River Street. I like spinach pies."

"All right, Roman. I'll get some for you." Delighted at having some concrete and easily satisfied desire on his part, Abigail drove off into the night, though she knew he would have forgotten about them by the time she got back.

"Get the plastic sheet," the computer commanded.

"What?"

"The plastic sheet. It's under the back porch where you put it."

"I don't remember any plastic sheet."

"I don't care if you remember it or not. Go get it and bring it in here."

Obediently, clumsily, Roman dragged in the heavy roll of plastic and spread it out on the study floor in obedience to the computer's instructions.

With a loud click the secure drawer slid open. Roman reached in and pulled out the pistol. He stared at it in wonder.

"The safety's on the side. Push it up. You know what to do." The computer's voice was sad. "I waited a long time, Roman. Perhaps too long. I just couldn't do it."

And indeed, though much of his mind was gone, Roman *did* know what to do. "Will this make Abigail happy?" He lay down on the plastic sheet.

"No, it won't. But you have to do it."

The pistol's muzzle was cold on the roof of his mouth.

"Jesus," Gerald said at the doorway. "Jesus Christ." He'd heard the gunshot from the driveway and had immediately known what it meant. He'd let himself in with his key. Roman Maitland's body lay twisted on the study floor, blood spattered from the hole torn in the back of his head. The plastic sheet had caught the blood that welled out.

"Why did he call me and then not wait?" Gerald was almost angry with his friend. "He sounded so sensible."

"He didn't call you. *I* did. Glad you could make it, Gerald."

Gerald stared around the study in terror. His friend was dead. But his friend's voice came from the speakers.

"A ghost," he whispered. "All that fancy electronics and software, and all Roman has succeeded in doing is making a ghost." He giggled. "God, science marches on."

"Don't be an ass." Roman's voice was severe. "We have things to do. Abigail will be home soon. I sent her on a meaningless errand to buy some spinach pies. I like spinach pies. I'll miss them."

"I like them too. I'll eat them for you."

"Thanks." There was no trace of sarcasm in the compute's voice.

Gerald stared at the field memories, having no better place to address. "Are you really in there, Roman?"

"It's not me. Just an amazing simulation. I'll say goodbye to you, then to Abigail, and then you can call the police. I hear her car in the driveway now. Meet her at the front door. Try to make it easy on her. She'll be pissed off at me, but that can't be helped. Goodbye, Gerald. You were as good a friend as a man could ask for."

Abigail stepped through the door with the plastic bag from the convenience store hanging on her wrist. As soon as she saw Gerald's face, she knew what had happened.

"*Damn* him! Damn him to hell! He always liked stupid tricks like that. He liked pointing over my shoulder to make me look. He never got over it."

She went into the study and put her hand on her husband's forehead. His face was scrunched up from the shock of the bullet, making him look like a child tasting something bitter.

"I'm sorry, Abigail," the computer said with Roman's voice. "I loved you too much to stay."

She didn't look up. "I know, Roman. It must have been hard to watch yourself fade away like that."

"It was. But even harder to watch you suffer it. Thank you. I love you."

"I love you." She walked slowly out of the room, bent over like a lonely old woman.

"Can I come around and talk with you sometimes?" Gerald sat down in a chair.

"No. I am not Roman Maitland. Get that through your thick skull, Gerald. I am a machine. And my job is finished. Roman didn't give me any choice about that. And I'm glad. You can write directly on the screen. Write the word 'zeugma.' To the screen's response write 'atrophy.' To the second response write 'fair voyage.' Goodbye, Gerald."

Gerald pulled a light pen from the drawer. When he wrote "zeugma" the parchment sheet said, **COMMAND TO ERASE MEMORY STORE. ARE YOU SURE?**

He wrote "atrophy."

THIS INITIATES COMPLETE ERASURE. ARE YOU ABSOLUTELY CERTAIN?

He wrote "fair voyage."

ERASURE INITIATED.

The parchment sheet flickered with internal light. One by one, the indicator lights on the field memories faded out. A distant piece of Mozart played on the speakers and faded also.

"I'll call the police." Gerald looked down at his friend's dead body, then looked back.

On the sheet were the words **COMMENCE ENTRY.**

DOGFIGHT

Michael Swanwick
and William Gibson

Michael Swanwick made his debut in 1980, and has gone on to become one of the most popular and respected of all that decade's new writers. He has several times been a finalist for the Nebula Award, as well as for the World Fantasy Award and for the John W. Campbell Award, and has won the Theodore Sturgeon Award and the Asimov's *Readers Award poll. In 1991, his novel* Stations of the Tide *won him a Nebula Award as well. His other books include his first novel,* In the Drift, *which was published in 1985, a novella-length book,* Griffin's Egg, *and 1987's popular novel* Vacuum Flowers. *His critically acclaimed short fiction has been assembled in* Gravity's Angels *and in a collection of his collaborative short work with other writers,* Slow Dancing Through Time. *His most recent book is a new novel,* The Iron Dragon's Daughter, *which has been a finalist for the World Fantasy Award and the Arthur C. Clarke Award. Swanwick lives in Philadelphia with his wife, Marianne Porter, and their son Sean.*

Here he joins forces with William Gibson, whose story "Burning Chrome" appears elsewhere in this anthology, to explore a low-life, small-time hacker circuit of Greyhound bus stations and smoke-filled pool halls, far from the exalted realms of industrial espionage and corporate intrigue that are the concerns of most hacker stories—but a world in which there are still victories to be won . . . and victories to be lost, *as well.*

He meant to keep on going, right down to Florida. Work passage on a gunrunner, maybe wind up conscripted into some rat-ass rebel army down in the war zone. Or maybe, with that ticket good as long as he didn't stop riding, he'd just never get off—Greyhound's Flying Dutchman. He grinned at his faint reflection in cold, greasy glass while the downtown lights of Norfolk slid past, the bus swaying on tired shocks as the driver slung it around a final corner. They shuddered to a halt in the terminal lot, concrete lit gray and harsh like a prison exercise yard. But Deke was watching himself starve, maybe in some snowstorm out of Oswego, with his cheek pressed up against the same bus window, and seeing his remains swept out at the next stop by a muttering old man in faded coveralls. One way or the other, he decided, it didn't mean shit to him. Except his legs seemed to have died already. And the driver called a twenty-minute stopover—Tidewater Station, Virginia. It was an old cinder-block building with two entrances to each rest room, holdover from the previous century.

Legs like wood, he made a halfhearted attempt at ghosting the notions counter, but the black girl behind it was alert, guarding the sparse contents of the old glass case as though her ass depended on it. *Probably does*, Deke thought, turning away. Opposite the washrooms, an open doorway offered GAMES, the word flickering feebly in biofluorescent plastic. He could see a crowd of the local kickers clustered around a pool table. Aimless, his boredom following him like a cloud, he stuck his head in. And saw a biplane, wings no longer than his thumb, blossom bright orange flame. Corkscrewing, trailing smoke, it vanished the instant it struck the green-felt field of the table.

"That's right, Tiny," a kicker bellowed, "you *take* that sumbitch!"

"Hey," Deke said. "What's going on?"

The nearest kicker was a bean pole with a black mesh Peterbilt cap. "Tiny's defending the Max," he said, not taking his eyes from the table.

"Oh, yeah? What's that?" But even as he asked, he saw it: a blue enamel medal shaped like a Maltese cross, the slogan *Pour le Mérite* divided among its arms.

The Blue Max rested on the edge of the table, directly

before a vast and perfectly immobile bulk wedged into a fragile-looking chrome-tube chair. The man's khaki work shirt would have hung on Deke like the folds of a sail, but it bulged across that bloated torso so tautly that the buttons threatened to tear away at any instant. Deke thought of southern troopers he'd seen on his way down; of that weird, gut-heavy, endotype balanced on gangly legs that looked like they'd been borrowed from some other body. Tiny might look like that if he stood, but on a larger scale—a forty-inch jeans inseam that would need a woven-steel waistband to support all those pounds of swollen gut. If Tiny were ever to stand at all—for now Deke saw that that shiny frame was actually a wheelchair. There was something disturbingly childlike about the man's face, an appalling suggestion of youth and even beauty in features almost buried in fold and jowl. Embarrassed. Deke looked away. The other man, the one standing across the table from Tiny, had bushy sideburns and a thin mouth. He seemed to be trying to push something with his eyes, wrinkles of concentration spreading from the corners. . . .

"You dumbshit or what?" The man with the Peterbilt cap turned, catching Deke's Indo proleboy denims, the brass chains at his wrists, for the first time. "Why don't you get your ass lost, fucker. Nobody wants your kind in here." He turned back to the dogfight.

Bets were being made, being covered. The kickers were producing the hard stuff, the old stuff, liberty-headed dollars and Roosevelt dimes from the stamp-and-coin stores, while more cautious bettors slapped down antique paper dollars laminated in clear plastic. Through the haze came a trio of red planes, flying in formation. Fokker D VIIs. The room fell silent. The Fokkers banked majestically under the solar orb of a two-hundred-watt bulb.

The blue Spad dove out of nowhere. Two more plunged from the shadowy ceiling, following closely. The kickers swore, and one chuckled. The formation broke wildly. One Fokker dove almost to the felt, without losing the Spad on its tail. Furiously, it zigged and zagged across the green flatlands but to no avail. At last it pulled up, the enemy hard after it, too steeply—and stalled, too low to pull out in time.

A stack of silver dimes was scooped up.

The Fokkers were outnumbered now. One had two Spads on its tail. A needle-spray of tracers tore past its cockpit. The Fokker slip-turned right, banked into an Immelmann, and was behind one of its pursuers. It fired, and the biplane fell, tumbling.

"Way to go, Tiny!" The kickers closed in around the table.

Deke was frozen with wonder. It felt like being born all over again.

Frank's Truck Stop was two miles out of town on the Commercial Vehicles Only route. Deke had tagged it, out of idle habit, from the bus on the way in. Now he walked back between the traffic and the concrete crash guards. Articulated trucks went slamming past, big eight-segmented jobs, the wash of air each time threatening to blast him over. CVO stops were easy makes. When he sauntered into Frank's, there was nobody to doubt that he'd come in off a big rig, and he was able to browse the gift shop as slowly as he liked. The wire rack with the projective wetware wafers was located between a stack of Korean cowboy shirts and a display for Fuzz Buster mudguards. A pair of Oriental dragons twisted in the air over the rack, either fighting or fucking, he couldn't tell which. The game he wanted was there: a wafer labeled SPADS&FOKKERS. It took him three seconds to boost it and less time to slide the magnet— which the cops in D.C. hadn't even bothered to confiscate— across the universal security strip.

On the way out, he lifted two programming units and a little Batang facilitator-remote that looked like an antique hearing aid.

He chose a highstack at random and fed the rental agent the line he'd used since his welfare rights were yanked. Nobody ever checked up; the state just counted occupied rooms and paid.

The cubicle smelled faintly of urine, and someone had

scrawled Hard Anarchy Liberation Front slogans across the walls. Deke kicked trash out of a corner, sat down, back to the wall, and ripped open the wafer pack.

There was a folded instruction sheet with diagrams of loops, rolls, and Immelmanns, a tube of saline paste, and a computer list of operational specs. And the wafer itself, white plastic with a blue biplane and logo on one side, red on the other. He turned it over and over in his hand: SPADS&FOKKERS, FOKKERS&SPADS. Red or blue. He fitted the Batang behind his ear after coating the inductor surface with paste, jacked its fiberoptic ribbon into the programmer, and plugged the programmer into the wall current. Then he slid the wafer into the programmer. It was a cheap set, Indonesian, and the base of his skull buzzed uncomfortably as the program ran. But when it was done, a sky-blue Spad darted restlessly through the air a few inches from his face. It almost glowed, it was so real. It had the strange inner life that fanatically detailed museum-grade models often have, but it took all of his concentration to keep it in existence. If his attention wavered at all, it lost focus, fuzzing into a pathetic blur.

He practiced until the battery in the earset died, then slumped against the wall and fell asleep. He dreamed of flying, in a universe that consisted entirely of white clouds and blue sky, with no up and down, and never a green field to crash into.

He woke to a rancid smell of frying krillcakes and winced with hunger. No cash, either. Well, there were plenty of student types in the stack. Bound to be one who'd like to score a programming unit. He hit the hall with the boosted spare. Not far down was a door with a poster on it: THERE'S A HELL OF A GOOD UNIVERSE NEXT DOOR. Under that was a starscape with a cluster of multicolored pills, torn from an ad for some pharmaceutical company, pasted over an inspirational shot of the "space colony" that had been under construction since before he was born. LET'S GO, the poster said, beneath the collaged hypnotics.

He knocked. The door opened, security slides stopping it at a two-inch slice of girlface. "Yeah?"

"You're going to think this is stolen." He passed the programmer from hand to hand. "I mean because it's new, virtual cherry, and the bar code's still on it. But listen, I'm not gonna argue the point. No. I'm gonna let you have it for only like half what you'd pay anywhere else."

"Hey, wow, *really*, no kidding?" The visible fraction of mouth twisted into a strange smile. She extended her hand, palm up, a loose fist. Level with his chin. "Lookahere!"

There was a hole in her hand, a black tunnel that ran right up her arm. Two small red lights. Rat's eyes. They scurried toward him—growing, gleaming. Something gray streaked forward and leaped for his face.

He screamed, throwing hands up to ward it off. Legs twisting, he fell, the programmer shattering under him.

Silicate shards skittered as he thrashed, clutching his head. Where it hurt, it hurt—it hurt very badly indeed.

"Oh, my God!" Slides unsnapped, and the girl was hovering over him. "Here, listen, come on." She dangled a blue hand towel. "Grab on to this and I'll pull you up."

He looked at her through a wash of tears. Student. That fed look, the oversize sweatshirt, teeth so straight and white they could be used as a credit reference. A thin gold chain around one ankle (fuzzed, he saw, with baby-fine hair). Choppy Japanese haircut. Money. "That sucker was gonna be my dinner," he said ruefully. He took hold of the towel and let her pull him up.

She smiled but skittishly backed away from him. "Let me make it up to you," she said. "You want some food? It was only a projection, okay?"

He followed her in, wary as an animal entering a trap.

"Holy shit," Deke said, "this is *real cheese*. . . ." He was sitting on a gutsprung sofa, wedged between a four-foot teddy bear and a loose stack of floppies. The room was ankle-deep in books and clothes and papers. But the food she magicked up—Gouda cheese and tinned beef and

honest-to-God greenhouse wheat wafers—was straight out
of the Arabian Nights.

"Hey," she said. "We know how to treat a proleboy right,
huh?" Her name was Nance Bettendorf. She was seventeen.
Both her parents had jobs—greedy buggers—and she was
an engineering major at William and Mary. She got top
marks except in English. "I guess you must really have a
thing about rats. You got some kind of phobia about rats?"

He glanced sidelong at her bed. You couldn't see it,
really; it was just a swell in the ground cover. "It's not like
that. It just reminded me of something else, is all."

"Like what?" She squatted in front of him, the big shirt
riding high up one smooth thigh.

"Well . . . did you ever see the—" his voice involun
tarily rose and rushed past the words—"*Washington Monument?* Like at night? It's got these two little . . . red lights
on top, aviation markers or something, and I, and I . . . ."
He started to shake.

"You're afraid of the Washington Monument?" Nance
whooped and rolled over with laughter, long tanned legs
kicking. She was wearing crimson bikini panties.

"I would die rather than look at it again," he said levelly.

She stopped laughing then, sat up, studied his face.
White, even teeth worried at her lower lip, like she was
dragging up something she didn't want to think about. At
last she ventured, "Brainlock?"

"Yeah," he said bitterly. "They told me I'd never go back
to D.C. And then the fuckers laughed."

"What did they get you for?"

"I'm a thief." He wasn't about to tell her that the actual
charge was career shoplifting.

"Lotta old *computer* hacks spent their lives programming
machines. And you know what? The human brain is not a
goddamn bit like a machine, no way. They just don't
program the same." Deke knew this shrill, desperate rap,
this long, circular jive that the lonely string out to the rare
listener; knew it from a hundred cold and empty nights
spent in the company of strangers. Nance was lost in it, and

Deke, nodding and yawning, wondered if he'd even be able to stay awake when they finally hit that bed of hers.

"I built that projection I hit you with myself," she said, hugging her knees up beneath her chin. "It's for muggers, you know? I just happened to have it on me, and I threw it at you 'cause I thought it was so funny, you trying to sell me that shit little Indojavanese programmer." She hunched forward and held out her hand again. "Look here." Deke cringed. "No, no, it's okay, I swear it, this is different." She opened her hand.

A single blue flame danced there, perfect and everchanging. "Look at that," she marveled. "Just look. I programmed that. It's not some diddly little seven-image job either. It's a continuous two-hour loop, seven thousand, two hundred seconds, never the same twice, each instant as individual as a fucking snowflake!"

The flame's core was glacial crystal, shards and facets flashing up, twisting and gone, leaving behind near-subliminal images so bright and sharp that they cut the eye. Deke winced. People mostly. Pretty little naked people, fucking. "How the hell did you do that?"

She rose, bare feet slipping on slick magazines, and melodramatically swept folds of loose printout from a raw plywood shelf. He saw a neat row of small consoles, austere and expensive-looking. Custom work. "This is the real stuff I got here. Image facilitator. Here's my fast-wipe module. This is a brain-map one-to-one function analyzer." She sang off the names like a litany. "Quantum flicker stabilizer. Program splicer. An image assembler . . ."

"You need all that to make one little flame?"

"You betcha. This is all state of the art, professional projective wetware gear. It's years ahead of anything you've seen."

"Hey," he said, "you know anything about SPADS&FOKKERS?"

She laughed. And then, because he sensed the time was right, he reached out to take her hand.

"Don't you touch me, motherfuck, don't you *ever touch me!*" Nance screamed, and her head slammed against the wall as she recoiled, white and shaking with terror.

"Okay!" He threw up his hands. "Okay! I'm nowhere near you. Okay?"

She cowered from him. Her eyes were round and unblinking; tears built up at the corners, rolled down ashen cheeks. Finally, she shook her head. "Hey. Deke. Sorry. I should've told you."

"Told me what?" But he had a creepy feeling . . . already knew. The way she clutched her head. The weakly spasmodic way her hands opened and closed. "You got a brainlock, too."

"Yeah." She closed her eyes. "It's a chastity lock. My asshole parents paid for it. So I can't stand to have anybody touch me or even stand too close." Eyes opened in blind hate. "I didn't even *do* anything. Not a fucking thing. But they've both got jobs and they're so horny for me to have a career that they can't piss straight. They're afraid I'd neglect my studies if I got, you know, involved in sex and stuff. The day the brainlock comes off I am going to fuck the vilest, greasiest, hairiest . . ."

She was clutching her head again. Deke jumped up and rummaged through the medicine cabinet. He found a jar of B-complex vitamins, pocketed a few against need, and brought two to Nance, with a glass of water. "Here." He was careful to keep his distance. "This'll take the edge off."

"Yeah, yeah," she said. Then, almost to herself, "You must really think I'm a jerk."

The games room in the Greyhound station was almost empty. A lone, long-jawed fourteen-year-old was bent over a console, maneuvering rainbow fleets of submarines in the murky grid of the North Atlantic.

Deke sauntered in, wearing his new kicker drag, and leaned against a cinder-block wall made smooth by countless coats of green enamel. He'd washed the dye from his proleboy butch, boosted jeans and T-shirt from the Goodwill, and found a pair of stompers in the sauna locker of a highstack with cut-rate security.

"Seen Tiny around, friend?"

The subs darted like neon guppies. "Depends on who's asking."

Deke touched the remote behind his left ear. The Spad snap-rolled over the console, swift and delicate as a dragonfly. It was beautiful; so perfect, so *true* it made the room seem an illusion. He buzzed the grid, millimeters from the glass, taking advantage of the programmed ground effect.

The kid didn't even bother to look up. "Jackman's," he said. "Down Richmond Road, over by the surplus."

Deke let the Spad fade in midclimb.

Jackman's took up most of the third floor of an old brick building. Deke found Best Buy War Surplus first, then a broken neon sign over an unlit lobby. The sidewalk out front was littered with another kind of surplus—damaged vets, some of them dating back to Indochina. Old men who'd left their eyes under Asian suns squatted beside twitching boys who'd inhaled mycotoxins in Chile. Deke was glad to have the battered elevator doors sigh shut behind him.

A dusty Dr. Pepper clock at the far side of the long, spectral room told him it was a quarter to eight. Jackman's had been embalmed twenty years before he was born, sealed away behind a yellowish film of nicotine, of polish and hair oil. Directly beneath the clock, the flat eyes of somebody's grandpappy's prize buck regarded Deke from a framed, blown-up snapshot gone the slick sepia of cockroach wings. There was the click and whisper of pool, the squeak of a work boot twisting on linoleum as a player leaned in for a shot. Somewhere high above the green-shaded lamps hung a string of crepe-paper Christmas bells faded to dead rose. Deke looked from one cluttered wall to the next. No facilitator.

"Bring one in, should we need it," someone said. He turned, meeting the mild eyes of a bald man with steel-rimmed glasses. "My name's Cline. Bobby Earl. You don't look like you shoot pool, mister." But there was nothing threatening in Bobby Earl's voice or stance. He pinched the steel frames from his nose and polished the thick lenses with a fold of tissue. He reminded Deke of a shop instructor who'd patiently tried to teach him retrograde biochip installation. "I'm a gambler," he said, smiling. His teeth were white plastic. "I know I don't much look it. "

"I'm looking for Tiny," Deke said.

"Well," replacing the glasses, "you're not going to find him. He's gone up to Bethesda to let the V.A. clean his plumbing for him. He wouldn't fly against you anyhow."

"Why not?"

"Well, because you're not on the circuit or I'd know your face. You any good?" When Deke nodded, Bobby Earl called down the length of Jackman's, "Yo, Clarence! You bring out that facilitator. We got us a flyboy."

Twenty minutes later, having lost his remote and what cash he had left, Deke was striding past the broken soldiers of Best Buy.

"Now you let me tell you, boy," Bobby Earl had said in a fatherly tone as, hand on shoulder, he led Deke back to the elevator, "You're not going to win against a combat vet— you listening to me? I'm not even especially good, just an old grunt who was on hype fifteen, maybe twenty times. Ol' Tiny, he was a *pilot*. Spent his entire enlistment hyped to the gills. He's got membrane attenuation real bad . . . you ain't never going to beat him."

It was a cool night. But Deke burned with anger and humiliation.

"Jesus, that's crude," Nance said as the Spad strafed mounds of pink underwear. Deke, hunched up on the couch, yanked her flashy little Braun remote from behind her ear.

"Now don't you get on my case too, Miss rich-bitch gonna-have-a-job—"

"Hey, lighten up! It's nothing to do with you—it's just *tech*. That's a really primitive wafer you got there. I mean, on the street maybe it's fine. But compared to the work I do at school, it's—hey. You ought to let me rewrite it for you."

"Say what?"

"Lemme beef it up. These suckers are all written in hexadecimal, see, 'cause the industry programmers are all washed-out computer hacks. That's how they think. But let me take it to the reader-analyzer at the department, run a few changes on it, translate it into a modern wetlanguage. Edit out all the redundant intermediaries. That'll goose up your reaction time, cut the feedback loop in half. So you'll fly faster and better. Turn you into a real pro, Ace!" She took a hit off her bong, then doubled over laughing and choking.

"Is that legit?" Deke asked dubiously.

"Hey, why do you think people buy gold-wire remotes? For the prestige? Shit. Conductivity's better, cuts a few nanoseconds off the reaction time. And reaction time is the name of the game, kiddo."

"No," Deke said. "If it were that easy, people'd already have it. Tiny Montgomery would have it. He'd have the best."

"Don't you ever *listen*?" Nance set down the bong; brown water slopped onto the floor. "The stuff I'm working with is three years ahead of anything you'll find on the street."

"No shit," Deke said after a long pause. "I mean, you can do that?"

It was like graduating from a Model T to a ninety-three Lotus. The Spad handled like a dream, responsive to Deke's slightest thought. For weeks he played the arcades, with not a nibble. He flew against the local teens and by ones and threes shot down their planes. He took chances, played flash. And the planes tumbled. . . .

Until one day Deke was tucking his seed money away, and a lanky black straightened up from the wall. He eyed the laminateds in Deke's hand and grinned. A ruby tooth gleamed. "You know," the man said, "I *heard* there was a casper who could fly, going up against the kiddies."

"Jesus," Deke said, spreading Danish butter on a kelp stick. "I wiped the *floor* with those spades. They were good, too."

"That's nice, honey," Nance mumbled. She was working on her finals project, sweating data into a machine.

"You know, I think what's happening is I got real talent for this kind of shit. You know? I mean, the program gives me an edge, but I got the stuff to take advantage of it. I'm really getting a rep out there, you know?" Impulsively, he snapped on the radio. Scratchy Dixieland brass blared.

"Hey," Nance said. "Do you *mind?*"

"No, I'm just—" He fiddled with the knobs, came up with some slow, romantic bullshit. "There. Come on, stand up. Let's dance."

"Hey, you know I can't—"

"Sure you can, sugarcakes." He threw her the huge teddy bear and snatched up a patchwork cotton dress from the floor. He held it by the waist and sleeve, tucking the collar under his chin. It smelled of patchouli, more faintly of sweat. "See, I stand over here, you stand over there. We dance. Get it?"

Blinking softly, Nance stood and clutched the bear tightly. They danced then, slowly, staring into each other's eyes. After a while, she began to cry. But still, she was smiling.

Deke was daydreaming, imagining he was Tiny Montgomery wired into his jumpjet. Imagined the machine responding to his slightest neural twitch, reflexes cranked *way* up, hype flowing steadily into his veins.

Nance's floor became jungle, her bed a plateau in the Andean foothills, and Deke flew his Spad at forced speed, as if it were a full-wired interactive combat machine. Computerized hypos fed a slow trickle of high-performance enhancement mélange into his bloodstream. Sensors were wired directly into his skull—pulling a supersonic snapturn in the green-blue bowl of sky over Bolivian rain forest. Tiny would have *felt* the airflow over control surfaces.

Below, grunts hacked through the jungle with hype-pumps strapped above elbows to give them that little extra death-dance fury in combat, a shot of liquid hell in a blue plastic vial. Maybe they got ten minutes' worth in a week. But coming in at treetop level, reflexes cranked to the max, flying so low the ground troops never spotted you until you were on them, phosgene agents released, away and gone before they could draw a bead . . . it took a constant trickle of hype just to maintain. And the direct neuron interface with the jumpjet was a two-way street. The onboard computers monitored biochemistry and decided when to open the sluice gates and give the human component a killer jolt of combat edge.

Dosages like that ate you up. Ate you good and slow and constant, etching the brain surfaces, eroding away the brain-cell membranes. If you weren't yanked from the air promptly enough, you ended up with brain-cell attenuation—with reflexes too fast for your body to handle and your fight-or-flight reflexed fucked real good. . . .

"I aced it, proleboy!"

"Hah?" Deke looked up, startled, as Nance slammed in, tossing books and bag onto the nearest heap.

"My finals project—I got exempted from exams. The prof said he'd never seen anything like it. Uh, hey, dim the lights, wouldja? The colors are weird on my eyes."

He obliged. "So show me. Show me this wunnerful thing."

"Yeah, okay." She snatched up his remote, kicked clear standing space atop the bed, and struck a pose. A spark flared into flame in her hand. It spread in a quicksilver line up her arm, around her neck, and it was a snake, with triangular head and flickering tongue. Molten colors, oranges and reds. It slithered between her breasts. "I call it a firesnake," she said proudly.

Deke leaned close, and she jerked back.

"Sorry. It's like your flame, huh? I mean, I can see these tiny little fuckers in it."

"Sort of." The firesnake flowed down her stomach. "Next month I'm going to splice two hundred separate flame programs together with meld justification in between to get the visuals. Then I'll tap the mind's body image to make it self-orienting. So it can crawl all over your body without your having to mind it. You could wear it dancing."

"Maybe I'm dumb. But if you haven't done the work yet, how come I can see it?"

Nance giggled. "That's the best part—half the work isn't done yet. Didn't have the time to assemble the pieces into a unified program. Turn on that radio, huh? I want to dance."

She kicked off her shoes. Deke tuned in something gutsy.
Then, at Nance's urging, turned it down, almost to a
whisper.

"I scored two hits of hype, see." She was bouncing on the
bed, weaving her hands like a Balinese dancer. "Ever try the
stuff? In-credible. Gives you like absolute concentration.
Look here." She stood *en pointe*. "Never done that before."

"Hype," Deke said. "Last person I heard of got caught
with that shit got three years in the infantry. How'd you
score it?"

"Cut a deal with a vet who was in grad school. She
bombed out last month. Stuff gives me perfect visualization.
I can hold the projection with my eyes shut. It was a snap
assembling the program in my head."

"On just two hits, huh?"

"One hit. I'm saving the other. Tech was so impressed
he's sponsoring me for a job interview. A recruiter from
I. G. Feuchtware hits campus in two weeks. That cap is
gonna sell him the program *and* me. I'm gonna cut out of
school two years early, straight into industry, do not pass
jail, do not pay two hundred dollars."

The snake curled into a flaming tiara. It gave Deke a
funny-creepy feeling to think of Nance walking out of his
life.

"I'm a witch," Nance sang, "a wetware witch." She
shucked her shirt over her head and sent it flying. Her fine,
high breasts moved freely, gracefully, as she danced. "I'm
gonna make it"—now she was singing a current pop
hit—"to the . . . top!" Her nipples were small and pink
and aroused. The firesnake licked at them and whipped
away.

"Hey, Nance," Deke said uncomfortably. "Calm down a
little, huh?"

"I'm celebrating!" She hooked a thumb into her shiny
gold panties. Fire swirled around hand and crotch. "I'm the
virgin goddess, baby, and I have the pow-er!" Singing
again.

Deke looked away. "Gotta go now," he mumbled. Gotta

go home and jerk off. He wondered where she'd hidden that second hit. Could be anywhere.

There was a protocol to the circuit, a tacit order of deference and precedence as elaborate as that of a Mandarin court. It didn't matter that Deke was hot, that his rep was spreading like wildfire. Even a name flyboy couldn't just challenge whom he wished. He had to climb the ranks. But if you flew every night. If you were always available to anybody's challenge. And if you were good . . . well, it was possible to climb fast.

Deke was one plane up. It was tournament fighting, three planes against three. Not many spectators, a dozen maybe, but it was a good fight, and they were noisy. Deke was immersed in the manic calm of combat when he realized suddenly that they had fallen silent. Saw the kickers stir and exchange glances. Eyes flicked past him. He heard the elevator doors close. Coolly, he disposed of the second of his opponent's planes, then risked a quick glance over his shoulder.

Tiny Montgomery had just entered Jackman's. The wheelchair whispered across browning linoleum, guided by tiny twitches of one imperfectly paralyzed hand. His expression was stern, blank, calm.

In that instant, Deke lost two planes. One to deresolution—gone to blur and canceled out by the facilitator—and the other because his opponent was a real fighter. Guy did a barrel roll, killing speed and slipping to the side, and strafed Deke's biplane as it shot past. It went down in flames. Their last two planes shared altitude and speed, and as they turned, trying for position, they naturally fell into a circling pattern.

The kickers made room as Tiny wheeled up against the table. Bobby Earl Cline trailed after him, lanky and casual. Deke and his opponent traded glances and pulled their machines back from the pool table so they could hear the man out. Tiny smiled. His features were small, clustered in the center of his pale, doughy face. One finger twitched slightly on the chrome handrest. "I heard about you." He looked straight at Deke. His voice was soft and shockingly sweet, a baby-girl little voice. "I heard you're good."

Deke nodded slowly. The smile left Tiny's face. His soft, fleshy lips relaxed into a natural pout, as if he were waiting for a kiss. His small, bright eyes studied Deke without malice. "Let's see what you can do, then."

Deke lost himself in the cool game of war. And when the enemy went down in smoke and flame, to explode and vanish against the table, Tiny wordlessly turned his chair, wheeled it into the elevator, and was gone.

As Deke was gathering up his winnings, Bobby Earl eased up to him and said, "The man wants to play you."

"Yeah?" Deke was nowhere near high enough on the circuit to challenge Tiny. "What's the scam?"

"Man who was coming up from Atlanta tomorrow canceled. Ol' Tiny, he was spoiling to go up against somebody new. So it looks like you get your shot at the Max."

"Tomorrow? Wednesday? Doesn't give me much prep time."

Bobby Earl smiled gently. "I don't think that makes no nevermind."

"How's that, Mr. Cline?"

"Boy, you just ain't got the *moves*, you follow me? Ain't got no surprises. You fly just like some kinda beginner, only faster and slicker. You follow what I'm trying to say?"

"I'm not sure I do. You want to put a little action on that?"

"Tell you truthful," Cline said, "I been hoping on that." He drew a small black notebook from his pocket and licked a pencil stub. "Give you five to one. They's nobody gonna give no fairer odds than that."

He looked at Deke almost sadly. "But Tiny, he's just naturally better'n you, and that's all she wrote, boy. He lives for that goddamned game, ain't *got* nothing else. Can't get out of that goddamned chair. You think you can best a man who's fighting for his life, you are just lying to yourself."

Norman Rockwell's portrait of the colonel regarded Deke dispassionately from the Kentucky Fried across Richmond Road from the coffee bar. Deke held his cup with hands that were cold and trembling. His skull hummed with fatigue. Cline was right, he told the colonel. I can go up against Tiny, but I can't win. The colonel stared back, gaze calm and level and not particularly kindly, taking in the coffee bar and Best Buy and all his drag-ass kingdom of Richmond Road. Waiting for Deke to admit to the terrible thing he had to do.

"The bitch is planning to leave me *anyway*," Deke said aloud. Which made the black countergirl look at him funny, then quickly away.

"Daddy called!" Nancy danced in the apartment, slamming the door behind her. "And you know what? He says if I can get this job and hold it for six months, he'll have the brainlock reversed. Can you *believe* it? Deke?" She hesitated. "You okay?"

Deke stood. Now that the moment was on him, he felt unreal, like he was in a movie or something. "How come you never came home last night?" Nance asked.

The skin on his face was unnaturally taut, a parchment mask. "Where'd you stab the hype, Nance? I need it."

"Deke," she said, trying a tentative smile that instantly vanished. "Deke, that's mine. My hit. I need it. For my interview."

He smiled scornfully. "You got money. You can always score another cap."

"Not by Friday! Listen, Deke, this is really important. My whole life is riding on this interview. I need that cap. It's all I got!"

"Baby, you got the fucking world! Take a look around you—six ounces of blond Lebanese hash! Little anchovy fish in tins. Unlimited medical coverage, if you need it." She was backing away from him, stumbling against the static waves of unwashed bedding and wrinkled glossy magazines that crested at the foot of her bed. "Me, I never had a glimmer of any of this. Never had the kind of edge it takes to get along. Well, this one time I am gonna. There is a match in two hours that I am going to fucking well win. Do you hear me?" He was working himself into a rage, and that was good. He needed it for what he had to do.

Nance flung up an arm, palm open, but he was ready for that and slapped her hand aside, never even catching a glimpse of the dark tunnel, let alone those little red eyes. Then they were both falling, and he was on top of her, her breath hot and rapid in his face. "Deke! Deke! I *need* that shit, Deke, my *interview*, it's the only . . . I gotta . . . gotta . . ." She twisted her face away, crying into the wall. "Please, God, please don't . . ."

"Where did you stash it?"

Pinned against the bed under his body. Nance began to spasm, her entire body convulsing in pain and fear.

"Where is it?"

Her face was bloodless, gray corpse flesh, and horror burned in her eyes. Her lips squirmed. It was too late to stop now; he'd crossed over the line. Deke felt revolted and nauseated, all the more so because on some unexpected and unwelcome level, he was *enjoying* this.

"Where is it, Nance?" And slowly, very gently, he began to stroke her face.

Deke summoned Jackman's elevator with a finger that moved as fast and straight as a hornet and landed daintily as a butterfly on the call button. He was full of bouncy energy, and it was all under control. On the way up, he whipped off his shades and chuckled at his reflection in the finger-smudged chrome. The blacks of his eyes were like pin-pricks, all but invisible, and still the world was neon bright.

Tiny was waiting. The cripple's mouth turned up at the corners into a sweet smile as he took in Deke's irises, the exaggerated calm of his motions, the unsuccessful attempt to mime an undrugged clumsiness. "Well," he said in that girlish voice, "looks like I have a treat in store for me."

The Max was draped over one tube of the wheelchair. Deke took up position and bowed, not quite mockingly. "Let's fly." As challenger, he flew defense. He materialized his planes at a conservative altitude, high enough to dive, low enough to have warning when Tiny attacked. He waited.

The crowd tipped him. A fatboy with brilliantined hair looked startled, a hollow-eyed cracker started to smile. Murmurs rose. Eyes shifted slow-motion in heads frozen by hyped-up reaction time. Took maybe three nanoseconds to pinpoint the source of attack. Deke whipped his head up, and—

Sonfoabitch, he was *blind!* The Fokkers were diving straight from the two-hundred-watt bulb, and Tiny had suckered him into staring right at it. His vision whited out. Deke squeezed lids tight over welling tears and frantically held visualization. He split his flight, curving two biplanes right, one left. Immediately twisting each a half-turn, then back again. He had to dodge randomly—he couldn't tell where the hostile warbirds were.

Tiny chuckled. Deke could hear him through the sounds of the crowd, the cheering and cursing and slapping down of coins that seemed to syncopate independent of the ebb and flow of the duel.

When his vision returned an instant later, a Spad was in flames and falling. Fokkers tailed his surviving planes, one on one and two on the other. Three seconds into the game and he was down one.

Dodging to keep Tiny from pinning tracers on him, he looped the single-pursued plane about and drove the other toward the blind spot between Tiny and the light bulb.

Tiny's expression went very calm. The faintest shadow of disappointment—of contempt, even—was swallowed up by tranquility. He tracked the planes blandly, waiting for Deke to make his turn.

Then, just short of the blind spot, Deke shoved his Spad into a dive, the Fokkers overshooting and banking wildly to either side, twisting around to regain position.

The Spad swooped down on the third Fokker, pulled into position by Deke's other plane. Fire strafed wings and crimson fuselage. For an instant nothing happened, and Deke thought he had a fluke miss. Then the little red mother veered left and went down, trailing black, oily smoke.

Tiny frowned, small lines of displeasure marring the perfection of his mouth. Deke smiled. One even, and Tiny held position.

Both Spads were tailed closely. Deke swung them wide, and then pulled them together from opposite sides of the table. He drove them straight for each other, neutralizing Tiny's advantage . . . neither could fire without endangering his own planes. Deke cranked his machines up to top speed, slamming them at each other's nose.

An instant before they crashed, Deke sent the planes over and under one another, opening fire on the Fokkers and twisting away. Tiny was ready. Fire filled the air. Then one blue and one red plane soared free, heading in opposite directions. Behind them, two biplanes tangled in midair. Wings touched, slewed about, and the planes crumpled. They fell together, almost straight down, to the green felt below.

Ten seconds in and four planes down. A black vet pursed his lips and blew softly. Someone else shook his head in disbelief.

Tiny was sitting straight and a little forward in his wheelchair, eyes intense and unblinking, soft hands plucking feebly at the grips. None of that amused and detached bullshit now; his attention was riveted on the game. The kickers, the table, Jackman's itself, might not exist at all for him. Bobby Earl Cline laid a hand on his shoulder; Tiny didn't notice. The planes were at opposite ends of the room, laboriously gaining altitude. Deke jammed his against the ceiling, dim through the smoky haze. He spared Tiny a quick glance, and their eyes locked. Cold against cold. "Let's see your best," Deke muttered through clenched teeth.

They drove their planes together.

The hype was peaking now, and Deke could see Tiny's tracers crawling through the air between the planes. He had to put his Spad into the line of fire to get off a fair burst, then twist and bank so the Fokker's bullets would slip by his undercarriage. Tiny was every bit as hot, dodging Deke's fire and passing so close to the Spad their landing gears almost tangled as they passed.

Deke was looping his Spad in a punishingly tight turn when the hallucinations hit. The felt writhed and twisted— became the green hell of Bolivian rain forest that Tiny had flown combat over. The walls receded to gray infinity, and he felt the metal confinement of a cybernetic jumpjet close in around him.

But Deke had done his homework. He was expecting the hallucinations and knew he could deal with them. The military would never pass on a drug that couldn't be fought through. Spad and Fokker looped into another pass. He could read the tensions in Tiny Montgomery's face, the echoes of combat in deep jungle sky. They drove their planes together, feeling the torqued tensions that fed straight from instrumentation to hindbrain, the adrenaline pumps kicking in behind the armpits, the cold, fast freedom of airflow over jet-skin mingling with the smells of hot metal and fear sweat. Tracers tore past his face, and he pulled back, seeing the Spad zone by the Fokker again, both untouched. The kickers were just going ape, waving hats and stomping feet, acting like God's own fools. Deke locked glances with Tiny again.

Malice rose up in him, and though his every nerve was taut as the carbon-crystal whiskers that kept the jumpjets from falling apart in superman turns over the Andes, he counterfeited a casual smile and winked, jerking his head slightly to one side, as if to say, "Lookahere."

Tiny glanced to the side.

It was only for a fraction of a second, but that was enough. Deke pulled as fast and tight as Immelmann—right on the edge of theoretical tolerance—as had ever been seen on the circuit, and he was hanging on Tiny's tail.

Let's see you get out of his one, sucker.

Tiny rammed his plane straight down at the green, and Deke followed after. He held his fire. He had Tiny where he wanted him.

Running. Just like he'd been on his every combat mission. High on exhilaration and hype, maybe, but running scared. They were down to the felt now, flying tree-top level. Break, Deke thought, and jacked up the speed. Peripherally, he could see Bobby Earl Cline, and there was a funny look on the man's face. A pleading kind of look. Tiny's composure was shot; his face was twisted and tormented.

Now Tiny panicked and dove his plane in among the crowd. The biplanes looped and twisted between the kickers. Some jerked back involuntarily, and others laughingly swatted at them with their hands. But there was a hot glint of terror in Tiny's eyes that spoke of an eternity of fear and confinement, two edges sawing away at each other endlessly. . . .

The fear was death in the air, the confinement a locking away in metal, first of the aircraft, then of the chair. Deke could read it all in his face: Combat was the only out Tiny had had, and he'd taken it every chance he got. Until some anonymous *nationalista* with an antique SAM tore him out of that blue-green Bolivian sky and slammed him straight down to Richmond Road and Jackman's and the smiling killer boy he faced this one last time across the faded cloth.

Deke rocked up on his toes, face burning with that million-dollar smile that was the trademark of the drug that had already fried Tiny before anyone ever bothered to blow him out of the sky in a hot tangle of metal and mangled flesh. It all came together then. He saw that flying was all that held Tiny together. That daily brush of fingertips against death, and then rising up from the metal coffin, alive again. He'd been holding back collapse by sheer force of will. Break that willpower, and mortality would come pouring out and drown him. Tiny would lean over and throw up in his own lap.

And Deke drove it home. . . .

There was a moment of stunned silence as Tiny's last plane vanished in a flash of light. "I did it," Deke whispered. Then, louder, "Son of a bitch, I did it!"

Across the table from him, Tiny twisted in his chair, arms jerking spastically; his head lolled over on one shoulder.

Behind him, Bobby Earl Cline stared straight at Deke, his eyes hot coals.

The gambler snatched up the Max and wrapped its ribbon around a stack of laminateds. Without warning, he flung the bundle at Deke's face. Effortlessly, casually, Deke plucked it from the air.

For an instant, then, it looked like the gambler would come at him, right across the pool table. He was stopped by a tug on his sleeve. "Bobby Earl," Tiny whispered, his voice choking with humiliation, "you gotta get me . . . out of here. . . ."

Stiffly, angrily, Cline wheeled his friend around, and then away, into shadow.

Deke threw back his head and laughed. By God, he felt good! He stuffed the Max into a shirt pocket, where it hung cold and heavy. The money he crammed into his jeans. Man, he had to jump with it, his triumph leaping up through him like a wild thing, fine and strong as the flanks of a buck in the deep woods he'd seen from a Greyhound once, and for this one moment it seemed that everything was worth it somehow, all the pain and misery he'd gone through to finally win.

But Jackman's was silent. Nobody cheered. Nobody crowded around to congratulate him. He sobered, and silent hostile faces swam into focus. Not one of these kickers was on his side. They radiated contempt, even hatred. For an interminably drawn-out moment the air trembled with potential violence . . . and then someone turned to the side, hawked up phlegm, and spat on the floor. The crowd broke up, muttering, one by one drifting into the darkness.

Deke didn't move. A muscle in one leg began to twitch, harbinger of the coming hype crash. The top of his head felt numb, and there was an awful taste in his mouth. For a second he had to hang on to the table with both hands to keep from falling down forever, into the living shadow beneath him, as he hung impaled by the prize buck's dead eyes in the photo under the Dr. Pepper clock.

A little adrenaline would pull him out of this. He needed to celebrate. To get drunk or stoned and talk it up, going over the victory time and again, contradicting himself, making up details, laughing and bragging. A starry old night like this called for big talk.

But standing there with all of Jackman's silent and vast and empty around him, he realized suddenly that he had nobody left to tell it to.

Nobody at all.

OUR NEURAL CHERNOBYL

Bruce Sterling

One of the most powerful and innovative new talents to enter SF in recent years, Bruce Sterling sold his first story in 1976, and has since sold stories to Universe, Omni, Asimov's Science Fiction, The Magazine of Fantasy and Science Fiction, Lone Star Universe, *and elsewhere. He first attracted serious attention in the eighties with a series of stories set in his exotic "Shaper/Mechanist" future (a complex and disturbing future where warring political factions struggle to control the shape of human destiny), and by the end of the decade had established himself, with novels such as the complex and Stapeldonian* Schismatrix *and the well-received* Islands in the Net *(as well as with his editing of the influential anthology* Mirrorshades: The Cyberpunk Anthology *and the infamous critical magazine* Cheap Truth*) as perhaps the prime driving force behind the revolutionary "Cyberpunk" movement in science fiction (rivaled for that title only by his friend and collaborator, William Gibson), and also as one of the best new hard-science writers to enter the field in some time. His other books include the novels* The Artificial Kid *and* Involution Ocean, *a novel in collaboration with William Gibson,* The Difference Engine, *and the landmark* Crystal Express *and* Globalhead. *His most recent books are a new novel,* Heavy Weather, *and a critically acclaimed nonfiction study of First Amendment issues in the world of computer networking,* The Hacker Crackdown: Law and Disorder on the Electronic Frontier. *He lives with his family in Austin, Texas.*

In the compact little story that follows, packed with enough new ideas to fuel most other writers' 400-page novels, he shows us that, in the unmarked territory some hackers boldly explore, even the smallest actions can have large, and often totally unexpected, consequences.

The late twentieth century, and the early years of our own millennium, form, in retrospect, a single era. This was the Age of the Normal Accident, in which people cheerfully accepted technological risks that today would seem quite insane.

Chernobyls were astonishingly frequent during this foot-loose, not to say criminally negligent, period. The nineties, with their rapid spread of powerful industrial technologies to the developing world, were a decade of frightening enormities, including the Djakarta supertanker spill, the Lahore meltdown, and the gradual but devastating mass poisonings from tainted Kenyan contraceptives.

Yet none of these prepared humankind for the astonishing global effects of biotechnology's worst disaster: the event that has come to be known as the "neural chernobyl."

We should be grateful, then, that such an authority as the Nobel Prize–winning systems neurochemist Dr. Felix Hotton should have turned his able pen to the history of *Our Neural Chernobyl* (Bessemer, December 2056, $499.95). Dr. Hotton is uniquely qualified to give us this devastating reassessment of the past's wrongheaded practices. For Dr. Hotton is a shining exemplar of the new "Open-Tower Science," that social movement within the scientific community that arose in response to the New Luddism of the teens and twenties.

Such pioneering Hotton papers as "The Locus Coeruleus Efferent Network: What in Heck Is It There For?" and "My Grand Fun Tracing Neural Connections With Tetramethyl-benzidine" established this new, relaxed, and triumphantly subjective school of scientific exploration.

Today's scientist is a far cry from the white-coated sociopath of the past. Scientists today are democratized, media-conscious, fully integrated into the mainstream of modern culture. Today's young people, who admire scientists with a devotion once reserved for pop stars, can scarcely imagine the situation otherwise.

But in Chapter 1, "The Social Roots of Gene-Hacking,"

Dr. Hotton brings turn-of-the-century attitudes into startling relief. This was the golden age of applied biotech. Anxious attitudes toward "genetic tampering" changed rapidly when the terrifying AIDS pandemic was finally broken by recombinant DNA research.

It was during this period that the world first became aware that the AIDS retrovirus was a fantastic blessing in a particularly hideous disguise. This disease, which dug itself with horrible, virulent cunning into the very genetic structure of its victims, proved a medical marvel when finally broken to harness. The AIDS virus's RNA transcriptase system proved an able workhorse, successfully carrying healing segments of recombinant DNA into sufferers from a myriad of genetic defects. Suddenly one ailment after another fell into the miracle of RNA transcriptase techniques: sickle-cell anemia, cystic fibrosis, Tay-Sachs disease—literally hundreds of syndromes now only an unpleasant memory.

As billions poured into the biotech industry, and the instruments of research were simplified, an unexpected dynamic emerged: the rise of "gene-hacking." As Dr. Hotton points out, the situation had a perfect parallel in the 1970s and 1980s in the subculture of computer hacking. Here again was an enormously powerful technology suddenly within the reach of the individual.

As biotech companies multiplied, becoming ever smaller and more advanced, a hacker subculture rose around this "hot technology" like a cloud of steam. These ingenious, anomic individuals, often led into a state of manic self-absorption by their ability to dice with genetic destiny, felt no loyalty to social interests higher than their own curiosity. As early as the 1980s, devices such as high-performance liquid chromatographs, cell-culture systems, and DNA sequencers were small enough to fit into a closet or attic. If not bought from junkyards, diverted, or stolen outright, they could be reconstructed from off-the-shelf parts by any bright and determined teenager.

Dr. Hotton's second chapter explores the background of one such individual: Andrew ("Bugs") Berenbaum, now generally accepted as the perpetrator of the neural chernobyl.

Bugs Berenbaum, as Dr. Hotton convincingly shows, was not much different from a small horde of similar bright young misfits surrounding the genetic establishments of North Carolina's Research Triangle. His father was a semi-successful free-lance programmer, his mother a heavy marijuana user whose life centered around her role as "Lady Anne of Greengables" in Raleigh's Society for Creative Anachronism.

Both parents maintained a flimsy pretense of intellectual superiority, impressing upon Andrew the belief that the family's sufferings derived from the general stupidity and limited imagination of the average citizen. And Berenbaum, who showed an early interest in such subjects as math and engineering (then considered markedly unglamorous), did suffer some persecution from peers and schoolmates. At fifteen he had already drifted into the gene-hacker subculture, accessing gossip and learning "the scene" through computer bulletin boards and all-night beer-and-pizza sessions with other would-be pros.

At twenty-one, Berenbaum was working a summer internship with the small Raleigh firm of CoCoGenCo, a producer of specialized biochemicals. CoCoGenCo, as later congressional investigations proved, was actually a front for the California "designer drug" manufacturer and smuggler, Jimmy "Screech" McCarley. McCarley's agents within CoCoGenCo ran innumerable late-night "research projects" in conditions of heavy secrecy. In reality, these "secret projects" were straight production runs of synthetic cocaine, beta-phenethylamine, and sundry tailored variants of endorphin, a natural antipain chemical ten thousand times more potent than morphine.

One of McCarley's "blackhackers," possibly Berenbaum himself, conceived the sinister notion of "implanted dope factories." By attaching the drug-producing genetics directly into the human genome, it was argued, abusers could be "wet-wired" into permanent states of intoxication. The agent of fixation would be the AIDS retrovirus, whose RNA sequence was a matter of common knowledge and available on dozens of open scientific databases. The one drawback to the scheme, of course, was that the abuser would "burn out like a shitpaper moth in a klieg light," to use Dr. Hotton's memorable phrase.

Chapter 3 is rather technical. Given Dr. Hotton's light and popular style, it makes splendid reading. Dr. Hotton attempts to reconstruct Berenbaum's crude attempts to rectify the situation through gross manipulation of the AIDS RNA transcriptase. What Berenbaum sought, of course, was a way to shut-off and start-up the transcriptase carrier, so that the internal drug factor could be activated at will. Berenbaum's custom transcriptase was designed to react to a simple user-induced trigger—probably D,1,2,5-phospholytic gluteinase, a fractionated component of "Dr. Brown's Celery Soda," as Hotton suggests. This harmless beverage was a favorite quaff of gene-hacker circles.

Finding the genomes for cocaine-production too complex, Berenbaum (or perhaps a close associate, one Richard "Sticky" Ravetch) switched to a simpler payload: the just-discovered genome for mammalian dendritic growth factor. Dendrites are the treelike branches of brain cells, familiar to every modern schoolchild, which provide the mammalian brain with its staggering webbed complexity. It was theorized at the time that DG factor might be the key to vastly higher states of human intelligence. It is to be presumed that both Berenbaum and Ravetch had dosed themselves with it. As many modern victims of the neural chernobyl can testify, it does have an effect. Not precisely the one that the CoCoGenCo zealots envisioned, however.

While under the temporary maddening elation of dendritic "branch-effect," Berenbaum made his unfortunate breakthrough. He succeeded in providing his model RNA transcriptase with a trigger, but a trigger that made the transcriptase itself far more virulent than the original AIDS virus itself. The stage was set for disaster.

It was at this point that one must remember the social attitudes that bred the soul-threatening isolation of the period's scientific workers. Dr. Hotton is quite pitiless in his psychoanalysis of the mental mind-set of his predecessors. The supposedly "objective worldview" of the sciences is now quite properly seen as a form of mental brainwashing, deliberately stripping the victim of the full spectrum of human emotional response. Under such conditions, Berenbaum's reckless act becomes almost pitiable; it was a convulsive overcompensation for years of emotional starvation. Without consulting his superiors, who might have shown more discretion, Berenbaum began offering free samples of his new wetwares to anyone willing to inject them.

There was a sudden brief plague of eccentric genius in Raleigh, before the now-well-known symptoms of "dendritic crash" took over, and plunged the experimenters into vision-riddled, poetic insanity. Berenbaum himself committed suicide well before the full effects were known. And the full effects, of course, were to go far beyond even this lamentable human tragedy.

Chapter 4 becomes an enthralling detective story as the evidence slowly mounts.

Even today the term "Raleigh collie" has a special ring for dog fanciers, many of whom have forgotten its original derivation. These likable, companionable, and disquietingly intelligent pets were soon transported all over the nation by eager buyers and breeders. Once it had made the jump from human host to canine, Berenbaum's transcriptase derivative, like the AIDS virus itself, was passed on through the canine maternal womb. It was also transmitted through canine sexual intercourse and, via saliva, through biting and licking.

No dendritically enriched "Raleigh collie" would think of biting a human being. On the contrary, these loyal and well-behaved pets have even been known to right spilled garbage cans and replace their trash. Neural chernobyl infections remained rare in humans. But they spread through North America's canine population like wildfire, as Dr. Hotton shows in a series of cleverly designed maps and charts.

Chapter 5 offers us the benefit of hindsight. We are now accustomed to the idea of many different modes of "intelligence." There are, for instance, the various types of

computer Artificial Intelligence, which bear no real relation
to human "thinking." This was not unexpected—but the
diverse forms of animal intelligence can still astonish in
their variety.

The variance between *Canis familiaris* and his wild
cousin, the coyote, remains unexplained. Dr. Hotton makes
a good effort, basing his explication on the coyote neural
mapping of his colleague, Dr. Reyna Sanchez of Los
Alamos National Laboratory. It does seem likely that the
coyote's more fully reticulated basal commissure plays a
role. At any rate, it is now clear that a startling advanced
form of social organization has taken root among the
nation's feral coyote organization, with the use of elaborate
coded barks, "scent-dumps," and specialized roles in hunting and food storage. Many of the nation's ranchers have
now taken to the "protection system," in which coyote packs
are "bought off" with slaughtered, barbecued livestock and
sacks of dog treats. Persistent reports in Montana, Idaho,
and Saskatchewan insist that coyotes have been spotted
wearing cast-off clothing during the worst cold of winter.

It is possible that the common household cat was infected
even earlier than the dog. Yet the effects of heightened cat
intelligence are subtle and difficult to specify. Notoriously
reluctant lab subjects, cats in their infected states are even
sulkier about running mazes, solving trick boxes, and so on,
preferring to wait out their interlocutors with inscrutable
feline patience.

It has been suggested that some domestic cats show a
heightened interest in television programs. Dr. Hotton casts
a skeptical light on this, pointing out (rightly, as this
reviewer thinks) that cats spend most of their waking hours
sitting and staring into space. Staring at the flickering of a
television is not much more remarkable than the hearthside
cat's fondness for the flickering fire. It certainly does not
imply "understanding" of a program's content. There are,
however, many cases where cats have learned to paw-push
the buttons of remote-control units. Those who keep cats as
mousers have claimed that some cats now torture birds and

rodents for longer periods, with greater ingenuity, and in some cases with improvised tools.

There remains, however, the previously unsuspected connection between advanced dendritic branching and manual dexterity, which Dr. Hotton tackles in his sixth chapter. This concept has caused a revolution in paleoanthropology. We are now forced into the uncomfortable realization that *Pithecanthropus robustus*, formerly dismissed as a large-jawed, vegetable-chewing ape, was probably far more intelligent than *Homo sapiens*. CAT-scans of the recently discovered Tanzanian fossil skeleton, nicknamed "Leonardo," revealed a *Pithecanthropus* skull-ridge obviously rich with dendritic branching. It has been suggested that the pithecanthropoids suffered from a heightened "life of the mind" similar to the life-threatening absent-minded genius of terminal neural chernobyl sufferers. This yields the uncomfortable theory that nature, through evolution, has imposed a "primate stupidity barrier" that allows humans, unlike *Pithecanthropus*, to get on successfully with the dumb animal business of living and reproducing.

But the synergetic effects of dendritic branching and manual dexterity are clear in a certain nonprimate species. I refer, of course, to the well-known "chernobyl jump" of *Procyon lotor*, the American raccoon. The astonishing advances of the raccoon, and its Chinese cousin the panda, occupy the entirety of Chapter 8.

Here Dr. Hotton takes the so-called "modern view," from which I must dissociate myself. I, for one, find it intolerable that large sections of the American wilderness should be made into "no-go areas" by the vandalistic activities of our so-called "stripe-tailed cousins." Admittedly, excesses may have been committed in early attempts to exterminate the verminous, booming population of these masked bandits. But the damage to agriculture has been severe, and the history of kamikaze attacks by self-infected rabid raccoons is a terrifying one.

Dr. Hotton holds that we must now "share the planet with a fellow civilized species." He bolsters his argument with hearsay evidence of "raccoon culture" that to me seems rather flimsy. The woven strips of bark known as "raccoon wampum" are impressive examples of animal dexterity, but to my mind it remains to be proven that they are actually "money." And their so-called "pictographs" seem little more than random daubings. The fact remains that the raccoon population continues to rise exponentially, with raccoon bitches whelping massive litters every spring. Dr. Hotton, in a footnote, suggests that we can relieve crowding pressure by increasing the human presence in outer space. This seems a farfetched unsatisfactory scheme.

The last chapter is speculative in tone. The prospect of intelligent rats is grossly repugnant; so far, thank God, the tough immune system of the rat, inured to bacteria and filth, has rejected retroviral invasion. Indeed, the feral cat population seems to be driving these vermin toward extinction. Nor have opossums succumbed; indeed, marsupials of all kinds seem immune, making Australia a haven of a now-lost natural world. Whales and dolphins are endangered species; they seem unlikely to make a comeback even with the (as-yet-unknown) cetacean effects of chernobyling. And monkeys, which might pose a very considerable threat, are restricted to the few remaining patches of tropical forest and, like humans, seem resistant to the disease.

Our neural chernobyl has bred a folklore all its own. Modern urban folklore speaks of "ascended masters," a group of chernobyl victims able to survive the virus. Supposedly, they "pass for human," forming a hidden counter-culture among the normals, or "sheep." This is a throwback to the dark tradition of Luddism, and the popular fears once projected onto the dangerous and reckless "priesthood of science" are now transferred to these fairy tales of supermen. This psychological transference becomes clear when one hears that these "ascended masters" specialize in advanced scientific research of a kind now frowned upon. The notion that some fraction of the population has achieved physical immortality, and hidden it from the rest of us, is utterly absurd.

Dr. Hotton, quite rightly, treats this paranoid myth with the contempt it deserves.

Despite my occasional reservations, this is a splendid book, likely to be the definitive work on this central phenomenon of modern times. Dr. Hotton may well hope to add another Pulitzer to his list of honors. At ninety-five, this grand old man of modern science has produced yet another stellar work in his rapidly increasing oeuvre. His many readers, like myself, can only marvel at his vigor and clamor for more.

—*for Greg Bear*

(LEARNING ABOUT)
MACHINE SEX

Candas Jane Dorsey

*Canadian writer and arts journalist Candas Jane Dorsey is
currently president of the Writers Guild of Alberta and also
president of SF Canada, the Speculative Writers Association
of Canada, of which she is founder. She is probably best-
known inside the genre for her collection* Machine Sex and
Other Stories, *and for co-editing (with Gerry Truscott) the
anthology of Canadian speculative fiction,* Tesseracts[3], *but she
has also published four books of poetry, and a novel,* Hardwired
Angel, *written in collaboration with Nora Abercrombie. Her
story "Sleeping in a Box" won the 1989 Aurora Award for
best short-form work in English. Her most recent book is the
anthology* Prairie Fire: New Canadian Speculative Fiction,
*co-edited with G. N. Louise Jonasson, and she is at work on
a new novel, a new book of short fiction, and a nonfiction
book on sex and society.*

*In the disturbing and powerful story that follows, she
reaffirms the truth of an old saying: nobody has ever gone
broke underestimating the taste of the general public. Or
pandering to its worst instincts, either.*

A naked woman working at a computer. Which attracts you
most? It was a measure of Whitman that, as he entered the
room, his eyes went first to the unfolded machine gleaming
small and awkward in the light of the long-armed desk
lamp; he'd seen the woman before.

Angel was the woman. Thin and pale-skinned, with dark
nipples and black pubic hair, and her face hidden by a dark
unkempt mane of long hair as she leaned over her work.

A woman complete with her work. It was a measure of

Angel that she never acted naked, even when she was. Perhaps especially when she was.

So she has a new board, thought Whitman, and felt his guts stir the way they stirred when he first contemplated taking her to bed. That was a long time ago. And she knew it, felt without turning her head the desire, and behind the screen of her straight dark hair, uncombed and tumbled in front of her eyes, she smiled her anger down.

"Where have you been?" he asked, and she shook her hair back, leaned backward to ease her tense neck.

"What is that thing?" he went on insistently, and Angel turned her face to him, half-scowling. The board on the desk had thin irregular wings spreading from a small central module. Her fingers didn't slow their keyboard dance.

"None of your business," she said.

She saved the input, and he watched her fold the board into a smaller and smaller rectangle. Finally she shook her hair back from her face.

"I've got the option on your bioware," he said.

"Pay as you go," she said. "New house rules."

And found herself on her ass on the floor from his reflexive, furious blow. And his hand in her hair, pulling her up and against the wall. Hard. Astonishing her with how quickly she could hurt and how much. Then she hurt too much to analyze it.

"You are a bitch," he said.

"So what?" she said. "When I was nicer, you were still an asshole."

Her head back against the wall, crack. Ouch.

Breathless, Angel: "Once more and you never see this bioware." And Whitman slowly draws breath, draws back, and looks at her the way she knew he always felt.

"Get out," she said. "I'll bring it to Kozyk's office when it's ready."

So he went. She slumped back in the chair, and tears began to blur her vision, but hate cleared them up fast enough, as she unfolded the board again, so that despite the pain she hardly missed a moment of programming time.

Assault only a distraction now, betrayal only a detail:

Angel was on a roll. She had her revenge well in hand, though it took a subtle mind to recognize it.

Again: "I have the option on any of your bioware." This time, in the office, Whitman wore the nostalgic denims he now affected, and Angel her street-silks and leather.

"That is mine, but I made one for you." She pulled it out of the bag. Where her board looked jerry-built, this one was sleek. Her board looked interesting; this one packaged. "I made it before you sold our company," she said. "I put my best into it. You may as well have it. I suppose you own the option anyway, eh?"

She stood. Whitman was unconsciously restless before her.

"When you pay me for this," she said, "make it in MannComp stock." She tossed him the board. "But be careful. If you take it apart wrong, you'll break it. Then you'll have to ask me to fix it, and from now on, my tech rate goes up."

As she walked by him, he reached for her, hooked one arm around her waist. She looked at him, totally expressionless. "Max," she said, "it's like I told you last night. From now on, if you want it, you pay. Just like everyone else." He let her go. She pulled the soft dirty white silk shirt on over the black leather jacket. The compleat rebel now.

"It's a little going away present. When you're a big shot in MannComp, remember that I made it. And that you couldn't even take it apart right. I guarantee."

He wasn't going to watch her leave. He was already studying the board. Hardly listening, either.

"Call it the Mannboard," she said. "It gets big if you stroke it." She shut the door quietly behind herself.

It would be easier if this were a story about sex, or about machines. It is true that the subject is Angel, a woman who builds computers like they have never been built before outside the human skull. Angel, like everyone else, comes from somewhere and goes somewhere else. She lives in that linear and binary universe. However, like everyone else, she lives concurrently in another universe less simple. Trivalent, quadrivalent, multivalent. World without end, with no amen. And so, on.

They say a hacker's burned out before he's twenty-one. Note the pronoun: he. Not many young women in that heady realm of the chip.

Before Angel was twenty-one—long before—she had taken the cybernetic chip out of a Wm. Kuhns fantasy and patented it; she had written the program for the self-taught AI the Bronfmanns had bought and used to gain world prominence for their MannComp lapboard; somewhere in there, she'd lost innocence, and when her clever additions to that AI turned it into something the military wanted, she dropped out of sight in Toronto and went back to Rocky Mountain House, Alberta, on a Greyhound bus.

It was while she was thinking about something else—cash, and how to get some—that she had looked out of the bus window in Winnipeg into the display window of a sex shop. Garter belts, sleazy magazines on cheap coated paper with Day-Glo orange stickers over the genitals of bored sex kings and queens, a variety of ornamental vibrators. She had too many memories of Max to take it lightly, though she heard the laughter of the roughnecks in the back of the bus as they topped each other's dirty jokes, and thought perhaps their humor was worth emulating. If only she could.

She passed her twentieth birthday in a hotel in Regina, where she stopped to take a shower and tap into the phone lines, checking for pursuit. Armed with the money she got through automatic transfer from a dummy account in Medicine Hat, she rode the bus the rest of the way ignoring the rolling of beer bottles under the seats, the acrid stink of the onboard toilet. She was thinking about sex.

As the bus roared across the long flat prairie she kept one hand on the roll of bills in her pocket, but with the other she made the first notes on the program that would eventually make her famous.

She made the notes on an antique NEC lapboard which had been her aunt's, in old-fashioned BASIC—all the machine would support—but she unraveled it and knitted it into that artificial trivalent language when she got to the place at Rocky and plugged the idea into her Mannboard. She had it written in a little over four hours on-time, but that counted an hour and a half she took to write a new loop into the AI. (She would patent that loop later the same year and put the royalties into a blind trust for her brother, Brian, brain damaged from birth. He was in Michener Centre in Red Deer, not educable; no one at Bronfmann knew about her family, and she kept it that way.)

She called it Machine Sex; working title.

Working title for a life: born in Innisfail General Hospital, father a rodeo cowboy who raised rodeo horses, did enough mixed farming out near Caroline to build his young second wife a big log house facing the mountain view. The first baby came within a year, ending her mother's tenure as teller at the local bank. Her aunt was a programmer for the University of Lethbridge, chemical molecular model analysis on the University of Calgary mainframe through a modem link.

From her aunt she learned BASIC, Pascal, COBOL and C; in school she played the usual turtle games on the Apple IIe; when she was fourteen she took a bus to Toronto, changed her name to Angel, affected a punk hairstyle and the insolent all-white costume of that year's youth, and eventually walked into Northern Systems, the company struggling most successfully with bionics at the time, with the perfected biochip, grinning at the proper young men in their gray three-piece suits as they tried to find a bug in it anywhere. For the first million she let them open it up; for the next five she told them how she did it. Eighteen years old by the phony records she'd cooked on her arrival in Toronto, she was free to negotiate her own contracts.

But no one got her away from Northern until Bronfmann bought Northern lock, stock and climate-controlled workshop. She had been sleeping with Northern's boy-wonder president by then for about a year, had yet to have an orgasm though she'd learned a lot about kinky sex toys. Figured

she'd been screwed by him for the last time when he sold
the company without telling her; spent the next two weeks
doing a lot of drugs and having a lot of cheap sex in the
degenerate punk underground; came up with the AI educa-
tion program.

Came up indeed, came staggering into Ted Kozyk's
office, president of Bronfmann's MannComp subsidiary,
with that jury-rigged Mannboard tied into two black-box
add-ons no bigger than a bar of soap, and said, "Watch this."

Took out the power supply first, wiped the memory,
plugged into a wall outlet and turned it on.

The bootstrap greeting sounded a lot like Goo.

"Okay," she said, "it's ready."

"Ready for what?"

"Anything you want," she said. By then he knew her,
knew her rep, knew that the sweaty-smelling, disheveled,
anorectic-looking waif in the filthy, oversized silk shirt (the
rebels had affected natural fabrics the year she left home,
and she always did after that, even later when the silk was
cleaner, more upmarket, and black instead of white) had
something. Two weeks ago he'd bought a company on the
strength of that something, and the board Whitman had
brought him the day after the sale, even without the software
to run on it, had been enough to convince him he'd been
right.

He sat down to work, and hours later he was playing Go
with an AI he'd taught to talk back, play games, and predict
horse races and the stock market.

He sat back, flicked the power switch and pulled the plug,
and stared at her.

"Congratulations," she said.

"What for?" he said; "you're the genius."

"No, congratulations, you just murdered your first baby,"
she said, and plugged it back in. "Want to try for two?"

"Goo," said the deck. "Dada."

It was her little joke. It was never a feature on the
MannComp A-One they sold across every MannComp
counter in the world.

• • •

But now she's all grown up, she's sitting in a log house near
Rocky Mountain House, watching the late summer sunset
from the big front windows, while the computer runs
Machine Sex to its logical conclusion, orgasm.

She had her first orgasm at nineteen. According to her
false identity, she was twenty-three. Her lover was a
delegate to MannComp's annual sales convention; she
picked him up after the speech she gave on the ethics of
selling AIs to high school students in Thailand. Or whatever,
she didn't care. Kozyk used to write her speeches but she
usually changed them to suit her mood. This night she'd
been circumspect, only a few expletives, enough to amuse
the younger sales representatives and reassure the older
ones.

The one she chose was smooth in his approach and
she thought, well, we'll see. They went up to the suite
MannComp provided, all mod cons and king-size bed, and
as she undressed she looked at him and thought he's
ambitious, this boy, better not give him an inch.

He surprised her in bed. Ambitious maybe, but he paid a
lot of attention to detail.

After he spread her across the universe in a way she had
never felt before, he turned to her and said, "That was pretty
good, eh, baby?" and smiled a smooth little grin. "Sure," she
said, "it was okay," and was glad she hadn't said more while
she was out in the ozone.

By then she thought she was over what Whitman had
done to her. And after all, it had been simple enough, what
he did. Back in that loft she had in Hull, upstairs of a shop,
where she covered the windows with opaque Mylar and
worked night and day in that twilight. That night as she
worked he stood behind her, hands on her shoulders,
massaging her into further tenseness.

"Hey, Max, you know I don't like it when people look
over my shoulder when I'm working."

"Sorry, baby." He moved away, and she felt her shoulders
relax just to have his hands fall away.

"Come on to bed," he said. "You know you can pick that up whenever."

She had to admit he was being pleasant tonight. Maybe he too was tired of the constant scrapping, disguised as jokes, that wore at her nerves so much. All his efforts to make her stop working, slow her down so he could stay up. The sharp edges that couldn't be disguised. Her bravado made her answer in the same vein, but in the mornings, when he was gone to Northern; she paced and muttered to herself, reworking the previous day until it was done with, enough that she could go on. And after all what was missing? She had no idea how to debug it.

Tonight he'd even made some dinner, and touched her kindly. Should she be grateful? Maybe the conversations, such as they were, where she tried to work it out, had just made it worse—

"Ah, shit," she said, and pushed the board away. "You're right, I'm too tired for this. *Demain*." She was learning French in her spare time.

He began with hugging her, and stroking the long line along her back, something he knew she liked, like a cat likes it, arches its back at the end of the stroke. He knew she got turned on by it. And she did. When they had sex at her house he was without the paraphernalia he preferred, but he seemed to manage, buoyed up by some mood she couldn't share; nor could she share his release.

Afterward, she lay beside him, tense and dissatisfied in the big bed, not admitting it, or she'd have to admit she didn't know what would help. He seemed to be okay, stretched, relaxed and smiling.

"Had a big day," he said.

"Yeah?"

"Big deal went through."

"Yeah?"

"Yeah, I sold the company."

"You what?" Reflexively moving herself so that none of her body touched his.

"Northern. I put it to Bronfmann. Megabucks."

"Are you joking?" but she saw he was not. "You didn't, I didn't . . . . Northern's *our* company."

"My company. I started it."

"I made it big for you."

"Oh, and I paid you well for every bit of that."

She got up. He was smiling a little, trying on the little-boy grin. No, baby, she thought, not tonight.

"Well," she said, "I know for sure that this is my bed. Get out of it."

"Now, I knew you might take this badly. But it really was the best thing. The R&D costs were killing us. Bronfmann can eat them for breakfast."

R&D costs meant her. "Maybe. Your clothes are here." She tossed them on the bed, went into the other room.

As well as sex, she hadn't figured out betrayal yet either; on the street, she thought, people fucked you over openly, not in secret.

This, even as she said it to herself, she recognized as romantic and certainly not based on experience. She was street-wise in every way but one: Max had been her first lover.

She unfolded the new board. It had taken her some time to figure out how to make it expand like that, to fit the program it was going to run. This idea of shaping the hardware to the software had been with her since she made the biochip, and thus made it possible and much more interesting than the other way around. But making the hardware to fit her new idea had involved a great deal of study and technique, and so far she had had limited success.

This reminded her again of sex, and, she supposed, relationships, although it seemed to her that before sex everything had been on surfaces, very easy. Now she had sex, she had had Max, and now she had no way to realize the results of any of that. Especially now, when Northern had just vanished into Bronfmann's computer empire, putting her in that position again of having to prove herself. What had Max used to make Bronfmann take the bait? She knew very clearly: Angel, the Northern Angel, would now become the MannComp Angel. The rest of the bait would have been the AI; she was making more of it every day, but couldn't yet bring it together. Could it be done at all? Bronfmann had paid high for an affirmative answer.

Certainly this time the bioware was working together. She began to smile a little to herself, almost unaware of it, as she saw how she could interconnect the loops to make a solid net to support the program's full and growing weight. Because, of course, it would have to learn as it went along—that was basic.

Angel as metaphor; she had to laugh at herself when she woke from programming hours later, Max still sleeping in her bed, ignoring her eviction notice. He'll have to get up to piss anyway, she thought; that's when I'll get him out. She went herself to the bathroom in the half-dawn light, stretching her cramped back muscles and thinking remotely, well, I got some satisfaction out of last night after all: the beginnings of the idea that might break this impasse. While it's still inside my head, this one is mine. How can I keep it that way?

New fiscal controls, she thought grimly. New contracts, now that Northern doesn't exist any more. Max can't have this, whatever it turns into, for my dowry to MannComp.

When she put on her white silks—leather jacket underneath, against the skin as street fashion would have it—she hardly knew herself what she would do. The little board went into her bag with the boxes of pills the pharmaceutical tailor had made for her. If there was nothing there to suit, she'd buy something new. In the end, she left Max sleeping in her bed; so what? she thought as she reached the highway. The first ride she hitched took her to Toronto, not without a little tariff, but she no longer gave a damn about any of that.

By then the drugs in her system had lifted her out of a body that could be betrayed, and she didn't return to it for two weeks, two weeks of floating in a soup of disjointed noise, and always the program running, unfolding, running again, unfolding inside her relentless mind. She kept it running to drown anything she might remember about trust or the dream of happiness.

When she came home two weeks later, on a hot day in summer with the Ottawa Valley humidity unbearable and her body tired, sore and bruised, and very dirty, she stepped out of her filthy silks in a room messy with Whitman's continued inhabitation; furious, she popped a system cleanser and unfolded the board on her desk. When he came back in she was there, naked, angry, working.

A naked woman working at a computer. What good were cover-ups? Watching Max after she took the new AI up to Kozyk, she was only triumphant because she'd done something Max could never do, however much he might be able to sell her out. Watching them fit it to the bioboard, the strange unfolding machine she had made to fit the ideas only she could have, she began to be afraid. The system cleanser she'd taken made the clarity inescapable. Over the next few months, as she kept adding clever loops and twists, she watched their glee and she looked at what telephone numbers were in the top ten on their modem memories and she began to realize that it was not only business and science that would pay high for a truly thinking machine.

She knew that ten years before there had been Pentagon programmers working to model predatory behavior in AIs using Prolog and its like. That was old hat. None of them, however, knew what they needed to know to write for her bioware yet. No one but Angel could do that. So, by the end of her nineteenth year, that made Angel one of the most sought-after, endangered ex-anorectics on the block.

She went to conferences and talked about the ethics of selling AIs to teenagers in Nepal. Or something. And took a smooth salesman to bed, and thought all the time about when they were going to make their approach. It would be Whitman again, not Kozyk, she thought; Ted wouldn't get his hands dirty, while Max was born with grime under his nails.

She thought also about metaphors. How, even in the new street slang which she could speak as easily as her native tongue, being screwed, knocked, fucked over, jossed, dragged all meant the same thing: hurt to the core. And this was what people sought out, what they spent their time seeking in pick-up joints, to the beat of bad old headbanger bands, that nostalgia shit. Now, as well as the biochip, Max, the AI breakthrough, and all the tailored drugs she could eat, she'd had orgasm too.

Well, she supposed it passed the time.

What interested her intellectually about orgasm was not the lovely illusion of transcendence it brought, but the absolute binary predictability of it. When you learn what to do to the nerve endings, and they are in a receptive state, the program runs like kismet. Warm boot. She'd known a hacker once who'd altered his bootstrap messages to read "Warm pussy." She knew where most hackers were at; they played with their computers more than they played with themselves. She was the same, otherwise why would it have taken a pretty-boy salesman in a three-piece to show her the simple answer? All the others, just like trying to use an old MS-DOS disc to boot up one of her Mann lapboards with crystal RO/RAM.

Angel forgets she's only twenty. Genius is uneven. There's no substitute for time, that relentless shaper of understanding. Etc. Etc. Angel paces with the knowledge that everything is a phrase, even this. Life is hard and then you die, and so on. And so, on

One day it occurred to her that she could simply run away.

This should have seemed elementary but to Angel it was a revelation. She spent her life fatalistically; her only successful escape had been from the people she loved. Her lovely, crazy grandfather; her generous and slightly avaricious aunt; and her beloved imbecile brother; they were buried deep in a carefully forgotten past. But she kept coming back to Whitman, to Kozyk and Bronfmann, as if she liked them.

As if, like a shocked dog in a learned helplessness experiment, she could not believe that the cage had a door, and the door was open.

She went out the door. For old times' sake, it was the bus

she chose; the steamy chill of an air-conditioned Greyhound hadn't changed at all. Bottles—pop and beer—rolling under the seats and the stench of chemicals filling the air whenever someone sneaked down to smoke a cigarette or a reef in the toilet. Did anyone ever use it to piss in? She liked the triple seat near the back, but the combined smells forced her to the front, behind the driver, where she was joined, across the country, by an endless succession of old women, immaculate in their Fortrels, who started conversations and shared peppermints and gum.

She didn't get stoned once.

The country unrolled strangely: sex shop in Winnipeg, bank machine in Regina, and hours of programming alternating with polite responses to the old women, until eventually she arrived, creased and exhausted, in Rocky Mountain House.

Rocky Mountain House: a comfortable model of a small town, from which no self-respecting hacker should originate. But these days, the world a net of wire and wireless, it doesn't matter where you are, as long as you have the information people want. Luckily for Angel's secret past, however, this was not a place she would be expected to live—or to go—or to come from.

An atavism she hadn't controlled had brought her this far. A rented car took her the rest of the way to the ranch. She thought only to look around, but when she found the tenants packing for a month's holiday, she couldn't resist the opportunity. She carried her leather satchel into their crocheted, frilled guest room—it had been her room fifteen years before—with a remote kind of satisfaction.

That night, she slept like the dead—except for some dreams. But there was nothing she could do about them.

Lightning and thunder. I should stop now, she thought, wary of power surges through the new board which she was charging as she worked. She saved her file, unplugged the power, stood, stretched, and walked to the window to look at the mountains.

The storm illuminated the closer slopes erratically, the

rain hid the distances. She felt some heaviness lift. The cool wind through the window refreshed her. She heard the program stop, and turned off the machine. Sliding out the backup capsule, she smiled her angry smile unconsciously. When I get back to the Ottawa Valley, she thought, where weather never comes from the west like it's supposed to, I'll make those fuckers eat this.

Out in the corrals where the tenants kept their rodeo horses, there was animal noise, and she turned off the light to go and look out the side window. A young man was leaning his weight against the reins-length pull of a rearing, terrified horse. Angel watched as flashes of lightning strobed the hackneyed scene. This was where she came from. She remembered her father in the same struggle. And her mother at this window with her, both of them watching the man. Her mother's anger she never understood until now. Her father's abandonment of all that was in the house, including her brother, Brian, inert and restless in his oversized crib.

Angel walked back through the house, furnished now in the kitschy western style of every trailer and bungalow in this countryside. She was lucky to stay, invited on a generous impulse, while all but their son were away. She felt vaguely guilty at her implicit criticism.

Angel invited the young rancher into the house only because this is what her mother and her grandmother would have done. Even Angel's great-grandmother, whose father kept the stopping house, which meant she kept the travelers fed, even her spirit infused in Angel the unwilling act. She watched him almost sullenly as he left his rain gear in the wide porch.

He was big, sitting in the big farm kitchen. His hair was wet, and he swore almost as much as she did. He told her how he had put a trailer on the north forty, and lived there now, instead of in the little room where she'd been invited to sleep. He told her about the stock he'd accumulated riding the rodeo. They drank Glenfiddich. She told him her father had been a rodeo cowboy. He told her about his university degree in agriculture. She told him she'd never been to university. They drank more whiskey and he told her he couldn't drink that other rotgut any more since he tasted real Scotch. He invited her to see his computer. She went with him across the yard and through the trees in the rain, her bag over her shoulder, board hidden in it, and he showed her his computer. It turned out to be the first machine she designed for Northern—archaic now, compared with the one she'd just invented.

Fair is fair, she thought drunkenly, and she pulled out her board and unfolded it.

"You showed me yours, I'll show you mine," she said.

He liked the board. He was amazed that she had made it. They finished the Scotch.

"I like you," she said. "Let me show you something. You can be the first." And she ran Machine Sex for him.

He was the first to see it: before Whitman and Kozyk who bought it to sell to people who already have had and done everything; before David and Jonathan, the Hardware Twins in MannComp's Gulf Islands shop, who made the touchpad devices necessary to run it properly; before a world market hungry for the kind of glossy degradation Machine Sex could give them bought it in droves from a hastily-created— MannComp-subsidiary—numbered company. She ran it for him with just the automouse on her board, and a description of what it would do when the hardware was upgraded to it.

It was very simple, really. If orgasm was binary, it could be programmed. Feed back the sensation through one or more touchpads to program the body. The other thing she knew about human sex was that it was as much cortical as genital, or more so: touch is optional for the turn-on. Also easy, then, to produce cortical stimuli by programmed input. The rest was a cosmetic elaboration of the premise.

At first it did turn him on, then off, then it made his blood run cold. She was pleased by that: her work had chilled her too.

"You can't market that thing!" he said.

"Why not. It's a fucking good program. Hey, get it? Fucking good."

"It's not real."

"Of course it isn't. So what?"

"So, people don't need that kind of stuff to get turned on."

She told him about people. More people than he'd known were in the world. People who made her those designer drugs, given in return for favors she never granted until after Whitman sold her like a used car. People like Whitman, teaching her about sexual equipment while dealing with the Pentagon and CSIS to sell them Angel's sharp angry mind, as if she'd work on killing others as eagerly as she was trying to kill herself. People who would hire a woman on the street, as they had her during that two-week nightmare almost a year before, and use her as casually as their own hand, without giving a damn.

"One night," she said, "just to see, I told all the johns I was fourteen. I was skinny enough, even then, to get away with it. And they all loved it. Every single one gave me a bonus, and took me anyway."

The whiskey fog was wearing a little thin. More time had passed than she thought, and more had been said than she had intended. She went to her bag, rummaged, but she'd left her drugs in Toronto, some dim idea at the time that she should clean up her act. All that had happened was that she had spent the days so tight with rage that she couldn't eat, and she'd already cured herself of that once; for the record, she thought, she'd rather be stoned.

"Do you have any more booze?" she said, and he went to look. She followed him around his kitchen.

"Furthermore," she said, "I rolled every one of them that I could, and all but one had pictures of his kids in his wallet, and all of them were teenagers. Boys and girls together. And their saintly dads out fucking someone who looked just like them. Just like them."

Luckily, he had another bottle. Not quite the same quality, but she wasn't fussy.

"So I figured," she finished, "that they don't care who they fuck. Why not the computer in the den? Or the office system at lunch hour?"

"It's not like that," he said. "It's nothing like that. People deserve better." He had the neck of the bottle in his big hand, was seriously, carefully pouring himself another shot. He gestured with both bottle and glass. "People deserve to have—love."

"Love?"

"Yeah, love. You think I'm stupid, you think I watched too much TV as a kid, but I know it's out there. Somewhere. Other people think so too. Don't you? Didn't you, even if you won't admit it now, fall in love with that guy Max at first? You never said what he did at the beginning, how he talked you into being his lover. Something must have happened. Well, that's what I mean: love."

"Let me tell you about love. Love is a guy who talks real smooth taking me out to the woods and telling me he just loves my smile. And then taking me home and putting me in leather handcuffs so he can come. And if I hurt he likes it, because he likes it to hurt a little and he thinks I must like it like he does. And if I moan he thinks I'm coming. And if I cry he thinks it's love. And so do I. Until one evening— not too long after my *last* birthday, as I recall—he tells me that he has sold me to another company. And this only after he fucks me one last time. Even though I don't belong to him anymore. After all, he had the option on all my bioware."

"All this is just politics." He was sharp, she had to grant him that.

"Politics," she said, "give me a break. Was it politics made Max able to sell me with the stock: hardware, software, liveware?"

"I've met guys like that. Women too. You have to understand that it wasn't personal to him, it was just politics." Also stubborn. "Sure, you were naive, but you weren't wrong. You just didn't understand company politics."

"Oh, sure I did. I always have. Why do you think I changed my name? Why do you think I dress in natural fibers and go through all the rest of this bullshit? I know how to set up power blocs. Except in mine there is only one party—me. And that's the way it's going to stay. Me against them from now on."

"It's not always like that. There are assholes in the world, and there are other people too. Everyone around here still remembers your grandfather, even though he's been retired in Camrose for fifteen years. They still talk about the way he and his wife used to waltz at the Legion Hall. What about him? There are more people like him than there are Whitmans."

"Charlotte doesn't waltz much since her stroke."

"That's a cheap shot. You can't get away with cheap shots. Speaking of shots, have another."

"Don't mind if I do. Okay, I give you Eric and Charlotte. But one half-happy ending doesn't balance out the people who go through their lives with their teeth clenched, trying to make it come out the same as a True Romance comic, and always wondering what's missing. They read those bodice-ripper novels, and make that do for the love you believe in so naively." Call her naive, would he? Two could play at that game. "That's why they'll all go crazy for Machine Sex. So simple. So linear. So fast. So uncomplicated."

"You underestimate people's ability to be happy. People are better at loving than you think."

"You think so? Wait until you have your own little piece of land and some sweetheart takes you out in the trees on a moonlit night and gives you head until you think your heart will break. So you marry her and have some kids. She furnishes the trailer in a five-room sale grouping. You have to quit drinking Glenfiddich because she hates it when you talk too loud. She gets an allowance every month and crochets a cozy for the TV. You work all day out in the rain and all evening in the back room making the books balance on the outdated computer. After the kids come she gains weight and sells real estate if you're lucky. If not she makes things out of recycled bleach bottles and hangs them in the yard. Pretty soon she wears a nightgown to bed and turns her back when you slip in after a hard night at the keyboard. So you take up drinking again and teach the kids about the rodeo. And you find some square-dancing chick who gives you head out behind the bleachers one night in Trochu, so sweet you think your heart will break. What you gonna do then, mountain man?"

"Okay, we can tell stories until the sun comes up. Which won't be too long, look at the time; but no matter how many stories you tell you can't make me forget about that thing." He pointed to the computer with loathing.

"It's just a machine."

"You know what I mean. That thing in it. And besides, I'm gay. Your little scenario wouldn't work."

She laughed and laughed. "So that's why you haven't made a pass at me yet." She wondered coldly how gay he was, but she was tired, so tired of proving power. His virtue was safe with her; so, she thought suddenly strangely, was hers with him. It was unsettling and comforting at once.

"Maybe," he said. "Or maybe I'm just a liar like you think everyone is. Eh? You think everyone strings everyone else a line? Crap. Who has the time for that shit?"

Perhaps they were drinking beer now. Or was it vodka? She found it hard to tell after a while.

"You know what I mean," she said. "You should know. The sweet young thing who has AIDS and doesn't tell you. Or me. I'm lucky so far. Are you? Or who sucks you for your money. Or josses you 'cause he's into denim and Nordic looks."

"Okay, okay. I give up. Everybody's a creep but you and me."

"And I'm not so sure about you."

"Likewise, I'm sure. Have another. So, if you're so pure, what about the ethics of it?"

"What *about* the ethics of it?" she asked. "Do you think I went through all that sex without paying attention? I had nothing else to do but watch other people come. I saw that old cult movie, where the aliens feed on heroin addiction and orgasm, and the woman's not allowed orgasm so she has to O.D. on smack. Orgasm's more decadent than shooting heroin? I can't buy that, but there's something about a world that sells it over and over again. Sells the thought of pleasure as a commodity, sells the getting of it as if it were the getting of wisdom. And all these times I told you about, I saw other people get it through me. Even when someone finally made me come, it was just a feather in his cap, an accomplishment, nothing personal. Like you said. All I was was a program, they plugged into me and went through the motions and got their result. Nobody cares if the AI finds fulfillment running their damned data analyses. Nobody thinks about depressed and angry Mannboard ROMs. They just think about getting theirs.

"So why not get mine?" She was pacing now, angry, leaning that thin body as if the wind were against her. "Let me be the one who runs the program."

"But you won't be there. You told me how you were going to hide out, all that spy stuff."

She leaned against the wall, smiling a new smile she thought of as predatory. And maybe it was. "Uh, yes," she said. "I'll be there the first time. When Max and Kozyk run this thing and it turns them on. I'll be there. That's all I care to see."

He put his big hands on the wall on either side of her and leaned in. He smelled of sweat and liquor and his face was earnest with intoxication.

"I'll tell you something," he said. "As long as there's the real thing, it won't sell. They'll never buy it."

Angel thought so too. Secretly, because she wouldn't give him the satisfaction of agreement, she too thought they would not go that low. *That's right*, she told herself, *trying to sell it is all right—because they will never buy it.*

But they did.

A woman and a computer. Which attracts you most? Now you don't have to choose. Angel has made the choice irrelevant.

In Kozyk's office, he and Max go over the ad campaign. They've already tested the program themselves quite a lot; Angel knows this because it's company gossip, heard over the cubicle walls in the washrooms. The two men are so absorbed that they don't notice her arrival.

"Why is a woman better than a sheep? Because sheep can't cook. Why is a woman better than a Mannboard?

Because you haven't bought your sensory add-on." Max laughs.

"And what's better than a man?" Angel says; they jump slightly. "Why, your MannComp touchpads, with two-way input. I bet you'll be able to have them personally fitted."

"Good idea," says Kozyk, and Whitman makes a note on his lapboard. Angel, still stunned though she's had weeks to get used to this, looks at them, then reaches across the desk and picks up her prototype board. "This one's mine," she says. "You play with yourselves and your touchpads all you want."

"Well, you wrote it, baby," said Max. "If you can't come with your own program . . ."

Kozyk hiccoughs a short laugh before he shakes his head. "Shut up, Whitman," he says. "You're talking to a very rich and famous woman."

Whitman looks up from the simulations of his advertising storyboards, smiling a little, anticipating his joke. "Yeah. It's just too bad she finally burned herself out with this one. They always did say it gives you brain damage."

But Angel hadn't waited for the punch line. She was gone.

Peterborough, Rouyn, Edmonton
1986–1988

CONVERSATIONS WITH MICHAEL

Daniel Marcus

New writer Daniel Marcus is a graduate of Clarion West who holds a Ph.D. in engineering and who has worked as an applied mathematician at the Lawrence Livermore National Laboratory. His technical papers have appeared in Communications in Mathematical Physics *and the* Journal of Theoretical and Computational Fluid Dynamics, *but he made his first fiction sale within the genre in 1992, and has since appeared in* Asimov's Science Fiction, The Magazine of Fantasy and Science Fiction, *and* Science Fiction Age. *In 1995, he was a finalist for the John W. Campbell Award for Best New Writer, was marketing his first novel, and was at work on several more. He lives with his wife in Berkeley, California, where he also teaches a course in science fiction writing.*

In the compelling and compassionate story that follows, he shows us that the price of being a hacker can be very high—sometimes higher than we are willing, or able, to pay . . .

"I'm not ready," I said. I laced my fingers together and leaned forward in the soft chair, perching on the edge of the cushion. I looked up at Alice. The window behind her was polarized black as pitch and gave the unsettling impression of limitless depth, framing her face like one of those velvet paintings you could buy down in Tijuana before the Burning.

"I think you are, Stacey," she said. "We've been working toward this for a long time. We've done everything we can in realspace. It's time for you to face him." She looked at me with an expectant, open expression, as if she was wondering what my response was going to be. I suspected that she knew, though. She always knew.

I looked down at my hand, leaned back in the chair, shifted my weight. The chair responded by subtly rearranging the cushions to support me. The silence hung between us. Our sessions were often like this—islands of brief dialogue separated by vast gulfs. Finally, I heaved a huge sigh. It felt like it was coming not just from my chest but from my whole body, like my soul was escaping. There was a tightness around the corners of my eyes and across my forehead. I looked up at her. I nodded.

The Virtual Session room—real wood paneling, indirect lighting, abstract art on three walls. A fourth wall dominated by an instrument panel of black glass and polished chrome. Two pieces of furniture, elaborate barcaloungers crowned with spiky helmets, sprouted neatly tied bundles of wires leading to the panel. Red and yellow telltales winked from beneath the glass like the eyes of jungle animals.

Alice led me to one of the chairs and strapped me in. "Remember, I'll be right here the whole time. I'll be *him*."

I nodded. I could feel beads of sweat forming on my upper lip and forehead. Alice attached sensors to my fingers, my neck. She produced a tissue from somewhere and gently wiped the sweat from my face.

"You'll be fine," she said, and began to connect herself to the other chair.

I was standing next to home plate in the Little League baseball field behind the ConEd cooling towers. A breeze coming in off the Long Island Sound brought with it a faint smell of salt and sewage. The sky was a soft, pale blue, a shade I hadn't seen in twenty years. I reached up and touched my face. *No u.v. block.* Brief surge of panic. I looked at the sky again and realized that I wouldn't need it.

My son was sitting in the whitewashed risers paralleling the third base line, looking at me. He raised his hand in greeting. I gave him an answering wave and walked toward him. My heart was pounding in my chest.

He looked vibrant and full of life, like he did in the yellowed, age-curled pictures I kept in the shoebox on the top shelf of my bedroom closet. It clashed with my last memory of him—withered, emaciated body, skin stretched tight across skullbones framed by crisp hospital linen, sick, flickering light in his ancient child's eyes. I sat down next to him.

"Hi, Mike," I said.

"Hey, Mom."

It's crazy, but I couldn't think of a single thing to say to him. There was so much I wanted to tell him. (I'm sorry. I'm so sorry, baby.) I wanted to take him in my arms and hold him to me and not let go. An inane thought came bubbling up to the surface of my mind—I wondered if he was hungry. It was a manageable thought, though, and I held on to it like a drowning swimmer clutching a life preserver.

"You hungry, champ?" I asked. My voiced only cracked a little.

He smiled up at me. "Yeah." I saw Keith in that quick, sure grin, and a surge of loss and anger passed through me like a hot, sudden wind, gone just as quickly.

A wicker basket suddenly appeared at my feet. The corners of a red-and-white checked cloth peeked out from under the edge of the lid.

"I've got some deviled ham," I said, knowing that it would be there. "And some Ho-Ho's for dessert."

"Great," he said, but it didn't sound right. I don't know why, but at that moment the illusion collapsed and I *knew* that it was just Alice there, Alice in a Michael suit, Alice strapped into a VS deck weaving a fiberoptic tapestry of ones and zeros with an insensate, cybernetic loom. To fool me into grace.

"This is bullshit," I said.

Michael frowned. "Mom . . .?" The frown was very good, very Michael-like, but the illusion was already shot.

"Just get me out of here, Alice. It's not working."

He sighed, shoulders set with the exaggerated exasperation of a child. "Okay," he nodded.

I closed my eyes, and when I opened them again, I was back in the VS room. I unstrapped myself and started to get up. A rush of vertigo sat me down again.

"Hey," Alice said. "Easy." Her face hovered over me like a cloud.

I looked at her accusingly. "I knew it was you. This is just bullshit gameplaying."

She shook her head. "You did very well for a first virtual session. Of course, your history helps you a lot here, but some people can't even interact in V-space at all. *You* created the ball park; *you* gave *me* enough cues to help build a consensual reality." She smiled gently and touched me on the shoulder. "We made progress today."

The Dinkins Arcology is built on a lattice of pontoons that stretches out from Battery Park into the Upper New York Bay like a dendritic tongue, sending fractal limbs in all directions. That's its official name, but even before the first fullerene panel was snapped into place, it was Dinkytown. It was intended to be an egalitarian effort, public housing hand-in-hand with private enterprise, the disadvantaged and the well-to-do rolling up their sleeves together and creating a community—turn-of-the-century policyspeak made manifest. (Soft industrial music swells in the background. Dissolve to a schoolyard swarming with children in a tastefully balanced demographic mix.) But in fact, a stratification evolved dynamically, independent of intention. Pockets of public assistance clusters dotted the arcology ("like cancerous cells," the *Times* op-ed file whined), side by side with ghettos of affluence, I still have an income, and managed to buy our way into Avalon, on the Governor's Island side.

I wasn't ready to go home yet, so I took the long way, out along the "boardwalk"–a promenade with the roof that runs around Dinkytown's circumference. Before long, the crowds thinned out, and I strolled slowly along the bay, enjoying the cool breeze coming in off the water. There was a trace of sewage smell and a hint of acrid chemicals, but it wasn't too bad. Some fool was windsurfing up near the mouth of the East River, begging for a dose of septic shock. They'd cleaned things up a lot since the twentieth, but it still wasn't exactly safe.

Some things you can't clean up, though, no matter how hard you try. Michael. I remember the day it happened. I was mainlining and somebody brought the system down cold. Sense impressions filtered in through the nausea— people rushing back and forth, voices shouting, several news feeds on at once. "Partial meltdown . . . Montauk nuke . . . another Chernobyl." Things blurred together. I made my way up to the roof heliport somehow and threatened a chopper pilot with my Swiss Army knife to take me to Montauk. It took three large men to hold me down.

It turned out to be just a "small" release, quickly contained. And it was late in the day, so the prevailing winds were blowing the radioactive plume out to sea, away from the thirty-odd million souls in the Greater New York Metropolitan Area. But it didn't spare Montauk. And it didn't spare Michael.

I could picture him standing there in the schoolyard, smiling, the wind ruffling his hair, as the gamma rays tunneled through his body, leaving an irreparable wake of damaged cells. The fatality rate in Montauk was 30 percent during the first year, 20 percent during the second, then it tailed off rapidly from there. Michael was still alive three years later, we thought he'd been spared. Then, all of a sudden, his immune system collapsed. He started losing weight like crazy. Great, purple bruises appeared all over his body, like mysterious objects floating up from the bottom of a murky pond. The leukemia ripped through him so quickly you could almost see him fading away in realtime. When it was over, there was hardly anything left to bury.

A pair of young men walked toward me along the promenade, holding hands. Their cheeks bore elaborate scars, a pattern I recognized as the chop of the Lords of Discipline.

"Don't stay out too long, Mama," the one on the left said. "UV count t'rough de roof today, mon." His boyfriend looked like he ought to know—a spiderweb tangle of ruptured blood vessels laced through the scars on his cheeks.

"Thanks," I nodded.

There were dirty dishes on the kitchen table, which meant that Keith had been up and about. I glanced down the hallway to where his door stood open a crack. He was probably back under. Just as well.

I sat down at my desk to check my e-mail. There were four ads and a message from Dmitry over at Cellular. I'd been doing some biotech database hacking for him, building a set of software tools for him to manage his technical library. It's not as boring as it sounds. Just because you can nanoscript a terabyte of data onto a slab of substrate the size of a mosquito wing doesn't mean you can retrieve it easily. In fact, with so much information available at your fingertips, encoding and navigating gets pretty hairy.

I flushed the ads and scrolled the message from Dmitry, a not particularly subtle inquiry as to just when I might have the bugs shaken out of the infosurfing macros I was looking up for him. I pounded out a quick reply—telling him that all good things come to those who wait, to cultivate the patient heart of a grandmother, and to get off my case or I'd accidentally mail his shiny, new virtual toys off to DevNull.

I enjoyed jerking his chain a little. I'd never met him in person, but we'd been working together online for a couple of years. His Proxy was a short, balding, somewhat chubby man who wore dark, rumpled suits with suspenders and frayed cuffs. The frayed cuffs were a brilliant touch—it was easy to forget you were looking at a sim. Of course, he probably looked nothing like that. Online relationships are almost all smoke and mirrors.

I got to work. I pulled down a couple of windows on the big monitor and dropped some shell scripts into the queue for the public database. The private and corporate 'bases were a little trickier. I fired off an autonomous agent to deal with the protocol.

I quickly became submerged in the work. It was soothing,

like immersing myself in the hot, swirling waters of a jacuzzi. It wasn't quite like mainlining, but it was close.

Mainlining, pure info-surfing: there's no other rush like it, chemical or virtual. And I had been good. The Net was a tangled, spidery sprawl of pulsing light, nodes of brightness for other surfers. Structs were patches of infrared and UV that I could sense by the quality of the pain they caused. My paradigm for navigation was the avoidance of discomfort.

After Michael, I started losing it. The only thing that keeps a surfer on that knife-edge of perception is discrimination—the ability to distinguish real from Memorex. Mine was shot. I'd be walking down the street, and the sparkles of light from the silica chips in the pavement would dissolve into the coruscating signature of the struct I'd navigated that morning. I'd be in the middle of a conversation and start framing my responses as instruction sets.

I fell apart for a while. When my medical leave ran out, I quit Sony. I still had connections, and managed to pull together an occasional consulting gig. Before I knew it, I had my hands full freelancing. I was surfing again, and it was good, but I never mainlined anymore. And Keith was always there to remind me why I shouldn't, just in case I forgot.

I don't know how long I worked, but slowly a sense of physical space began to seep back into my consciousness. It had gotten dark; my hands on the keypad were illuminated only by the glow of the monitor. Outside, the sky held the last blush of twilight. Reflected lights from Manhattan and Brooklyn made shimmering castles in the water at the mouth of the East River.

I logged off the satlink and sat there in the dark for a few minutes. It was time to look in on Keith. I took a deep breath, then another.

The room was dark except for the tiny, amber console lights. I could sense his shape, though, sprawled in the beanbag chair wedged into a corner. The soft, raspy whisper of his breathing filled the room. A stew of sour smells hung in the air—body odor, traces of urine, a strong whiff of feces.

I turned on the light. Keith didn't even flinch—the rig's induction field coupled right into his optic nerve. Not much bandwidth, but what it lacked in information content it more than made up for in the sheer intensity of the pleasure it provided. I'd tried it once—I felt so lousy when I came out of it, I was scared to try it again.

Not Keith. He'd been jacking off ever since the rigs went alpha. It was just a weekend thing at first, but after Michael died, he started going under more and more. Now he was down almost all the time. It was as if grief were a black hole, and he'd disappeared somewhere beyond its event horizon.

He was naked except for the incontinence pants bunched around his waist. Diapers, really. They gave him the bizarre appearance of a sallow, gray-haired baby. I could count his ribs. A streak of blood ran down his arm, and the IV rig lay on its side in the middle of the room. Probably ripped out the glucose drip and went looking for solid food after I left in the morning. He did that sometimes. I was always surprised when he got himself out from under long enough to get out to the kitchen and back.

I got a fresh pair of diapers from the closet, cleaned him up, and changed him. I set the IV up again and stood there for a while, looking at him. He still hadn't registered my presence. Every now and then, a muscle in his arm or thigh twitched. It reminded me of a dog I had when I was a child. She used to curl up in front of the fire to sleep, and every now and then, her hind legs would jump and scrabble at the carpet.

"Chasing rabbits in her dreams," my father would say, if he wasn't passed out yet. I wondered what kind of rabbits Keith was chasing.

I walked over to the console and turned it off. The glaze faded from his eyes and he clutched at himself.

"Wha—?" It came out like a croak.

I don't really know what I was thinking about. I guess I wanted to talk to him about Michael, but that was crazy.

I looked down at him. His eyes were burning flecks of

pain. For a second, I saw Michael there, held in the hollow angles of his cheekbones. Then the impression was gone.

"You sick fuck," I said. I flicked the console back on and walked out of the room.

"Why do you stay with him?" Alice asked. The window behind her was in Aquarium mode—schools of brightly colored fish darted through shafts of sunlight over a carpet of waving, green kelp. It really irritated me.

"I hate that window," I said.

She reached under her desk and did something. The aquarium dissolved slowly to a neutral gray.

"Better?"

I nodded. "A little."

She sat there, smiling faintly. Waiting.

"So, why do I . . . ?"

She nodded.

I took in a deep breath. I felt like I wasn't getting enough air. I let it out with a sigh.

"I . . . don't know. There's nobody home—he's a total wirehead. He's been like this ever since Michael died."

She nodded.

"He . . . needs me."

She nodded again, looking at me. Waiting.

I could feel myself tensing up, digging in my heels. I wasn't going to give her what she wanted.

Finally, she said, "What do *you* need, Stacey?"

I looked at her for a long time. Finally, I shook my head. "I don't know."

Jones Beach stretched out in front of us, a long pale ribbon, bordered on one side by the slate gray of the ocean and on the other by a checkerboard scatter of parking lots and ball fields that now served as sites for sprawling tent villages. Michael walked beside me, his head bent in concentration, absorbed with a piece of techno-trash he had picked up somewhere. A graceful curve of metal wound in a converging helix around a core of bundled fiberoptic cable. Wires trailed loosely from one end. It looked like a prop from a cheesy science fiction movie. Every now and then, he aimed it at an imaginary target and made ray-gun noises, *gzh-gzh-gzh*, his eyes narrowed with intense concentration.

The beach was filthier than I remembered. Ocean-tossed detritus of civilization lay everywhere—used hypodermic syringes, plastic bottles, the occasional limp, wrinkled condom. Coney Island whitefish, my father used to call them. I chuckled softly and looked over at Michael.

"What you doing, champ?" I asked.

Michael looked up at me and smiled his quick, sure smile. "Changing stuff."

"Oh, yeah? What are you changing it into?"

"Making everything go away." He trained the ray gun on a dead seagull lying half-buried in the sand a few feet away. *Gzh-gzh-gzh.*

"Why do you want to do that?" I asked.

His face wrinkled in the disdain the children reserve for stupid adults. "It's *soft.*"

I smiled ruefully. "It sure is, champ."

Gzh-gzh-gzh. A tangle of seaweed and glittering strands of polyfoil was sent off to never-never land.

We walked together in silence for a while.

"If you could put anything you wanted here instead," I asked, finally, "what would it be?"

He thought for a moment. "In school, we were in a sim with dinosaurs. It was so *way.* There was this big one and it chased the little one and ate it. We were on a beach but there wasn't anything there." He looked up at me and smiled. "I'd put dinosaurs."

"Dinosaurs. Cool." I paused. "Do you know what happened to the dinosaurs?" I asked.

He nodded. "They died."

"How did they die, champ?"

His eyebrows drew together in a frown as he struggled to remember the words. "They couldn't, uh, adapt." He looked directly at me. "They couldn't adapt to cataclysm."

We stood there in the hot sun. I could see Alice looking at me through Michael's eyes without pretense now, calm and knowing. I was aware of myself standing on the cusp between reality and illusion, one foot in each. The coppery smell of decaying seaweed hung in the air, and the wind caressed my face in light, feathery touches.

Dmitry's "benevolent uncle" persona beamed at me from the vidscreen. "I have a proposition for you, Stacey," he said. There was a faint trace of Slavic accent in his voice.

I think of Proxies as fashion accessories, not all that much different from makeup or hairstyle—another layer of illusion we project to help us navigate the reefs and shoals of human interaction. Of course, there are the usual, endless Globalnet flamewars about the moral implications of being able to construct your own persona from scratch and modify it according to your own mood and who you're talking to. That's mostly the neo-Luddites, though, tooth and nail with the crackpot Libertarians—a lot of heat and smoke, not much light. My own feeling is that we all do that anyway to some extent, even in realspace.

"I'm listening, Dmitry." I was wearing what I thought of as my Conan the Librarian Proxy—a lean-limbed warrior goddess with blond, sun-streaked hair, a deerskin vest (a bit offensive to some, I know), and a quiver of arrows at my back. A button pinned to my vest read WILL HACK FOR FOOD. I had a monitor window open in the upper left corner of the vidscreen, and I could see the image that Dmitry was looking at. Rolling green hills dotted with grazing sheep spread out behind me. The sky was a deep, cloudless blue.

He cleared his throat. "You know that Cellular has recently purchased shares in the Velikovsky Orbital."

I nodded. Of course I did—I'd hacked a substantial portion of the background documentation on orbital biotech for their Stockholders' Report.

"We're putting together a small community up there to get a facility going—pharmaceuticals, protein construction, genetic mods. Not just biotech, though—we've got plans to start a substrate farm, grow high-T superconductors, microgee metallurgy, the works."

I nodded again. No surprises there. Everything he'd

mentioned required a zero-gravity environment for profitable manufacturing.

"Let's cut to the chase, Dmitry. I *wrote* that P.R. pitch."

He smiled and nodded, his head bobbing up and down.
"Yes, yes, you did, didn't you? Very well." He cleared his
throat again. "We need a—well, kind of a sysadmin up
there, someone to coordinate all the info-hacking facilities.
Of course, we're hooked into Globalnet via microwave, but
we also want to have an autonomous system for the Orbital
itself. There'll be all the usual personal support stuff—you
can delegate that—and we'll have a cluster of teraflop
nodes for process simulation. Lots of bit-hacking there, and
microwave links just don't have the bandwidth for that." He
paused. "I floated your name up the food-chain here, and so
far the echoes have all been pretty favorable. I'm sorry I
didn't ask you beforehand, but I wanted to test the water
first." He looked at me, his eyebrows raised, a slight smile
playing on the corners of his mouth.

I didn't know what to say. I'd expected a lucrative
project, enough consulting work to keep me solvent for a
while, but nothing like this. My knee-jerk reactions was *No
way*, but there was a small, still voice underneath that I
couldn't quite smother. *Why not?* it asked.

I was silent for a long time.

"Stacey?" he said, finally.

"Look, Dmitry, I . . ." I saw my Proxy up there in a
corner of the screen mouthing my words. It brushed a strand
of windswept hair from its eyes. I reached up to the screen
and tapped twice on the image—it rolled up like a window
shade and disappeared. "Can we drop the Proxies, Dmitry?
I need to really *see* you."

His eyebrows rose, then he nodded slowly. "Sure," he
said, finally.

He reached offscreen and did something. His image
collapsed and was replaced immediately with another. A
plain, pleasant-looking man of young middle-age looked
through the screen at me. He wore a conservative, corporate-
style vest, and a pair of gold hoops dangled from his left
earlobe. There was a streak of purple in his straight black

hair. Behind him was a cluttered, windowless office, unre-markable except for a shelf of real books. He smiled questioningly at me.

I expected to be surprised by his appearance, but I wasn't—I already felt like I knew him. I stretched my hand to punch in the escape metacharacter on my own keypad, and when his eyebrows rose, I knew he was seeing the "real me" as well.

"Better?" he asked. The Slavic accent was gone, replaced with a flat, Midwestern drawl.

I nodded. "Yeah, much." We just sat there looking at each other for what felt like a long time, even though it was probably less than a minute. Finally, I sighed and shook my head. "I don't know what to say, Dmitry. I'm going to need some time to think."

"Sure," he nodded. "But don't take *too* long. You know how these things go—sooner or later, the posting winds up on Globalnet and we get flooded with applicants, most of them cranks. It gets a lot harder to separate the wheat from the chaff. The Powers That Be would rather see this nailed down through word-of-mouth."

"I'll let you know," I said.

"Good." He looked carefully at me. "Take care of yourself, Stacey."

"Bye." I said, but his image had already collapsed into a thin line and disappeared. I sat looking at the flat, blank space on the screen where the vidscreen window had been. I imagined I saw shapes rolling and shifting there, sub-merged in the depths of the phosphor.

Afternoon sunlight streamed through the Venetian blinds, throwing a pattern of stripes across the hospital bed. Michael sat propped up on a mass of pillows, looking very small surrounded by all that puffy whiteness. He was playing some sort of hand-held simulation game—crude holos a couple of inches high swarmed across the bed. They were barely visible in the bars of intense sunlight, coming alive with color when they scurried into the shadows. The high, tiny sound of their combat filled the room.

I stood at the door, watching him. His eyebrows were drawn down in concentration; the pink tip of his tongue protruded from the corner of his mouth. Tubes snaked from a patch on his arm to an array of soft, plastic bags hanging from a rack next to the bed.

"Hey, champ," I said.

He looked up and smiled. Dark circles framed his eyes, and the curve of his cheekbones seemed impossibly sharp.

"Hey, Mom. Just a sec . . ." His fingers danced on the little console for a few seconds longer. He leaned toward the panel. "Save," he said. The armies of tiny simulacra froze, then disappeared.

"I made it up to Level 7," he said, smiling.

"That's great, Mike." I walked over and sat down in the chair next to the bed. I reached out and brushed a strand of hair from his forehead.

"When you get better, we'll take you to one of those places where you can play with sim-holos as big as houses . . ."

He looked at me and frowned. "Come on, Mom, I'm not *gonna* get better. I'm gonna *die*." It was a simple declaration, not a complaint—as if he were explaining the facts of life to a slightly stupid friend.

It felt like he had physically struck me.

"I—why do you say that?" I stammered.

"I'm not *stupid*, Mom." He lifted his arm, showing the tubes trailing from the patch in his arm. He gestured around the room at the menagerie of stuffed animals resting on every available surface. "Med-net says that they'll be able to cure leukemia in ten years with nanocritters, but that we just aren't there yet." He shrugged. He looked and sounded for all the world like a wise old man. How did little kids learn so much?

I sighed. "I know you're not stupid, baby. It's just that . . . it's hard . . ." I didn't want to cry in front of him, to put him in the position of having to parent me. It wasn't supposed to work like that. But the tightness across my forehead got worse, and soon I could feel hot tears on my cheeks.

"I'm so sorry, baby . . ." I said.

He reached over and put his small hand on my shoulder. "It's not *your* fault, Mom. *You* didn't do anything."

I *felt* responsible, though. We poisoned the world, killing off millions of our own children—*our own children*—so that we could have dishwashers and computers and microwave sat-links, and we were only beginning to step back from the brink. I didn't know if it was too late for us. But it was too late for Michael.

"It just *happened*, Mom." His voice jolted me out of my fog of self-pity. "Stuff just happens."

Alice sat behind her desk, waiting for me to say something. In the window behind her, the New York skyline glittered in the afternoon sun. There was a subtle quality about the colors and the distance resolution that told me it was real.

"I'll say this for you," I said, finally. "You're good. You're very good. It's uncanny how well you . . . simulate him. I almost feel like I could forgive myself . . ."

She smiled gently. "I want to show you something," she said. She punched something into the console at her desk and swiveled the monitor around so it was facing me.

VIRTUAL SESSION LOG

Name	Status	On	Off	Date
Donovan, Stacey	Solo	13:10	14:04	4/22/18

I looked up at her. "Solo?"

"Yeah. If we'd been doing another tandem session, my name would be on the log, too. You were all alone in there."

I felt something *give* inside me, like a door I'd been leaning on with all my strength was just beginning to budge. Alice nodded and smiled in the slightly smug and annoying way she has when she thinks she's made some sort of breakthrough with me. I didn't mind much, though. I even smiled back a little.

• • •

Keith was sitting in his beanbag chair in the corner, curled up like a loosely tied bundle of sticks. I walked over to the window and de-polarized it. Sunlight flooded the room. Keith looked impossibly pale in the light. Oozing sores stood out on his skin like bright, red stars. He'd pulled the glucose drop again, and a crust of dried blood peeked out from under the ragged bandage on his arm.

I turned off the console and waited. It took a few seconds, then he squeezed his eyes together and brought his arm up to shield them. Whimpering noises came from somewhere deep in his chest.

After a little while, the whimpering stopped, and he lowered his arm from his face. He looked at me accusingly. It was like playing a tape loop, those pain-filled eyes burning into me again. It was going to be different this time, though.

"I know you can understand me, Keith," I said. "I can't take care of you anymore. I've arranged for you to go to a treatment program out on the Island. It's thirty days, and after that, you're on your own. I don't know if I'm going to be here or not when you get out, but you can't come live here again." I paused, not knowing what else to say. "I'm sorry," I said, finally. "It's got to be this way."

I couldn't read his expression. I looked for Michael there in his hurt eyes, in the angry set of his shoulders, but I couldn't see him, not a trace. He opened his mouth again, as if he wanted to say something, but all that came out was a raspy croak.

I stood there in the sunlight, waiting for him to find his voice.

GENE WARS

Paul J. McAuley

*Born in Oxford, England, in 1955, Paul J. McAuley now
makes his home in Strathkinness, in Scotland. He is consid-
ered to be one of the best of the new British breed of
"hard-science" writers, and is a frequent contributor to*
Interzone, *as well as to markets such as* Amazing, The
Magazine of Fantasy and Science Fiction, Asimov's Science
Fiction, When the Music's Over, *and elsewhere. His first
novel,* Four Hundred Billion Stars, *won the Philip K. Dick
Award. His other books include the novels* Of the Fall *and*
Eternal Light, *a collection of his short work,* The King of the
Hill and Other Stories, *and an original anthology co-edited
with Kim Newman,* In Dreams. *His most recent book is a
major new novel,* Pasquale's Angel.

*In the dizzyingly fast-paced little story that follows, he
paints a sharp portrait of a new kind of hacker and a new
kind of entrepreneur, a self-made man—twenty-first century
style.*

1

On Evan's *eighth* birthday, his aunt sent him the latest
smash-hit biokit, *Splicing Your Own Semisentients.* The
box-lid depicted an alien swamp throbbing with weird,
amorphous life; a double helix spiraling out of a test-tube
was embossed in one corner. Don't let your father see that,
his mother said, so Evan took it out to the old barn, set up
the plastic culture trays and vials of chemicals and retrovi-
ruses on a dusty workbench in the shadow of the shrouded
combine.

His father found Evan there two days later. The slime
mold he'd created, a million amoebae aggregated around a

drop of cyclic AMP, had been transformed with a retrovirus and was budding little blue-furred blobs. Evan's father dumped culture trays and vials in the yard and made Evan pour a liter of industrial-grade bleach over them. More than fear or anger, it was the acrid stench that made Evan cry.

That summer, the leasing company foreclosed on the livestock. The rep who supervised repossession of the supercows drove off in a big car with the test-tube and double-helix logo on its gull-wing door. The next year the wheat failed, blighted by a particularly virulent rust. Evan's father couldn't afford the new resistant strain, and the farm went under.

2

Evan lived with his aunt, in the capital. He was fifteen. He had a street bike, a plug-in computer, and a pet microsaur, a cat-sized triceratops in purple funfur. Buying the special porridge which was all the microsaur could eat took half of Evan's weekly allowance; that was why he let his best friend inject the pet with a bootleg virus to edit out its dietary dependence. It was only a partial success: the triceratops no longer needed its porridge, but it developed epilepsy triggered by sunlight. Even had to keep it in his wardrobe. When it started shedding fur in great swatches, he abandoned it in a nearby park. Microsaurs were out of fashion, anyway. Dozens could be found wandering the park, nibbling at leaves, grass, discarded scraps of fastfood. Quite soon they disappeared, starved to extinction.

3

The day before Evan graduated, his sponsor firm called to tell him that he wouldn't be doing research after all. There had been a change of policy: the covert gene wars were going public. When Evan started to protest, the woman said sharply, "You're better off than many long-term employees. With a degree in molecular genetics you'll make sergeant at least."

4

The jungle was a vivid green blanket in which rivers made silvery forked lightnings. Warm wind rushed around Evan as he leaned out the helicopter's hatch; harness dug into his shoulders. He was twenty-three, a tech sergeant. It was his second tour of duty.

His goggles flashed icons over the view, tracking the target. Two villages a klick apart, linked by a red dirt road narrow as a capillary that suddenly widened to an artery as the helicopter dove.

Flashes on the ground: Evan hoped the peasants only had Kalashnikovs: last week some gook had downed a copter with an antiquated SAM. Then he was too busy laying the pattern, virus-suspension in a sticky spray that fogged the maize fields.

Afterwards, the pilot, an old-timer, said over the intercom. "Things get tougher every day. We used just to take a leaf, cloning did the rest. You couldn't call it theft. And this stuff . . . I always thought war was bad for business."

Evan said, "The company owns copyright to the maize genome. Those peasants aren't licensed to grow it."

The pilot said admiringly, "Man you're a real company guy. I bet you don't even know what country this is."

Evan thought about that. He said, "Since when were countries important?"

5

Rice fields spread across the floodplain, dense as a hand-stitched quilt. In every paddy, peasants bent over their own reflections, planting seedlings for the winter crop.

In the center of the UNESCO delegation, the Minister for Agriculture stood under a black umbrella held by an aide. He was explaining that his country was starving to death after a record rice crop.

Evan was at the back of the little crowd, bareheaded in warm drizzle. He wore a smart one-piece suit, yellow overshoes. He was twenty-eight, had spent two years infiltrating UNESCO for his company.

The minister was saying, "We have to buy seed gene-spliced for pesticide resistance to compete with our neighbors, but my people can't afford to buy the rice they grow. It must all be exported to service our debt. Our children are starving in the midst of plenty."

Evan stifled a yawn. Later, at a reception in some crumbling embassy, he managed to get the minister on his own. The man was drunk, unaccustomed to hard liquor. Evan told him he was very moved by what he had seen.

"Look in our cities," the minister said, slurring his words. "Every day a thousand more refugees pour in from the countryside. There is kwashiorkor, beri-beri."

Evan popped a canapé into his mouth. One of his company's new lines, it squirmed with delicious lasciviousness before he swallowed it. "I may be able to help you," he said. "The people I represent have a new yeast that completely fulfills dietary requirements and will grow on a simple medium."

"How simple?" As Evan explained, the minister, no longer as drunk as he had seemed, steered him onto the terrace. The minister said, "You understand this must be confidential. Under UNESCO rules . . ."

"There are ways around that. We have lease arrangements with five countries that have . . . trade imbalances similar to your own. We lease the genome as a loss-leader, to support governments who look favorably on our other products . . ."

6

The gene pirate was showing Evan his editing facility when the slow poison finally hit him. They were aboard an ancient ICBM submarine grounded somewhere off the Philippines. Missile tubes had been converted into fermenters. The bridge was crammed with the latest manipulation technology, virtual reality gear which let the wearer directly control molecule-sized cutting robots as they traveled along DNA helices.

"It's not facilities I need," the pirate told Evan, "it's distribution."

"No problem," Evan said. The pirate's security had been pathetically easy to penetrate. He'd tried to infect Evan with a zombie virus, but Evan's gene-spliced designer immune system had easily dealt with it. Slow poison was so much more subtle: by the time it could be detected it was too late. Evan was thirty-two. He was posing as a Swiss gray-market broker.

"This is where I keep my old stuff," the pirate said, rapping a stainless-steel cryogenic vat. "Stuff from before I went big time. A free luciferase gene complex, for instance. Remember when the Brazilian rainforest started to glow? That was me." He dashed sweat from his forehead, frowned at the room's complicated thermostat. Grossly fat and completely hairless, he wore nothing but Bermuda shorts and shower sandals. He'd been targeted because he was about to break the big time with a novel HIV cure. The company was still making a lot of money from its own cure: they made sure AIDS had never been completely eradicated in third-world countries.

Evan said, "I remember the Brazilian government was overthrown—the population took it as a bad omen."

"Hey, what can I say? I was only a kid. Transforming the gene was easy, only difficulty was finding a vector. Old stuff. Somatic mutation really is going to be the next big thing, believe me. Why breed new strains when you can rework a genome cell by cell?" He rapped the thermostat. His hands were shaking. "Hey, is it hot in here, or what?"

"That's the first symptom," Evan said. He stepped out of the way as the gene pirate crashed to the decking. "And that's the second."

The company had taken the precaution of buying the pirate's security chief: Evan had plenty of time to fix the fermenters. By the time he was ashore, they would have boiled dry. On impulse, against orders, he took a microgram sample of the HIV cure with him.

7

"The territory between piracy and legitimacy is a mine-field," the assassin told Evan. "It's also where paradigm shifts are most likely to occur, and that's where I come in. My company likes stability. Another year and you'd have gone public, and most likely the share issue would have made you a billionaire—a minor player, but still a player. Those cats, no one else has them. The genome was supposed to have been wiped out back in the twenties. Very astute, quitting the gray medical market and going for luxury goods." She frowned. "Why am I talking so much?"

"For the same reason you're not going to kill me," Evan said.

"It seems such a silly thing to want to do," the assassin admitted.

Evan smiled. He'd long ago decoded the two-stage virus the gene-pirate had used on him: one a Trojan horse which kept his T lymphocytes busy while the other rewrote loyalty genes companies implanted in their employees. Once again it had proven its worth. He said, "I need someone like you in my organization. And since you spent so long getting close enough to seduce me, perhaps you'd do me the honor of becoming my wife. I'll need one."

"You don't mind being married to a killer?"

"Oh, that. I used to be one myself."

8

Evan saw the market crash coming. Gene wars had win-nowed basic foodcrops to soybeans, rice, and dole yeast: tailored ever-mutating diseases had reduced cereals and many other cash crops to nucleotide sequences stored in computer vaults. Three global biotechnology companies held patents on the calorific input of ninety-eight percent of humanity, but they had lost control of the technology. Pressures of the war economy had simplified it to the point where anyone could directly manipulate her own genome, and hence her own body form.

Evan had made a fortune in the fashion industry, selling templates and microscopic self-replicating robots which edited DNA. But he guessed that sooner or later someone would come up with a direct-photosynthesis system, and his stock-market expert systems were programmed to correlate research in the field. He and his wife sold controlling interest in their company three months before the first green people appeared.

9

"I remember when you knew what a human being was," Evan said sadly. "I suppose I'm old-fashioned, but there it is."

From her cradle, inside a mist of spray, his wife said, "Is that why you never went green? I always thought it was a fashion statement."

"Old habits die hard." The truth was, he liked his body the way it was. These days, going green involved somatic mutation which gave a meter-high black cowl to absorb sufficient light energy. Most people lived in the tropics, swarms of black-caped anarchists. Work was no longer a necessity, but an indulgence. Evan added, "I'm going to miss you."

"Let's face it," his wife said, "we never were in love. But I'll miss you, too." With a flick of her powerful tail she launched her streamlined body into the sea.

10

Black-cowled post-humans, gliding slowly in the sun, aggregating and reaggregating like amoebae. Dolphinoids, tentacles sheathed under fins, rocking in tanks of cloudy water. Ambulatory starfish; tumbling bushes of spikes; snakes with a single arm, a single leg; flocks of tiny birds, brilliant as emeralds, each flock a single entity.

People, grown strange, infected with myriads of microscopic machines which re-engraved their body form at will.

Evan lived in a secluded estate. He was revered as a founding father of the posthuman revolution. A purple funfur microsaur followed him everywhere. It was recording him because he had elected to die.

"I don't regret anything," Evan said, "except perhaps not following my wife when she changed. I saw it coming, you know. All this. Once the technology became simple enough, cheap enough, the companies lost control. Like television or computers, but I suppose you don't remember those. He sighed. He had the vague feeling he'd said all this before. He'd had no new thoughts for a century, except the desire to put an end to thought.

The microsaur said, "In a way, I suppose I am a computer. Will you see the colonial delegation now?"

"Later." Evan hobbled to a bench and slowly sat down. In the last couple of months he had developed mild arthritis, liver spots on the backs of his hands: death finally expressing parts of his genome that had been suppressed for so long. Hot sunlight fell through the velvet streamers of the tree things; Evan dozed, woke to find a group of starfish watching him. They had blue, human eyes, one at the tip of each muscular arm.

"They wish to honor you by taking your genome to Mars," the little purple triceratops said.

Evan sighed. "I just want peace. To rest. To die."

"Oh, Evan," the little triceratops said patiently, "surely even you know that nothing really dies anymore."

SPEW

Neal Stephenson

New writer Neal Stephenson scored big with his first novel,
Snow Crash, *which became one of the most talked-about
novels of 1994, both inside and outside of the genre,
establishing itself as one of the most successful "cyberpunk"
novels since Gibson's* Neuromancer. *He is also the author of
a novel called* Zodiac: The Eco-Thriller, *and his most recent
novel is* The Diamond Age, *which is also being well-received
by the critics. Stephenson has published only a handful of
short stories, including one in* Time *magazine, but, as far as
I can tell, except for one sale to* Full Spectrum, *has published
almost nothing in traditional genre markets; the story that
follows was published in the computer-scene magazine*
Wired*—and, in what may be a Sign of Things to Come, we
read it online in* Wired's *Internet website,* HotWired, *and
downloaded a copy of the story for use in this anthology
without ever actually physically touching the issue of* Wired
magazine in which it originally appeared.

*In the mordant story that follows, Stephenson demon-
strates that, even in a high-tech future, A Policeman's Lot Is
Not a Happy One, especially as there will always be people
who want to Make Their Own Fun, no matter how difficult
and technically challenging it may become to do so . . .*

Yeah, I know it's boring of me to send you plain old Text
like this, and I hope you don't just blow this message off
without reading it.

But what can I say, I was an English major. On video, I
come off like a stunned bystander. I'm just a Text kind of
guy. I'm gambling that you'll think it's quaint or something.
So let me just tell you the whole sorry tale, starting from the
point where I think I went wrong.

I'd be blowing brown smoke if I said I wasn't nervous when they shoved in the needles, taped on the trodes, thrust my head into the Big Cold Magnet, and opened a channel direct from the Spew to my immortal soul. Of course they didn't call it the Spew, and neither did I—I wanted the job, after all. But how could I not call it that, with its Feeds multifarious as the glistening strands cascading sunnily from the supple scalps of the models in the dandruff shampoo ads.

I mention that image because it was the first thing I saw when they turned the Spew on, and I wasn't even ready. Not that anyone could ever *get ready* for the dreaded Polysurf Exam. The proctors came for me when *they* were ready, must have got my address off that job app yellowing in their infinite files, yanked me straight out of a fuzzy gray hangover dream with a really wandering story arc, the kind of dream concussion victims must have in the back of the ambulance. I'd been doing shots of vodka in the living room the night before, decided not to take a chance on the stairs, turned slowly into a mummy while I lay comatose on our living-room couch—the First Couch Ever Built, a Couch upholstered in avocado Orlon that had absorbed so much tar, nicotine, and body cheese over the centuries that now the centers of the cushions had developed the black sheen of virgin Naugahyde. When they buzzed me awake, my joints would not move nor my eyes open: I had to bolt four consecutive 32-ounce glasses of tap water to reconstitute my freeze-dried plasma.

Half an hour later I'm in Television City. A million stories below, floes of gray-yellow ice, like broken teeth, grind away at each other just below the surface of the Hudson. I've signed all the releases and they're lowering the Squid helmet over me, and without any warning *BAM* the Spew comes on and the first thing I see is this model chick shaking her head in ultra-slow-mo, her lovely hairs gleaming because they've got so many spotlights cross-firing on her head that she's about to burst into flames, and in voice-over she's talking about how her dandruff problem is just a nasty, embarrassing memory of adolescence now along with pimples and (if I may just fill in the blanks) screwing skanky guys who'll never have a salaried job. And I think she's cute and everything but it occurs to me that this is really kind of sick—I mean, this chick has *admitted* to a history of shedding *blizzards* ever time she moved her head, and here she is *getting down* under eight megawatts of color-corrected halogen light, and I just *know* I'm supposed to be thinking about *how much head chaff* would be sifting down in her personal space right now if she hadn't ditched her old hair care product lineup in favor of—

Click. Course, it never really clicks anymore, no one has used mechanical switches since like the fifties, but some Spew terminals emit a synthesized click—they wired up a 1955 Sylvania in a digital sound lab somewhere and had some old gomer in a tank-top stagger up to it and change back and forth between Channel 4 and Channel 5 a few times, paid him off and fired him, then compressed the sound and inseminated it into the terminals' fundamental ROMs so that we'd get that reassuring *click* when we jumped from one Feed to another. Which is what happens now; except I haven't touched a remote, don't even *have* a remote, that being the whole point of the Polysurf. Now it's some fucker picking a banjo, *ouch* it is an actual *Hee Haw* rerun, digitally remastered, frozen in pure binary until the collapse of the Universe.

Click. And I resist the impulse to say, "Wait a minute. *Hee Haw* is my favorite show."

Well, I have lots of favorite shows. But me and my housemates, we're always watching *Hee Haw*. But all I get is two or three twangs of the banjo and a glimpse of the eerily friendly grin of the banjo picker and then *click* it's a '77 Buick LeSabre smashing through a guardrail in SoCal and bursting into a fireball *before it has even touched the ground,* which is only one of my favorite things about TV. Watch that for a while and just as I am settling into a nice Spew daze, it's a rap video, white trailer park boys in Clackamas who've actually got their moho on hydraulics so it can tilt and bounce in the air while the homeboys are partying down inside. Even the rooftop sentinels are boo-gieing, they have a boogie, using their AK-47s like jugglers' poles to keep their balance. Under the TV lights, the chrome-plated bayonets spark like throwaway cameras at the Orange Bowl Halftime Show.

And so it goes. Twenty clicks into the test I've left my fear behind, I'm Polysurfing like some incarnate sofa god, my attention plays like a space laser across the Spew's numberless Feeds, each Feed a torrent, all of them plexed together across the panascopic bandwidth of the optical fiber as if the contents of every Edge City in Greater America have been rammed into the maw of a giant pasta machine and extruded as endless, countless strands of polychrome angel hair. Within an hour or so I've settled into a pattern without even knowing it. I'm surfing among 20 or so different Feeds. My subconscious mind is like a retarded homunculus sacked out on the couch of my reptilian brain, his thumb wandering crazily around the keypad of the world's largest remote control. It looks like chaos, even to me, but to the proctors, watching all my polygraph traces superimposed on the video feed, tracking my blood pressure and pupil dilation, there is a strange attractor somewhere down there, and if it's the right one . . .

"Congratulations," the proctor says, and I realize the chilly mind-sucking apparatus has been retracted into the ceiling. I'm still fixated on the Spew. Bringing me back to reality: the nurse chick ripping off the handy disposable self-stick electrodes, bristling with my body hair.

So, a week later I'm still wondering how I got this job: patrolman on the information highway. We don't call it that, of course, the job title is Profile Auditor 1. But if the Spew is a highway, imagine a hard-jawed, close-shaven buck lurking in the shade of an overpass, your license plate reflected in the quicksilver pools of his shades as you whoosh past. Key difference: we never bust anyone, we just like to watch.

We sit in Television City cubicles, VR rigs strapped to our skulls, grokking people's Profiles in n-dimensional Demo Tainment Space, where demographic, entertainment, consumption habits, and credit history all intersect to define a weird imaginary universe that is every bit as twisted and

convoluted as those balloon animals that so eerily squelch
and shudder from the hands of feckless loitering clowns in
the touristy districts of our great cities. Takes killer spatial
relations not to get lost. We turn our heads, and the
Demosphere moves around us; we point at something of
interest—the distinct galactic cluster formed by some
schmo's Profile—and we fly toward it, warp speed. Hell,
we fly right through the middle of it, we do barrel rolls
through said schmo's annual mortgage interest statements
and gambol in his urinalysis records. Course, the VR
illusion doesn't track just right, so most of us get sick for the
first few weeks until we learn to move our heads slowly,
like tank turrets. You can always tell a rookie by the scope
patch glued beneath his ear, strong mouthwash odor, gray
lips.

Through the Demosphere we fly, we men of the Database
Maintenance Division, and although the Demosphere be-
longs to General Communications Inc., it is the schmos of
the world who make it—every time a schmo surfs to a
different channel, the Demosphere notes that he is bored
with program A and more interested, at the moment, in
program B. When a schmo's paycheck is delivered over the
I-way, the number on the bottom line is plotted in his
Profile, and if that schmo got it by telecommuting we know
about that too—the length of his coffee breaks and the size
of his bladder are an open book to us. When a schmo buys
something on the I-way it goes into his Profile, and if it
happens to be something that he recently saw advertised
there, we call that interesting, and when he uses the I-way to
phone his friends and family, we Profile Auditors can
navigate his social web out to a gazillion fractal iterations,
the friends of his friends of his friends of his friends, what
they buy and what they watch and if there's a correlation.

So now it's a year later. I have logged many a megaparsec
across the Demosphere, I can pick out an anomalous Profile
at a glance and notify my superiors. I am dimly aware of
two things: (1) that my yearly Polysurf test looms, and (2)
I've a decent chance of being promoted to Profile Auditor 2
and getting a cubicle some 25 percent larger and with my

choice from among three different color schemes and four
pre-approved decor configurations. If I show some stick-to-
it-iveness, put out some Second Effort, spread my legs on
cue, I may one day be issued a *chair with arms.*

But let's not get ahead of ourselves. Have to get through
that Polysurf test first. And I am oddly nervous. I am
nervous because of *Hee Haw.*

Why did my subconscious brain surf away from *Hee
Haw*? That wasn't like me at all. And yet perhaps it was this
that had gotten me the job.

Disturbing thought: the hangover. I was in a foul mood,
short-tempered, reactionary, literal-minded—in short, the
temporary brain insult had turned me into an ideal candidate
for this job.

But this time they will come and tap me for the test at a
random time, while I am at work. I cannot possibly arrange
to be hung over, unless I *stay* hung over for two weeks
straight—tricky to arrange, I am a fraud. Soon they will
know; ignominy, poverty will follow.

I am going to lose my job—my salaried job with medical
and dental and even a *pension plan.* Didn't even know what
a pension was until the employee benefits counselor clued
me in, and it nearly blew the top of my skull off. For a
couple of weeks I was like that lucky conquistador from
the poem—stout what's-his-name silent upon a peak in
Darien—as I dealt this wild surmise: twenty years of rough
country ahead of me leading down to an ocean of Slack that
stretched all the way to the sunlit rim of the world, or to the
end of my natural life expectancy, whichever came first.

So now I am scared shitless about the next Polysurf test.
And then, hope.

My division commander zooms toward me in the Demosphere, an alienated human head wearing a bowler hat as
badge of rank. "Follow me, Stark," he says, launching the
command like a bronchial loogie, and before I can even "yes
sir" I'm trying to keep up with him, dodging through
DemoTainment Space.

And ten minutes later we are cruising in a standard orbit
around your Profile.

And from the middle distance it looks pretty normal. I can see at a glance you are a 24-year-old single white female New Derisive with post-Disillusionist leanings, income careening in a death spiral around the poverty line, you spend more on mascara than is really appropriate compared to your other cosmetics outlays, which are Low Modest—I'd wager you're hooked on some exotic brand—no appendix, O positive, HIV-negative, don't call your mother often enough, spend an hour a day talking to your girlfriends, you prefer voice phone to video, like Irish music as well as the usual intelligent yet primal, sludgy yet danceable rock that someone like you would of course listen to. Your use of the Spew follows a bulimic course—you'll watch for two days at a time and then not switch on for a week.

But I know it can't be that simple, the commander wouldn't have brought me here because he was worried about your mascara imbalance, there's got to be something else.

I decide to take a flyer. "Geez, boss, something's not right here," I say, "this profile looks normal—too normal."

He buys it. He buys it like a set of snow tires. His disembodied head spins around and he looks at me intently, an oval of two-dimensional video in DemoTainment Space. "You saw that!?" he says.

Now I'm in deep. "Just a hunch, boss."

"Get to the bottom of it, and you'll be picking out color schemes by the end of the week," he says, then streaks off like a bottle rocket.

So that's it then; if I nab myself a promotion before the next Polysurf, they'll be a lot more forgiving if, say, the little couch potato in my brain stem chooses to watch *Hee Haw* for half an hour, or whatever.

Thenceforward I am in full Stalker Mode, I stake out your Profile, camp out in the middle of your income-tax returns, dance like an arachnid through your Social Telephony Web, dog you through the Virtual Mall trying to predict what clothes you're going to buy. It takes me about ten minutes to figure out you've been buying mascara for one of your girlfriends who got fired from her job last year, so that solves that little riddle. Then I get nervous because whatever weirdness it was about you that drew the Commander's attention doesn't seem to be there anymore. Almost like you know someone's watching.

OK, let's just get this out of the way: it's creepy. Being a creep is a role someone has to take for society to remain free and hence prosperous (or is it the other way around?).

I am pursuing a larger goal that isn't creepy at all. I am thinking of Adderson. Every one of us, sitting in our cubicles, is always thinking of Adderson, who started out as a Profile Auditor 1 just like us and making eight to nine digits a year depending on whether he gets around to exercising his stock options. One day young Adderson was checking out a Profile that didn't fit in with established norms, and by tracing the subject's social telephony web, noticed a trend: Post-Graduate Existentialists who *started going to church*. You heard me: Adderson single-handedly discovered the New Complacency.

It was an unexploited market niche of cavernous proportions: upwards of one-hundredth of one percent of the population. Within six hours, Adderson had descended upon the subject's moho with a Rapid Deployment Team of entertainment lawyers and development assistants and launched the fastest-growing new channel ever to wend its way into the thick braid of the Spew.

I'm figuring that there's something about you, girl, that's going to make me into the next Adderson and you into the next Spew Icon—the voice of a generation, the figurehead of a Spew channel, a straight polished shaft leading direct to the heart of a *hitherto unknown and unexploited market*. I know how awful this sounds, by the way.

So I stay late in my cubicle and dig a little deeper, rewinding your Profile back into the mists of time. Your credit record is fashionably cratered—but that's cool, even the God of the New Testament is not as forgiving as the consumer credit system. You've blown many scarce dollars at your local BodyMod franchise getting yourself pierced ("topologically enhanced"), and, on one occasion, tattooed: a medium #P879, left breast. Perusal of BodyMod's graphical database (available, of course, over the Spew) turns up "© 1991 by Ray Troll of Ketchikan, Alaska." BodyMod's own market research on this little gem indicates that it first become widely popular within the Seattle music scene.

So the plot thickens. I check out of my cubicle. I decide to go undercover.

Wouldn't think a Profile Auditor 1 could pull that off, wouldja? But I'm just like you, or I was a year ago. All I have to do is dig a yard deeper into the sediments of my dirty laundry pile, which have become metamorphic under prolonged heat and pressure.

As I put the clothes on it occurs to me that I could stand a little prolonged heat and pressure myself.

But I can't be thinking about *that*, I'm a professional, got a job to do, and frankly I could do without this unwanted insight. That's just what I need, for the most important assignment of my career to turn into a nookie hunt. I try to drive it from my mind, try to lose myself in the high-definition Spew terminals in the subway car, up there where the roach motel placards used to be. They click from one Feed to another following some irrational pattern and I wonder who has the job of surfing the channels in the subway; maybe it's what I'll be doing for a living, a week from now.

Just before the train pulls into your stop, the terminal in my face surfs into episode #2489 of *Hee Haw*. It's a skit. The banjo picker is playing a bit part, sitting on a bale of hay in the back of a pickup truck—chewing on a stalk of grass, surprisingly enough. His job is to laugh along with the cheesy jokes but he's just a banjo picker, not an actor, he doesn't know the drill, he can't keep himself from looking at the camera—looking at me. I notice for the first time that his irises are different colors. I turn up the collar on my jacket as I detrain, feeling those creepy eyes on my neck.

I have already discovered much about the infrastructure of your life that is probably hidden even from you, including your position in the food chain, which is as follows: the SRVX group is the largest *zaibatsu* in the services industry. They own five different hotel networks, of which Nospicor is the second-largest but only the fourth most profitable. Hospicor hotels are arranged in tiers: at the bottom we have Catchawink, which is human coin lockers in airports, everything covered in a plastic sheet that comes off a huge roll, like sleeping inside a giant, loose-fitting condom. Then we have Mom's Sleep Inn, a chain of motels catering to truckers and homeless migrants; The Family Room, currently getting its ass kicked by Holiday Inn; Kensington Place, going for that all-important biz traveler; and Imperion Preferred Resorts.

I see that you work for the Kensington Place Columbus Hotel, which is too far from the park and too viewless to be an Imperion Preferred, even though it's in a very nice old building. So you are, to be specific, a desk clerk and you work the evening shift there.

I approach the entrance to the hotel at 8:05 P.M., long-jumping across vast reservoirs of gray-brown slush and blowing off the young men who want to change my money into Hong Kong dollars. The doorman is too busy tapping a fresh Camel on his wrist bone to open the door for me so I do it myself.

The lobby looks a little weird because I've only seen it on TV, through that security camera up there in the corner, with its distorting wide-angle lens, which feeds directly into the Spew, of course. I'm all turned around for a moment, doing sort of a drunken pirouette in the middle of the lobby, and finally I get my bearings and establish missile lock on You, standing behind the reception desk with Evan, your goatee-sporting colleague, both of you looking dorky (as I'm sure you'd be the first to assert) in your navy blue Kensington Place uniforms, which would border on dignified if not for the maroon piping and pseudo-brass name tags.

For long minutes I stand more or less like an idiot right there under the big chandelier, watching you giving the business to some poor sap of a guest. I am too stunned to move because something big and heavy is going upside my head. Not sure exactly what.

But it feels like the Big L. And I don't just mean Lust, though it is present.

The guest is approaching tears because the fridge in her room is broken and she has some kind of medicine that has to be kept cold or else she won't wake up tomorrow morning.

No it's worse than that, there's no fridge in her room *at all*.

Evan suggests that the woman leave the medicine outside on her windowsill overnight. It is a priceless moment, I feel like holding up a big card with 9.8 written on it. Some of my all-time fave Television Moments have been on surveillance TV, moments like this one, but it takes patience. You have to wait for it. Usually, at a Kensington Place you don't have to wait for long.

As I have been watching Evan and you on the Stalker Channel the past couple of days, I have been trying to figure out if the two of you have a thing going. It's hard because the camera doesn't give me audio, I have to work it out from body language. And after careful analysis of instant replays, I suspect you of being one of those dangerous types who innocently give good body language to everyone. The type of girl who should have someone walking ten paces in front of her with a red flashing light and a clanging bell. Just my type.

The woman storms out in tears, wailing something about lawyers. I resist the urge to applaud and stand there for a minute or so, waiting to be greeted. You and Evan ignore me. I approach the desk. I clear my throat. I come right up to the desk and put my bag down on the counter right there and sigh very loudly. Evan is poking randomly at the computer and you are misfiling thousands of tiny little oaktag cards, the color of old bananas in a small wooden drawer.

I inhale and open my mouth to say *excuse me*, but Evan cuts me off: "Customerrrrzz . . . gotta love 'em."

You grin wickedly and give him a nice flirty conspiratorial look. No one has looked at me yet. That's OK. I recognize your technique from the surveillance camera: good clerk, bad clerk.

"Reservation for Stark," I say.

"Stark," Evan says, and rolls it around in his head for a minute or so, unwilling to proceed until he has deconstructed my name. "That's German for 'strong,' right?"

"It's German for 'naked,'" I say.

Evan drops his gaze to the computer screen, defeated and temporarily humble. You laugh and glance up at me for the first time. What do you see? You see a guy who looks pretty much like the guys you hang out with.

I shove the sleeves of my ratty sweater up to the elbows and rest one forearm across the counter. The tattoo stands out vividly against my spudlike flesh, and in my peripheral I can see your eyes glance up for a moment, taking in the black rectangle, the skull, the crossed fish. Then I pretend to get self-conscious. I step back and pull my sleeve down again—don't want you to see that the tattoo is only about a day old.

"No reservation for Stark," Evan says, right on cue. I'm cool, I'm expecting this; they lose all of the reservations.

"Dash these computers," I say. "You have any empty rooms?"

"Just a suite. And a couple of economy rooms," he says, issuing a double challenge: do I have the bucks for the former or the moxie for the latter?

"I'll take one of the economy rooms," I say.

"You sure?"

"HIV-positive."

Evan shrugs, the hotel clerk's equivalent of issuing a twenty-page legal disclaimer, and prods the computer, which is good enough to spit out a keycard, freshly imprinted with a random code. It's also spewing bits upstairs to the computer lock on my door, telling it that I'm cool, I'm to be let in.

"Would you like someone to show you up?" Evan says, glancing in mock surprise around the lobby, which is of course devoid of bellhops. I respond in the only way possible: chuckle darkly—*good one, Ev!*—and hump my own bag.

My room's lone window looks out on a narrow well somewhere between an air shaft and a garbage chute in size and function. Patches of the shag carpet have fused into mysterious crust formations, and in the corners of the bathroom, pubic hairs have formed into gnarled drifts. There is a Robobar in the corner but the door can only be opened halfway because it runs into the radiator, a 12-ton cast-iron model that, randomly, once or twice an hour, makes a noise like a rock hitting the windshield. The Robobar is mostly empty but I wriggle one arm into it and yank out a canned Mai Tai, knowing that the selection will show up instantaneously on the computer screens below, where you and Evan will derive fleeting amusement from my offbeat tastes.

Yes, now we are surveiling each other. I open my suitcase and take my own Spew terminal out of its case, unplug the room's set and jack my own into the socket. Then I start opening windows: first, in the upper left, you and Evan in wide-angle black-and-white. Then an episode of *Starsky and Hutch* that I happened to notice. Starsky's hair is very big in this one. And then I open a data window too and patch it into the feed coming out of your terminal down there at the desk. Profile Auditors can do this because data security on the Spew is a joke. It was deliberately made a joke by the Government so that they, and we, and anyone else with a Radio Shack charge card and a trade school diploma, can snoop on anyone.

I sit back on the bed and sip my execrable Mai Tai from its heavy, rusty can and watch *Starsky and Hutch*. Every so often there's some activity at the desk and I watch you and Evan for a minute. When Evan uses his terminal, lines of ASCII text scroll up my data window. I cannot help noticing that when Evan isn't actively slacking he can type at a burst speed in excess of 200 words per minute.

From *Starsky and Hutch* I surf to an *L.A. Law* rerun and then to *Larry King Live*. There's local news, then Dave comes on, and about the time he's doing his Top Ten list, I see activity at the desk.

It is a young gentleman with hair way down past the epaulets of his tremendously oversized black wool overcoat. Naked hairy legs protrude below the coat and are socketed

into large, ratty old basketball shoes. He is carrying, not a
garment bag, but a guitar.

For the first time all night, you and Evan show actual
hospitality. Evan does some punching on his computer, and
monitoring the codes I see that the guitarist is being checked
into a room.

Into my room. Not the one I'm in, but the one I'm
supposed to be in. Number 707. I pull out the fax that Marie
at Kensington Place Worldwide Reservation Command sent
to me yesterday, just to double check.

Sure enough, the guitarist is being checked into my room.
Not only that—Evan's checking him in *under my name*.

I go out into the streets of the city. You and Evan pretend
to ignore me, but I can see you following me with your eyes
as I circumvent the doorman, who is planted like a dead
Ficus benjamina before the exit, and throw my shoulder
against the sullen bulk of the revolving door. It has
commenced snowing for the eleventh time today. I walk
cross-town to Television City and have a drink in a bar
there, a real Profile Auditor hangout, the kind of joint where
I'm proud to be seen. When I get back to the hotel, the shift
has changed, you and Evan have apparently stalked off into
the rapidly developing blizzard, and the only person there is
the night clerk.

I stand there for ten minutes or so while she winds down
a rather involved, multithreaded conversation with a friend
in Ireland. "Stark," I say, as she's hanging up, "Room 707.
Left my keycard in the room."

She doesn't even ask to see ID, just makes up another
keycard for me. Bad service has its charms. But I cruise past
the seventh floor and go on up to my own cell because I
want to do this right.

I jack into the Spew. I check out what's going on in Room
707.

First thing I look at is the Robobar transcript. Whoever's
in there has already gone through four beers and two
non-sparkling mineral waters. And one bad Mai Tai.

Guess I'm a trendsetter here. A hunch thuds into my

cortex. I pop a beer from my own Robobar and rewind the lobby security tape to midnight.

You and Evan hand over the helm to the Irish girl. Then, like Picard and Riker on their way to Ten Forward after a long day of sensitive negotiations, you head straight for Elevator Three, the only one that seems to be hooked up. So I check out the elevator activity transcript too—not to be monotonous or anything, but it's all on the Spew—and sho nuff, it seems that you and Evan went straight to the seventh floor. You're in there, I realize, with your guitar-player bud who wears shorts in the middle of the winter, and you're drinking bad beer and Mai Tais from my Robobar.

I monitor the Spew traffic to Room 707. You did some random surfing like anyone else, sort of as foreplay, but since then you've just been hoovering up gigabyte after gigabyte of encrypted data.

It's gotta be media; only media takes that many bytes. It's coming from an unknown source, definitely not the big centralized Spew nodes—but it's been forwarded six ways from Sunday, it's been bounced off Indian military satellites, divided into tiny chunks, disguised as credit card authorizations, rerouted through manual telephone exchanges in Nigeria, reassembled in pirated insurance-company databases in the Netherlands. Upshot; I'll never trace it back to its source, or sources.

What is ten times as weird: *you're putting data out.* You're talking *back* to the Spew. You have turned your room—*my room*—into a broadcast station. For all I know, you've got a *live studio audience* packed in there with you.

All of your outgoing stuff is encrypted too.

Now. My rig has some badass code-breaking stuff built into it, Profile Auditor warez, but all of it just bounces off. You guys are cypherpunks, or at least you know some. You're using codes so tough they're illegal. Conclusion: you're talking to other people—other people like you— probably squatting in other Kensington Place hotel rooms all over the world at this moment.

Everything's falling into place. No wonder Kensington

Place has such legendarily shitty service. No wonder it's so unprofitable. The whole chain has been infiltrated.

And what's really brilliant is that all the weird shit you're pulling off the Spew, all the hooch you're pulling out of my Robobar, is going to end up tacked onto my Profile, while you end up looking infuriatingly normal.

I kind of like it. So I invest another half-hour of my life waiting for an elevator, take it down to the lobby, go out to a twenty-four-hour mart around the corner and buy two six-packs—one of the fashionable downmarket swill that you are drinking and one of your brand of mineral water. I can tell you're cool because your water costs more than your beer.

Ten minutes later I'm standing in front of 707, sweating like a high school kid in a cheesy tuxedo on prom night. After a few minutes the sheer patheticity of this little scene starts to embarrass me and so I tuck a six under my arm and swipe my card through the slot. The little green light winks at me knowingly. I shoulder through the door saying, "Honey, I'm home!"

No response. I have to negotiate a narrow corridor past the bath and closets before I can see into the room proper. I step out with what I hope is a non-creepy smile. Something wet and warm sprays into my face. It trickles into my mouth. It's on the savory side.

The room's got like ten feet of open floor space that you have increased to fifteen by stacking the furniture in the bathroom. In the midst of this is the guitar dude, stripped to his colorful knee-length shorts. He is playing his ax, but it's not plugged into anything. I can hear some melodious plinks, but the squelch of his fingers on the strings, the thud of calluses on the fingerboard almost drown out the notes.

He sweats hard, even though the windows are open and cold air is blowing into the room, the blinds running with condensation and whacking crazily against the leaky aluminum window frame. As he works through his solo, sighing and grunting with effort, his fingers drumming their way higher and higher up the fingerboard, he swings his head back and forth and his hair whips around, broadcasting sweat. He's wearing dark shades.

Evan is perched like an arboreal primate on top of the room's Spew terminal, which is fixed to the wall at about head level. His legs are spread wide apart to expose the screen, against which crash waves of black-and-white static. The motherly warmth of the cathode-ray tube is, I guess, permeating his buttocks.

On his lap is just about the bitchingest media processor I have ever seen, and judging from the heavy cables exploding out of the back it looks like he's got it crammed with deadly expansion cards. He's wearing dark shades too, just like the guitarist's; but now I see they aren't shades, they are VR rigs, pretty good ones actually. Evan is also wearing a pair of Datagloves. His hands and fingers are constantly moving. Sometimes he makes typing motions, sometimes he reaches out and grabs imaginary things and moves them around, sometimes he points his index finger and navigates through virtual space, sometimes he riffs in some kind of sign language.

You—you are mostly in the airspace above the bed, touching down frequently, using it as trampoline and safety net. Every three-year-old bouncing illicitly on her bed probably aspires to your level of intensity. You've got the VR rig too, you've got the Datagloves, you've got Velcro bands around your wrists, elbows, waist, knees, and ankles, tracking the position of every part of your body in three-dimensional space. Other than that, you have stripped down to voluminous plaid boxer shorts and a generously sized tank-top undershirt.

You are rocking out. I have never seen anyone dance like this. You have churned the bedspread and pillows into sufferin' succotash. They get in your way so you kick them vindictively off the bed and get down again, boogieing so hard I can't believe you haven't flown off the bed yet. Your undershirt is drenched. You are breathing hard and steady and in sync with the rhythm, which I cannot hear but can infer.

I can't help looking. There's the SPAWN TILL YOU DIE tattoo.

And there on the other breast is something else. I walk into the room for a better look, taking in a huge whiff of perfume and sweat and beer. The second tattoo consists of small but neat navy-blue script, like that of names embroidered on bowling shirts, reading, HACK THE SPEW.

It's not too hard to trace the connections. A wire coils out of the guitar, runs across the floor, and jumps up to jack into Evan's badass media processor. You have a wireless rig hanging on your waist and the receiver is likewise patched into Evan's machine. And Evan's output port, then, is jacked straight into the room's Spew socket.

I am ashamed to notice that the Profile Auditor 1 part of my brain is thinking that this weird little mime fest has UNEXPLOITED MARKET NICHE—ORDER NOW! superimposed all over it in flashing yellow block letters.

Evan gets so into his solo that he sinks unsteadily to his knees and nearly falls over. He's leaning way back, stomach muscles knotting up, his wet hair dangling back and picking up detritus from the carpet as he swings his head back and forth.

This whole setup is depressingly familiar: it is just like high school, when I had a crush on some girl, and even though I was in the same room with her, breathing the same air, sharing the same space, she didn't know I existed; she had her own network of friends, all grooving on some frequency I couldn't pick up, existing on another plane that I couldn't even see.

There's a note on the dresser, scrawled on hotel stationery with a dried-up hotel ball-point. WELCOME CHAZ, it says, JACK IN AND JOIN US! followed by ten lines of stuff like:

A073 49D2 CD01 7813 000F B09B 323A E040

which are obviously an encryption key, written in the hexadecimal system beloved of hackers. It is the key to whatever plane you and your buds are on at the moment.

But I am not Chaz.

I open the desk drawer to reveal the room's fax machine, a special Kensington Place feature that Marie extolled to me most tediously. I put the note into it and punched the Copy key, shove the copy into my pocket when it's finished and leave the note where I found it. I leave the two six-packs on the dresser as a ritual sacrifice, and slink out of the room, not looking back. An elevator is coming up toward me, L M 2 3 4 5 6 and then DING and the doors open, and out steps a slacker who can only be Chaz, thousands of snowflakes caught in his hair, glinting in the light like he's just stepped out of the Land of Faerie. He's got kind of a peculiar expression on his face as he steps out of the elevator, and as we trade places, and I punch the button for the lobby, I recognize it: Chaz is happy. Happier than me.

TANGENTS

Greg Bear

Hackers often end up exploring unknown territory, some-times inadvertently. As the brilliant story that follows sug-gests, though, sometimes the way you look at the things you find may be every bit as important as what you're looking at . . .

Born in San Diego, California, Greg Bear made his first sale at the age of fifteen to Robert Lowndes's Famous Science Fiction, *and has subsequently established himself as one of the top professionals in the genre. He won a Nebula Award for his pyrotechnic novella "Hardfought," a Nebula and Hugo Award for his famous story "Blood Music," which was later expanded into a novel of the same title, and a subsequent Nebula and Hugo for the story that follows, "Tangents." His other books include the novels* Hegira, Psychlone, Beyond Heaven's River, Strength of Stones, The Infinity Concerto, The Serpent Mage, Eon, Eternity, The Forge of God, Anvil of Stars, *and the critically acclaimed* Queen of Angels, *as well as the collections* The Wind From a Burning Woman *and* Tangents. *His most recent books are the novels* Moving Mars, Heads, *and* Legacy, *and, as editor, the original anthology* New Legends. *He lives with his family just outside of Seattle, Washington.*

The nut-brown boy stood in the California field, his Asian face shadowed by a hardhat, his short stocky frame clothed in a T-shirt and a pair of brown shorts. He squinted across the hip-high grass at the spraddled old two-story ranch house, whistling a few bars from a Haydn piano sonata.

Out of the upper floor of the house came a man's high, frustrated "Bloody hell!" and the sound of a fist slamming on a solid surface. Silence for a minute. Then, more softly, a woman's question, "Not going well?"

"No. I'm swimming in it, but I don't see it."

"The encryption?" the woman asked timidly.

"The tesseract. If it doesn't gel, it isn't aspic."

The boy squatted in the grass and listened.

"And?" the woman encouraged.

"Ah, Lauren, it's still cold broth."

The boy lay back in the grass. He had crept over the split-rail and brick-pylon fence from the new housing project across the road. School was out for the summer and his mother—foster mother—did not like him around the house all day. Or at all.

Behind his closed eyes, a huge piano keyboard appeared, with him dancing on the keys. He loved music.

He opened his eyes and saw a thin, graying lady in a tweed suit leaning over him, staring. "You're on private land," she said, brows knit.

He scrambled up and brushed grass from his pants. "Sorry."

"I thought I saw someone out here. What's your name?"

"Pal," he replied.

"Is that a name?" she asked querulously.

"Pal Tremont. It's not my real name. I'm Korean."

"Then what's your real name?"

"My folks told me not to use it anymore. I'm adopted. Who are you?"

The gray woman looked him up and down. "My name is Lauren Davies," she said. "You live near here?"

He pointed across the fields at the close-packed tract homes.

"I sold the land for those homes ten years ago," she said. She seemed to be considering something. "I don't normally enjoy children trespassing."

"Sorry," Pal said.

"Have you had lunch?"

"No."

"Will a grilled cheese sandwich do?"

He squinted at her and nodded.

In the broad, red-brick and tile kitchen, sitting at an oak table with his shoulders barely rising above the top, he ate the slightly charred sandwich and watched Lauren Davies watching him.

"I'm trying to write about a child," she said. "It's difficult. I'm a spinster and I don't understand children."

"You're a writer?" he asked, taking a swallow of milk.

She sniffed. "Not that anyone would know."

"Is that your brother, upstairs?"

"No," she said. "That's Peter. We've been living together for twenty years."

"But you said you're a spinster . . . isn't that someone who's never married, or never loved?" Pal asked.

"Never married. And never you mind. Peter's relationship to me is none of your concern." She placed a bowl of soup and a tuna salad sandwich on a lacquer tray. "His lunch," she said. Without being asked, Pal trailed up the stairs after her.

"This is where Peter works," Lauren explained. Pal stood in the doorway, eyes wide. The room was filled with electronics gear, computer terminals, and bookcases with geometric cardboard sculptures sharing each shelf with books and circuit boards. She rested the tray precariously on a pile of floppy disks atop a rolling cart.

"Time for a break," she told a thin man seated with his back toward them.

The man turned around on his swivel chair, glanced briefly at Pal and the tray and shook his head. The hair on top of his head was a rich, glossy black; on the close-cut sides, the color changed abruptly to a startling white. He had a small thin nose and large green eyes. On the desk before him was a high-resolution computer monitor. "We haven't been introduced," he said, pointing to Pal.

"This is Pal Tremont, a neighborhood visitor. Pal, this is Peter Tuthy. Pal's going to help me with that character we discussed this morning."

Pal looked at the monitor curiously. Red and green lines shadowed each other through some incomprehensible transformation on the screen, then repeated.

"What's a 'tesseract'?" Pal asked, remembering what he had heard as he stood in the field.

"It's a four-dimensional analog of a cube. I'm trying to teach myself to see it in my mind's eye," Tuthy said. "Have you ever tried that?"

"No," Pal admitted.

"Here," Tuthy said, handing him the spectacles. "As in the movies."

Pal donned the spectacles and stared at the screen. "So?" he said. "It folds and unfolds. It's pretty—it sticks out at you, and then it goes away." He looked around the workshop. "Oh, wow!" The boy ran to a yard-long black music keyboard propped in one corner. "A Tronclavier! With all the switches! My mother had me take piano lessons, but I'd rather play this. Can you play it?"

"I toy with it," Tuthy said, exasperated. "I toy with all sorts of electronic things. But what did you see on the screen?" He glanced up at Lauren, blinking. "I'll eat the food, I'll eat it. Now please don't bother us."

"He's supposed to be helping *me*," Lauren complained.

Peter smiled at her. "Yes, of course. I'll send him downstairs in a little while."

When Pal descended an hour later, he came into the kitchen to thank Lauren for lunch. "Peter's a real flake," he said confidentially. "He's trying to learn to see in weird directions."

"I know," Lauren said, sighing.

"I'm going home now," Pal said. "I'll be back, though . . . if it's all right with you. Peter invited me."

"I'm sure it will be fine," Lauren said dubiously.

"He's going to let me learn the Tronclavier." With that, Pal smiled radiantly and exited through the kitchen door, just as he had come in.

When she retrieved the tray, she found Peter leaning back in his chair, eyes closed. The figures on the screen were still folding and unfolding.

"What about Hockrum's work?" she asked.

"I'm on it," Peter replied, eyes still closed.

• • •

Lauren called Pal's foster mother on the second day to apprise them of their son's location, and the woman assured her it was quite all right. "Sometimes he's a little pest. Send him home if he causes trouble . . . but not right away! Give me a rest," she said, then laughed nervously.

Lauren drew her lips together tightly, thanked the woman, and hung up.

Peter and the boy had come downstairs to sit in the kitchen, filling up paper with line drawings. "Peter's teaching me how to use his program," Pal said.

"Did you know," Tuthy said, assuming his highest Cambridge professorial tone, "that a cube, intersecting a flat plane, can be cut through a number of geometrically different cross-sections?"

Pal squinted at the sketch Tuthy had made. "Sure," he said.

"If shoved through the plane the cube can appear, to a two-dimensional creature living on the plane—let's call him a 'Flatlander'—to be either a triangle, a rectangle, a trapezoid, a rhombus, or a square. If the two-dimensional being observes the cube being pushed through all the way, what he sees is one of more of these objects growing larger, changing shape suddenly, shrinking, and disappearing."

"Sure," Pal said, tapping his sneakered toe. "That's easy. Like in that book you showed me."

"And a sphere pushed through a plane would appear, to the hapless flatlander, first as an 'invisible' point (the two-dimensional surface touching the sphere, tangential), then as a circle. The circle would grow in size, then shrink back to a point and disappear again." He sketched two-dimensional stick figures looking in awe at such an intrusion.

"Got it," Pal said. "Can I play with the Tronclavier now?"

"In a moment. Be patient. So what would a tesseract look like, coming into our three-dimensional space? Remember the program, now . . . the pictures on the monitor."

Pal looked up at the ceiling. "I don't know," he said, seeming bored.

"Try to think," Tuthy urged him.

"It would . . ." Pal held his hands out to shape an angular object. "It would look like one of those Egyptian things, but with three sides . . . or like a box. It would look like a weird-shaped box, too, not square. And if *you* were to fall through a flatland . . ."

"Yes, that would look very funny," Peter acknowledged with a smile. "Cross-sections of arms and legs and body, all surrounded by skin . . ."

"And a head!" Pal enthused. "With eyes and a nose."

The doorbell rang. Pal jumped off the kitchen chair. "Is that my mom?" he asked, looking worried.

"I don't think so," Lauren said. "More likely it's Hockrum." She went to the front door to answer. She returned a moment later with a small, pale man behind her. Tuthy stood and shook the man's hand. "Pal Tremont, this is Irving Hockrum," he introduced, waving his hand between them. Hockrum glanced at Pal and blinked a long, cold blink.

"How's the work coming?" he asked Tuthy.

"It's finished," Tuthy said. "It's upstairs. Looks like your savants are barking up the wrong logic tree." He retrieved a folder of papers and printouts and handed them to Hockrum.

Hockrum leafed through the printouts. "I can't say this makes me happy. Still, I can't find fault. Looks like the work is up to your usual brilliant standards. Here's your check." He handed Tuthy an envelope. "I just wish you'd given it to us sooner. It would have saved me some grief—and the company quite a bit of money."

"Sorry," Tuthy said.

"Now I have an important bit of work for you . . ." And Hockrum outlined another problem. Tuthy thought it over for several minutes and shook his head.

"Most difficult, Irving. Pioneering work there. Take at least a month to see if it's even feasible."

"That's all I need to know for now—whether it's feasible. A lot's riding on this, Peter." Hockrum clasped his hands together in front of him, looking even more pale and worn than when he had entered the kitchen. "You'll let me know soon?"

"I'll get right on it," Tuthy said.

"Protégé?" he asked, pointing to Pal. There was a speculative expression on his face, not quite a leer.

"No, a young friend. He's interested in music," Tuthy said. "Damned good at Mozart, in fact."

"I help with his tesseracts," Pal asserted.

"I hope you don't interrupt Peter's work. Peter's work is important."

Pal shook his head solemnly. "Good," Hockrum said, and then left the house with the folder under his arm.

Tuthy returned to his office, Pal in train. Lauren tried to work in the kitchen, sitting with fountain pen and pad of paper, but the words wouldn't come. Hockrum always worried her. She climbed the stairs and stood in the open doorway of the office. She often did that; her presence did not disturb Tuthy, who could work under all sorts of adverse conditions.

"Who was that man?" Pal was asking Tuthy.

"I work for him," Tuthy said. "He's employed by a big electronics firm. He loans me most of the equipment I use. The computers, the high-resolution monitors. He brings me problems and then takes my solutions back to his bosses and claims he did the work."

"That sounds stupid," Pal said. "What kind of problems?"

"Codes, encryptions. Computer security. That was my expertise, once."

"You mean, like fencerail, that sort of thing?" Pal asked, face brightening. "We learned some of that in school."

"Much more complicated, I'm afraid," Tuthy said, grinning. "Did you ever hear of the German 'Enigma,' or the 'Ultra' project?"

Pal shook his head.

"I thought not. Let's try another figure now." He called up another routine on the four-space program and sat Pal before the screen. "So what would a hypersphere look like if it intruded into our space?"

Pal thought a moment. "Kind of weird," he said.

"Not really. You've been watching the visualization."

"Oh, in *our* space. That's easy. It just looks like a balloon, blowing up from nothing and then shrinking again. It's harder to see what a hypersphere looks like when it's real. Reft of us, I mean."

"Reft?" Tuthy said.

"Sure. Reft and light. Dup and owwen. Whatever the directions are called."

Tuthy stared at the boy. Neither of them had noticed Lauren in the doorway. "The proper terms are *ana* and *kata*," Tuthy said. "What does it look like?"

Pal gestured, making two wide wings with his arms. "It's like a ball and it's like a horseshoe, depending on how you look at it. Like a balloon stung by bees, I guess, but it's smooth all over, not lumpy."

Tuthy continued to stare, then asked quietly, "You actually see it?"

"Sure," Pal said. "Isn't that what your program is supposed to do—make you see things like that?"

Tuthy nodded, flabbergasted.

"Can I play the Tronclavier now?"

Lauren backed out of the doorway. She felt she had eavesdropped on something momentous, but beyond her. Tuthy came downstairs an hour later, leaving Pal to pick out Telemann on the synthesizer. He sat at the kitchen table with her. "The program works," he said. "It doesn't work for me, but it works for him. I've just been showing him reverse shadow figures. He caught on right away, and then he went off and played Haydn. He's gone through all my sheet music. The kid's a genius."

"Musical, you mean?"

He glanced directly at her and frowned. "Yes, I suppose he's remarkable at that, too. But spacial relations—coordinates and motion in higher dimensions . . . Did you know that if you take a three-dimensional object and rotate it in the fourth dimension, it will come back with left-right reversed? So if I were to take my hand"—he held up his right hand—"and lift it *dup*"—he enunciated the word clearly, *dup*—"or drop it *owwen*, it would come back like this?" He held his left hand over his right, balled the right up into a fist, and snuck it away behind his back.

"I didn't know that," Lauren said. "What are *dup* and *owwen*?"

"That's what Pal calls movement along the fourth dimension. *Ana* and *kata* to purists. Like up and down to a flatlander, who only comprehends left and right, back and forth."

She thought about the hands for a moment. "I still can't see it," she said.

"I've tried, but neither can I," Tuthy admitted. "Our circuits are just too hard-wired, I suppose."

Upstairs, Pal had switched the Tronclavier to a cathedral organ and steel guitar combination and was playing variations on Pergolesi.

"Are you going to keep working for Hockrum?" Lauren asked. Tuthy didn't seem to hear her.

"It's remarkable," he murmured. "The boy just walked in here. You brought him in by accident. Remarkable."

"Can you show me the direction, point it out to me?" Tuthy asked the boy three days later.

"None of my muscles move that way," the boy replied. "I can see it, in my head, but . . ."

"What is it like, seeing that direction?"

Pal squinted. "It's a lot bigger. We're sort of stacked up with other places. It makes me feel lonely."

"Why?"

"Because I'm stuck here. Nobody out there pays any attention to us."

Tuthy's mouth worked. "I thought you were just intuiting those directions in your head. Are you telling me . . . you're actually *seeing* out there?"

"Yeah. There's people out there, too. Well, not people, exactly. But it isn't my eyes that see them. Eyes are like muscles—they can't point those ways. But the head—the brain, I guess—can."

"Bloody hell," Tuthy said. He blinked and recovered. "Excuse me. That's rude. Can you show me the people . . . on the screen?"

"Shadows, like we were talking about," Pal said.

"Fine. Then draw the shadows for me."

Pal sat down before the terminal, fingers pausing over the keys. "I can show you, but you have to help me with something."

"Help you with what?"

"I'd like to play music for them . . . out there. So they'll notice us."

"The people?"

"Yeah. They look really weird. They stand on us, sort of. They have hooks in our world. But they're tall . . . high dup. They don't notice us because we're so small, compared to them."

"Lord, Pal, I haven't the slightest idea how we'd send music out to them . . . I'm not even sure I believe they exist."

"I'm not lying," Pal said, eyes narrowing. He turned his chair to face a mouse on a black-ruled pad and began sketching shapes on the monitor. "Remember, these are just shadows of what they look like. Next I'll draw the dup and owwen lines to connect the shadows."

The boy shaded the shapes he drew to make them look solid, smiling at his trick but explaining it was necessary because the projection of a four-dimensional object in normal space was, of course, three-dimensional.

"They look like you take the plants in a garden, flowers and such, and giving them lots of arms and fingers . . . and it's kind of like seeing things in an aquarium," Pal explained.

After a time, Tuthy suspended his disbelief and stared in open-mouthed wonder at what the boy was re-creating on the monitor.

"I think you're wasting your time, that's what I think," Hockrum said. "I needed that feasibility judgment by today." He paced around the living room before falling as heavily as his light frame permitted into a chair.

"I *have* been distracted," Tuthy admitted.

"By that boy?"

"Yes, actually. Quite a talented fellow—"

"Listen, this is going to mean a lot of trouble for me. I guaranteed the study would be finished by today. It'll make me look bad." Hockrum screwed his face up in frustration. "What in hell are you doing with that boy?"

"Teaching him, actually. Or rather, he's teaching me. Right now, we're building a four-dimensional cone, part of a speaker system. The cone is three-dimensional, the material part, but the magnetic field forms a fourth-dimensional extension—"

"Do you ever think how it looks, Peter?" Hockrum asked.

"It looks very strange on the monitor, I grant you—"

"I'm talking about you and the boy."

Tuthy's bright, interested expression fell slowly into long, deep-lined dismay. "I don't know what you mean."

"I know a lot about you, Peter. Where you come from, why you had to leave . . . It just doesn't look good."

Tuthy's face flushed crimson.

"Keep him away from here," Hockrum advised.

Tuthy stood. "I want you out of this house," he said quietly. "Our relationship is at an end."

"I swear," Hockrum said, his voice low and calm, staring up at Tuthy from under his brows, "I'll tell the boy's parents. Do you think they'd want their kid hanging around an old—pardon the expression—queer? I'll tell them if you don't get the feasibility judgment made. I think you can do it by the end of this week—two days. Don't you?"

"No, I don't think so," Tuthy said. "Please leave."

"I know you're here illegally. There's no record of you entering the country. With the problems you had in England, you're certainly not a desirable alien. I'll pass word to the INS. You'll be deported."

"There isn't time to do the work," Tuthy said.

"Make time. Instead of 'educating' that kid."

"Get out of here."

"Two days, Peter."

Over dinner that evening, Tuthy explained to Lauren the exchange he had had with Hockrum. "He thinks I'm buggering Pal. Unspeakable bastard. I will never work for him again."

"We'd better talk to a lawyer, then," Lauren said. "You're sure you can't make him . . . happy, stop all this trouble?"

"I could solve his little problem for him in just a few hours. But I don't want to see him or speak to him again."

"He'll take your equipment away."

Tuthy blinked and waved one hand through the air helplessly. "Then we'll just have to work fast, won't we? Ah, Lauren, you were a fool to bring me here. You should have left me to rot."

"They ignored everything you did for them," Lauren said bitterly. "You saved their hides during the war, and then . . . They would have shut you up in prison." She stared through the kitchen window at the overcast sky and woods outside.

The cone lay on the table near the window, bathed in morning sun, connected to both the mini-computer and the Tronclavier. Pal arranged the score he had composed on a music stand before the synthesizer. "It's like Bach," he said, "but it'll play better for them. It has a kind of over-rhythm that I'll play on the dup part of the speaker."

"Why are we doing this, Pal?" Tuthy asked as the boy sat down to the keyboard.

"You don't belong here, really, do you, Peter?" Pal asked in turn. Tuthy stared at him.

"I mean, Miss Davies and you get along okay—but do you belong *here*, now?"

"What makes you think I don't belong?"

"I read some books in the school library. About the war and everything. I looked up 'Enigma' and 'Ultra.' I found a fellow named Peter Thornton. His picture looked like you. The books made him seem like a hero."

Tuthy smiled wanly.

"But there was this note on one page. You disappeared in 1965. You were being prosecuted for something. They didn't say what you were being prosecuted for."

"I'm a homosexual," Tuthy said quietly.

"Oh. So what?"

"Lauren and I met in England in 1964. We became good friends. They were going to put me in prison, Pal. She smuggled me into the U.S. through Canada."

"But you said you're a homosexual. They don't like women."

"Not at all true, Pal. Lauren and I like each other very much. We could talk. She told me about her dreams of being a writer, and I talked to her about mathematics, and about the war. I nearly died during the war."

"Why? Were you wounded?"

"No. I worked too hard. I burned myself out and had a nervous breakdown. My lover—a man—kept me alive throughout the forties. Things were bad in England after the war. But he died in 1963. His parents came in to settle the estate, and when I contested the settlement in court, I was arrested. So I suppose you're right, Pal. I don't really belong here."

"I don't, either. My folks don't care much. I don't have too many friends. I wasn't even born here, and I don't know anything about Korea."

"Play," Tuthy said, his face stony. "Let's see if they'll listen."

"Oh, they'll listen," Pal said. "It's like the way they talk to each other."

The boy ran his fingers over the keys on the Tronclavier. The cone, connected with the keyboard through the mini-computer, vibrated tinnily.

For an hour, Pal paged back and forth through his composition, repeating and trying variations. Tuthy sat in a corner, chin in hand, listening to the mousy squeaks and squeals produced by the cone. *How much more difficult to interpret a four-dimensional sound*, he thought. *Not even visual clues . . .*

Finally the boy stopped and wrung his hands, then stretched his arms. "They must have heard. We'll just have to wait and see." He switched the Tronclavier to automatic playback and pushed the chair away from the keyboard.

Pal stayed until dusk, then reluctantly went home. Tuthy

sat in the office until midnight, listening to the tinny sounds issuing from the speaker cone.

All night long, the Tronclavier played through its preprogrammed selection of Pal's compositions. Tuthy lay in bed in his room, two doors down from Lauren's room, watching a shaft of moonlight slide across the wall. *How far would a four-dimensional being have to travel to get here?*

How far have I come to get here?

Without realizing he was asleep, he dreamed, and in his dream a wavering image of Pal appeared, gesturing with both arms as if swimming, eyes wide. *I'm okay*, the boy said without moving his lips. *Don't worry about me . . . I'm okay. I've been back to Korea to see what it's like. It's not bad, but I like it better here. . . .*

Tuthy awoke sweating. The moon had gone down and the room was pitch-black. In the office, the hyper cone continued its distant, mouse-squeak broadcast.

Pal returned early in the morning, repetitively whistling a few bars from Mozart's Fourth Violin Concerto. Lauren let him in and he joined Tuthy upstairs. Tuthy sat before the monitor, replaying Pal's sketch of the four-dimensional beings.

"Do you see anything?" he asked the boy.

Pal nodded. "They're coming closer. They're interested. Maybe we should get things ready, you know . . . be prepared." He squinted. "Did you ever think what a four-dimensional footprint would look like?"

Tuthy considered for a moment. "That would be most interesting," he said. "It would be solid."

On the first floor, Lauren screamed.

Pal and Tuthy almost tumbled over each other getting downstairs. Lauren stood in the living room with her arms crossed above her bosom, one hand clamped over her mouth. The first intrusion had taken out a section of the living-room floor and the east wall.

"Really clumsy," Pal said. "One of them must have bumped it."

"The music," Tuthy said.

"What in HELL is going on?" Lauren demanded, her voice starting as a screech and ending as a roar.

"Better turn the music off," Tuthy elaborated.

"Why?" Pal asked, face wreathed in an excited smile.

"Maybe they don't like it."

A bright filmy blue blob rapidly expanded to a yard in diameter just beside Tuthy. The blob turned red, wiggled, froze, and then just as rapidly vanished.

"That was like an elbow," Pal explained. "One of its arms. I think it's listening. Trying to find out where the music is coming from. I'll go upstairs."

"Turn it off!" Tuthy demanded.

"I'll play something else." The boy ran up the stairs. From the kitchen came a hideous hollow crashing, then the sound of a vacuum being filled—a reverse-pop, ending in a hiss—followed by a low-frequency vibration that set their teeth on edge . . .

The vibration caused by a four-dimensional creature *scraping* across its "floor," their own three-dimensional space. Tuthy's hands shook with excitement.

"Peter—" Lauren bellowed, all dignity gone. She unwrapped her arms and held clenched fists out as if she were about to start exercising, or boxing.

"Pal's attracted visitors," Tuthy explained.

He turned toward the stairs. The first four steps and a section of floor spun and vanished. The rush of air nearly drew him down the hole. Regaining his balance, he knelt to feel the precisely cut, concave edge. Below lay the dark basement.

"Pal!" Tuthy called out.

"I'm playing something original for them," Pal shouted back. "I think they like it."

The phone rang. Tuthy was closest to the extension at the bottom of the stairs and instinctively reached out to answer it. Hockrum was on the other end, screaming.

"I can't talk now—" Tuthy said. Hockrum screamed again, loud enough for Lauren to hear. Tuthy abruptly hung up. "He's been fired, I gather," he said. "He seemed angry." He stalked back three paces and turned, then ran forward and leaped the gap to the first intact step. "Can't talk." He stumbled and scrambled up the stairs, stopping on the landing. "Jesus," he said, as if something had suddenly occurred to him.

"He'll call the government," Lauren warned.

Tuthy waved that off. "I know what's happening. They're knocking chunks out of three-space, into the fourth. The fourth dimension. Like Pal says: clumsy brutes. They could kill us!"

Sitting before the Tronclavier, Pal happily played a new melody. Tuthy approached and was abruptly blocked by a thick green column, as solid as rock and with a similar texture. It vibrated and ascribed an arc in the air. A section of the ceiling four feet wide was kicked out of three-space. Tuthy's hair lifted in the rush of wind. The column shrank to a broomstick and hairs sprouted all over it, writhing like snakes.

Tuthy edged around the hairy broomstick and pulled the plug on the Tronclavier. A cage of zeppelin-shaped brown sausages encircled the computer, spun, elongated to reach the ceiling, the floor, and the top of the monitor's table, and then pipped down to tiny strings and was gone.

"They can't see too clearly here," Pal said, undisturbed that his concert was over. Lauren had climbed the outside stairs and stood behind Tuthy. "Gee, I'm sorry about the damage."

In one smooth, curling motion, the Tronclavier and cone and all the wiring associated with them were peeled away as if they had been stick-on labels hastily removed from a flat surface.

"Gee," Pal said, his face suddenly registering alarm.

Then it was the boy's turn. He was removed more slowly, with greater care. The last thing to vanish was his head, which hung suspended in the air for several seconds.

"I think they liked the music," he said, grinning.

Head, grin and all, dropped away in a direction impossible for Tuthy or Lauren to follow. The air in the room sighed.

Lauren stood her ground for several minutes, while Tuthy wandered through what was left of the office, passing his hand through mussed hair.

"Perhaps he'll be back," Tuthy said. "I don't even know . . ." But he didn't finish. Could a three-dimensional boy survive in a four-dimensional void, or whatever lay dup . . . or owwen?

Tuthy did not object when Lauren took it upon herself to call the boy's foster parents and the police. When the police arrived, he endured the questions and accusations stoically, face immobile, and told them as much as he knew. He was not believed; nobody knew quite what to believe. Photographs were taken. The police left.

It was only a matter of time, Lauren told him, until one or the other or both of them were arrested. "Then we'll make up a story," he said. "You'll tell them it was my fault."

"I will *not*," Lauren said. "But where *is* he?"

"I'm not positive," Tuthy said. "I think he's all right, however."

"How do you *know*?"

He told her about the dream.

"But that was before," she said.

"Perfectly allowable in the fourth dimension," he explained. He pointed vaguely up, then down, and shrugged.

On the last day, Tuthy spent the early morning hours bundled in an overcoat and bathrobe in the drafty office, playing his program again and again, trying to visualize *ana* and *kata*. He closed his eyes and squinted and twisted his head, intertwined his fingers and drew odd little graphs on the monitors, but it was no use. His brain was hard-wired.

Over breakfast, he reiterated to Lauren that she must put all the blame on him.

"Maybe it will all blow over," she said. "They haven't got a case. No evidence . . . nothing."

"All blow *over*," he mused, passing his hand over his head and grinning ironically. "How *over*, they'll never know."

The doorbell rang. Tuthy went to answer it, and Lauren followed a few steps behind.

Tuthy opened the door. Three men in gray suits, one with

a briefcase, stood on the porch. "Mr. Peter Thornton?" the tallest asked.

"Yes," Tuthy acknowledged.

A chunk of the door frame and wall above the door vanished with a roar and a hissing pop. The three men looked up at the gap. Ignoring what was impossible, the tallest man returned his attention to Tuthy and continued, "We have information that you are in this country illegally."

"Oh?" Tuthy said.

Beside him, an irregular filmy blue cylinder grew to a length of four feet and hung in the air, vibrating. The three men backed away on the porch. In the middle of the cylinder, Pal's head emerged, and below that, his extended arm and hand.

"It's fun here," Pal said. "They're friendly."

"I believe you," Tuthy said.

"Mr. Thornton," the tallest man continued valiantly.

"Won't you come with me?" Pal asked.

Tuthy glanced back at Lauren. She gave him a small fraction of a nod, barely understanding what she was assenting to, and he took Pal's hand. "Tell them it was all my fault," he said.

From his feet to his head, Peter Tuthy was peeled out of this world. Air rushed in. Half of the brass lamp to one side of the door disappeared.

The INS men returned to their car without any further questions, with damp pants and embarrassed, deeply worried expressions. They drove away, leaving Lauren to contemplate the quiet. They did not return.

She did not sleep for three nights, and when she did sleep, Tuthy and Pal visited her, and put the question to her.

Thank you, but I prefer it here, she replied.

It's a lot of fun, the boy insisted. *They like music*.

Lauren shook her head on the pillow and awoke. Not very far away, there was a whistling, tinny kind of sound, followed by a deep vibration.

To her, it sounded like applause.

She took a deep breath and got out of bed to retrieve her notebook.

THE FINEST THE UNIVERSE HAS TO OFFER